Praise for

"Fresh, heartfelt, an[d]  miss debut that feels l[ike]... —*BuzzFeed*

"The novel depicts the challenge of navigating two cultures, both of which Yinka is a part of and apart from. In her commitment to being her whole self and true to her faith and ideals, Yinka writes a prayer for *herself*, a rallying cry to which we can all shout, 'Amen!'" —NPR

"So modern and fresh. Like Bridget Jones, Yinka is a lovable and relatable disaster—which is to say, she isn't actually a disaster at all... I adore her."
—Emily Henry, #1 *New York Times* bestselling author of *Funny Story*

"A story that includes a little bit of everything... funny, relatable, witty, yet poignant... reinforce[s] the importance of surrounding oneself with a supportive community." —Taraji P. Henson, *Oprah Daily*

"Blackburn's debut novel is incredibly relatable for anybody whose family members frequently question their relationship status. In *Yinka, Where Is Your Huzband?* a thirty-something Nigerian woman attempts to find herself a wedding date and learns some valuable lessons about life and love." —*Marie Claire*

"Turns traditional elements of romantic comedy on its head, discussing love and how it can weave its way between two cultures."
—*The Washington Post*

"If... *Yinka, Where Is Your Huzband?* was to become a TV sitcom, it could run episode after episode, season after season, without losing steam

on story material. Cheeky and entertaining, the novel . . . packs in a whole lot of cross-cultural drama and social commentary with an easygoing, conversational style. Add romantic and professional mishaps, and complicated relationships . . . and you have the makings of comedic gold."
—*Star Tribune*

"In the end, what matters most in *Yinka, Where Is Your Huzband?* is not your marital status but self-love, love of family, and a broader sense of connection. And maybe you'll find something better than a happily-ever-after fairy tale." —Mabinty Quarshie, *USA Today*

"An uplifting and entertaining story you won't want to put down."
—*HuffPost*

"A delightful romantic comedy that refuses to play by the genre's rules."
—*POPSUGAR*

"A great foray into Nigerian-style rom-com territory with a lovable and unconventional heroine. Although Yinka considers herself traditional, this book feels very modern and has great humor." —*Book Riot*

"With poignant themes of identity and independence, Blackburn's buoyant look at contemporary courtship is a sure conversation starter for book clubs." —*BookPage*

"A laugh-out-loud story of self-discovery, set against the world of contemporary dating . . . Fans of Uzma Jalaluddin and Sonya Lalli will delight in this story of a one-of-a-kind woman learning how to love one of the most important people in her life: herself." —*Booklist*

"A sassy, spirited story." —*Kirkus Reviews*

"Blackburn's lighthearted tone helps deliver heavy thoughts on colorism, the tension of cultural differences, and the benefits of therapy, as the story moves toward a happy ending on all fronts. This delivers loads of entertainment and a dollop of enlightenment."
—*Publishers Weekly*

"Blackburn's Bridget Jones–esque debut is a sensitive, humorous chronicle of a young woman's journey of self-discovery. . . . Readers who like the novels of Marian Keyes and Cecelia Ahern will find much to enjoy here."
—*Library Journal*

"*Yinka, Where Is Your Huzband?* was a total joy to read—it's hilarious, insightful, and so uplifting. Yinka is the most lovable character I've come across in a long time—I was cheering her on for every step of her journey."
—Beth O'Leary, international bestselling author of *The Wake-Up Call*

"Beautifully observed, warm and deeply human, *Yinka, Where Is Your Huzband?* is a meditation on family and friendship, on love and self-love. Feel-good, funny, and clever, it's got smash-hit written all over it!"
—Josie Silver, #1 *New York Times* bestselling author of *One Day in December*

"*Yinka, Where Is Your Huzband?* is a beautiful, bighearted story about friendship, family, and love. Yinka's charming voice draws you in and her journey toward self-acceptance will make you stay. A fun and relatable read."
—Emiko Jean, *New York Times* bestselling author of *Mika in Real Life*

"Warm and fun and sweet, great on female friendships and extended families."
—Marian Keyes, international bestselling author of *My Favorite Mistake*

"Blackburn deftly immerses us in the life of a lovable Yinka as she straddles two cultures in her search for a 'huzband.' Smart, sophisticated, and fresh, this is the 'girl gets herself' type of story I love to read!"
—Jayne Allen, author of *Black Girls Must Die Exhausted*

"A warm, witty, and joyful novel bursting with charm and unforgettable characters, this is a story about friendship, family, romance, and the most important quest of all—loving and accepting yourself."
—Lauren Ho, author of *Last Tang Standing*

"Spreadsheets, meddling aunties, and makeovers . . . *Yinka, Where Is Your Huzband?* is a delightful journey of a British Nigerian woman longing to find love, and to love herself. Reader, you'll root for Yinka the whole way."
—Patricia Park, author of *Re Jane*

"Blackburn writes with a witty tenderness and absorbing fluidity that brings Yinka, the most lovable character you'll meet, to rich life. I cheered for her, cringed for her, and rooted for her all the way. A fabulously fresh debut guaranteed to warm your heart. Loved it!"
—Lọlá Ákínmádé Åkerström, international bestselling author of *In Every Mirror She's Black*

"Glorious debut! Read it over two nights and loved it!"
—Nikki May, author of *Wahala*

"Bitingly funny and relatable . . . A gorgeous, easy read, but with real depth to its punchy chapters. . . . An extraordinary debut from one of the rising talents in contemporary fiction."
—Lizzy Dent, author of *The Summer Job*

penguin books

THE RE-WRITE

Lizzie Damilola Blackburn is a British Nigerian charity worker–turned-author who grew up in south London and now lives with her husband and young son in Milton Keynes. Her debut novel, *Yinka, Where Is Your Huzband?*, was selected by Nobel Peace Prize laureate Malala Yousafzai as a Literati book club pick. Blackburn was also a runner-up for a Diverse Book Award (UK) in 2023. *The Re-Write* is her second novel.

ALSO BY
LIZZIE DAMILOLA BLACKBURN

Yinka, Where Is Your Huzband?

The Re-Write

a novel

Lizzie Damilola Blackburn

PENGUIN BOOKS

PENGUIN BOOKS
An imprint of Penguin Random House LLC
1745 Broadway, New York, NY 10019
penguinrandomhouse.com

Copyright © 2025 by Elizabeth Damilola Blackburn Ltd.

Penguin Random House values and supports copyright.
Copyright fuels creativity, encourages diverse voices, promotes free
speech, and creates a vibrant culture. Thank you for buying an authorized
edition of this book and for complying with copyright laws by not reproducing,
scanning, or distributing any part of it in any form without permission. You are
supporting writers and allowing Penguin Random House to continue to publish
books for every reader. Please note that no part of this book may be used
or reproduced in any manner for the purpose of training artificial
intelligence technologies or systems.

Set in Granjon LT Std

LIBRARY OF CONGRESS CATALOGING-IN-PUBLICATION DATA
Names: Blackburn, Lizzie Damilola, author.
Title: The re-write : a novel / Lizzie Damilola Blackburn.
Description: New York : Penguin Books, 2025.
Identifiers: LCCN 2024044516 (print) | LCCN 2024044517 (ebook) |
ISBN 9780593299050 (trade paperback) | ISBN 9780593299043 (ebook)
Subjects: LCGFT: Romance fiction. | Humorous fiction. | Novels.
Classification: LCC PR6102.L3343 R49 2025 (print) |
LCC PR6102.L3343 (ebook) | DDC 823/.92—dc23/eng/20240924
LC record available at https://lccn.loc.gov/2024044516
LC ebook record available at https://lccn.loc.gov/2024044517

First published in Great Britain by Penguin Books,
an imprint of Penguin Random House UK, 2025
Published in Penguin Books (USA) 2025

Printed in the United States of America
1st Printing

The authorized representative in the EU for product safety and compliance is
Penguin Random House Ireland, Morrison Chambers, 32 Nassau Street,
Dublin D02 YH68, Ireland, https://eu-contact.penguin.ie.

To my darling son:

Thank you for being my inner and outer motivation.
You have been with me the entire journey since the very beginning.

And to all the writers who doubt themselves—don't.

The Re-Write

THE DAILY BIZ

Who is *The Villa* star Wale Bandele? Meet the south London contestant whose biggest turnoff is badly bitten fingernails.

It's June. And that can only mean one thing. *The Villa* is back.

Now in its sixth season, the popular reality dating show will see ten sexy singletons compete to be the last couple standing in a bid to win a five-figure cash prize. Over the course of ten weeks, the singletons will live together in a luxurious villa in Ibiza for a summer of dating, challenges, and, of course, hot, sizzling drama.

A Liverpudlian hairdresser, a grime artist, and a Taylor Swift body double have all been confirmed for this year's lineup. This includes 25-year-old British Nigerian Wale Bandele, a charity fundraising officer from Camberwell. Ahead of his departure, we interviewed Wale to find out everything from his celebrity crush to what he's looking for in the villa.

Tell us, how did you get on the show?

I was waiting to get a tattoo—I have eight now—when this woman walked up to me. We got chatting, she revealed she was a producer, and yeah, the rest is history.

Who is your celebrity crush?

Oh, Nia Long, without a shadow of a doubt. Remember when she had that sexy pixie cut way back when she was on *The Fresh Prince*? Yeah, I fell in love with her then.

What is your biggest turnoff?

Bad hygiene. And bitten fingernails. There's something about a girl who takes pride in her nails that does it for me.

What are you looking for in the villa?

Honestly? I'm open to all sorts so long as she's confident and has good chat.

Last question, how would your ex describe you?

(Laughs) Err . . . next question.

The Villa will air next Monday at 9 p.m. on TV6. Join the conversation #TheVilla

1

Eleven weeks later... August

My heart can't take another rejection.

This thought keeps coming to mind as I wait in a quiet restaurant in Covent Garden. My agent emailed me to catch up over lunch, so I'm assuming she has news for me—whether it's good or bad, I don't know.

"Water?"

A smiley waiter fills the two glasses on the table. The aroma of freshly made buttery waffles, which under normal circumstances would make me hungry, is now making me sick to my stomach.

And then a lump the size of a cough sweet lodges itself in my throat.

Directly ahead of me on the widescreen TV is my ex-boyfriend, Wale. A rerun episode of *The Villa: The Reunion* is on.

My lips quiver but I manage to hold it together.

Six months down the drain. Just like that.

The producers play a reel of Wale's highlights from the five weeks he was on the show before being voted off by the public—not that I was keeping track. They've set it to the tune of Mariah Carey's "Heartbreaker," which couldn't be more fitting.

They show his entrance:

"What's happening, people! My name is Wale and I'm from south London!"

His first connection with a Geordie lass called Sally:

"Yeah, you're a sweet one, still."

They show how he breaks her heart, before swiftly coupling up with Taleesha and doing the exact same thing. This happens quite a few times. Going from one girl to the other. Going from piping hot to ice cube cold, until he is paired up with Kelechi—a stunning British Nigerian model with rich chocolate skin and big eyes. When they hit it off, I'd switched off. I could no longer watch as the love of my life fell into the arms of somebody else. But, despite avoiding the show, it was almost impossible to dodge Black Twitter. Every day, Wale and Kelechi, or "Walechi" as they were called, inundated my news feed. They were #couplegoals #BlackLove #YorubaAndIgboKingAndQueen. Until, one day, a different hashtag was trending: #GetWaleOut #FBoy #WaleIsTrashBinHim.

It seemed as though Mr. Pretty Boy had broken Kelechi's heart too.

The reel comes to an end. Wale is met with a few lone boos from the audience. Kelechi gives him an earful; his attempt to defend himself is drowned out.

A pang of sympathy fills my empty stomach. *No, Temi, he deserves this. See this as your gift.* Now the world can see Wale for who he really is.

Shaking my head, I continue to watch. Wale is fumbling; they sound like excuses.

"Oh, please. Give it a rest," I say to myself.

And right into my agent's face.

I was so busy watching the reunion, I didn't even see her walk in.

Mayee looks over at the screen, then at me. "You're a fan?" she says, hanging the chain of her diamond-quilted Chanel bag over the back of her chair.

I scrunch up my nose.

"Urgh, no." (I've watched nearly all six seasons of *The Villa* and could most likely win trivia on it.)

"Well, good thing I'm sitting with my back toward the TV, then," she says. "Don't judge. Guilty pleasure."

My brows quirk. Oh, we could have bonded over that.

If there's any literary agent who is known by one name alone, it's

Mayee. She's the Madonna of publishing. With nearly two decades of experience under her belt, she represents all of the biggest award-winning, best-selling romance authors. I'm lucky to be on her books, let alone sharing the same oxygen; I got rejected by twelve agents before she signed me. I cannot. F. This. Up.

Remembering that we're now on hugging terms, I clamber to my feet and wrap my arms around her. Mayee's tall frame makes me feel even shorter than I already am.

"You look well," she says as I ruefully give my tank top a quick *yoink*.

Shakira must be doing a fabulous job concealing my eye bags because I barely slept a wink last night, worried stiff about this meeting. Shakira is one of my many beautiful pairs of prescription glasses—nude polygonal frames with silver rhinestones along the side temples. Hey, some people name their cars. I name my eyewear.

"Thanks for meeting with me," Mayee says after we slide into our seats. She's wearing one of those chic, military-style blazers, and on a less terrifying day, I'd be asking where it's from. "It's been a while since we've last met in person, hasn't it?"

"It has."

Over the last few months, Mayee has broken bad news over the phone and via email. This is why today could be different.

While she studies the menu, I study her body language—honestly, the woman is impossible to read. The waiter comes over and takes our order.

"So," Mayee says. The TV behind cuts to an ad break. "I've got some news."

Under the table, my thighs start to sweat. I can hear myself breathing through my nose.

Mayee places her interlocked hands on the table, her stiletto-shaped nails crimson red. "As you know, for the past, what, eight, nine months now, I've been submitting your manuscript to editors at a number of publishing houses. And I've recently heard back from Paxton."

Despite her attempts to maintain a neutral tone, I can tell that the news is bad. A familiar, dull ache spreads under my ribs.

Rejected. Again.

Mayee gives me a moment to absorb the news before she resumes. "I know this is not what you want to hear," she carries on, her voice softening, "but the feedback from Paxton was the same. The editor *loved* your writing. *Loved* the Black, plus-size representation. But, sadly, she didn't think the concept would appeal to the market. So, we need to make a decision."

My lungs contract. There's a finality in her tone.

"I'm so sorry, Temi, but we're going to have to draw a line under *Wildest Dreams*."

2

I started writing *Wildest Dreams* about four years ago. I was eighteen and on the cusp of starting uni to study English lit. Devouring *The Time Traveler's Wife* over the summer sparked the idea. A quirky romcom, *Wildest Dreams* follows a plus-size British Nigerian woman who has the ability to live out two separate lives—one in reality and the other in her dreams—and consequently finds herself caught in a love triangle between a dashing phantom and her college crush.

At uni, when I wasn't studying or turning down parties and social events, I was tucked away in the library or in my room, chipping away at my manuscript, using tips I had picked up from creative writing books and the internet to improve my draft. I became so fixated on getting *Wildest Dreams* published that after I failed to pass my six-month probation period at my first job post uni—I worked as a junior ghost editor at a minuscule ghostwriting company called Bonsai—I didn't even bother trying to find another full-time role. Instead, since last autumn, I've been working at a call center, trying to flog sustainable bamboo tissue subscriptions to customers who'll barely give me two seconds of their time. My rationale—as I explained to my concerned-looking parents—was that I needed a job with flexible hours that would give me time to write, finish my manuscript, and later edit it when it got sold. I needed to go all in and chase my dreams while the stakes were still relatively low.

This is why I can't get my head around what Mayee is saying now. Had all my sacrifice and hard work been for nothing? Did I miss out on a once-in-a-lifetime uni experience and a foot on the corporate ladder for a delusion? It can't have been in vain.

"But what about Ocean?" I cry, grasping at straws. Ocean Books is the world's biggest publisher. My dream publisher. "We haven't heard back from all of the editors yet. Can you chase them up?"

Before I've even reached the end of my sentence, Mayee is shaking her head.

"As you know, I submitted your manuscript to multiple editors at Ocean, and have now heard back with passes from all but one. I'm afraid it hasn't received the interest we were hoping for—"

"Here you go!"

The waiter has returned and, with a flourish, he places our food and drinks on the table. A hotness creeps into the backs of my eyes. *I will not cry, I will not cry.* My manuscript wasn't good enough for a top agent like Mayee to sell. I can't let her think that I haven't got the steel for this business.

"But we saw this coming, didn't we?" She looks down to cut her cinnamon-dusted waffle, and I quickly swipe my finger under my eyes. "That's why, as soon as we got our first 'no,' I told you to start working on another book. How is *Love Drive* coming along?"

Oh, shit!

I hope my face hasn't given me away.

Love Drive is the novel I told Mayee I'd start when she set me this assignment over eight months ago. So far, I've only written one chapter. Okay, half a chapter. It's not because *Love Drive* has a bad plot—risk-averse actress makes a bet with a daredevil stunt driver to live on the edge for a month and ends up falling head over heels for him despite being a commitment-phobe—it's just . . . *Wildest Dreams* is my baby! I never thought I would have to let her go—for goodness' sake, I only needed one "yes"! And Mayee hadn't given me a hard deadline to send her my new manuscript by, so I thought, like me, she was betting all her chips on it too.

I can now see that stalling wasn't the wisest thing to do.

My brain ticks. I stuff a skewerful of sliced bananas into my mouth, washing it down with a gulp of blueberry margarita.

"Oh, you know." I attempt a casual laugh. "It's going."

Mayee frowns. "What? Going well? Going badly? And how far along are you now?" I'm in the hot seat. "When I checked in a few months ago, you made it seem like you were on a roll. Although you have been a bit cryptic about your writing process, which is fine if having a bit of space is how you prefer to work. But in order for me to support you, Temi, I'm going to need an update."

"I'm about halfway," a voice says suddenly.

A voice that came out of my mouth.

The mouth of an idiot.

Mayee's eyes light up. "Oh, fantastic. You're further ahead than I thought."

Way to go, Temi.

"Can you send me what you've got?"

I neck the rest of my cocktail. I desperately need another. My brain is running at fiber-optic speed. There is no way I can tell Mayee the truth. "Well, the thing is, there's this part that I'm dying to write. I would *love* to send you my manuscript once that's done. It's a twist!" *Great, now I have to think of a twist.* "I promise you it'll be worth the wait."

There's a clatter as Mayee sets down her knife and fork. She reaches for her napkin and dabs it against the corners of her matte red lips, appearing both sophisticated and intimidating at the same time.

"How long do you need?"

My gut twists.

If I say another nine months—which is probably what I do need—I can't guarantee that she won't rip up my contract and ditch me right on the spot. But if I say nine days . . . can I write half a friggin' novel in a little over a week? That's, like, 40,000 words!

Then again, I have blitzed a novel before . . .

My eyes pan to the TV screen. There's a wide shot of all the cast members on the set of *The Villa*, with the host looking spectacular in a figure-hugging lime dress. Unlike the other contestants, who are grinning widely with their veneer-white teeth, Wale is slumped on his stool toward the back.

Hold up, should I tell Mayee about *that* manuscript? The one I wrote in the space of four weeks, spurred by a frenzy of red-hot, vengeful rage? The one about how a cold-hearted boy-man (Wayne) ditched his hopelessly romantic, anxiety-ridden girlfriend (Sophie) when she was at her most vulnerable moment after being rejected for twelve-plus acting gigs, then went on to appear on a reality TV dating show?! The one that I've titled *The Ultimate Payback*, where the protagonist writes an exposé about her ex, getting her sweet, sweet revenge.

"Temi?"

I blink rapidly.

Mayee is poker-faced. "How about the week commencing the sixteenth of September? Which would give you about a month."

"Perfect." I grin. *Fuck-fuck-fuck-fuck.*

With one swift motion, Mayee pulls out her phone, locking the deadline in her diary. She gestures to the waiter for the bill.

"I'm so sorry but I'm going to have to shoot off. My day is packed." The waiter returns with a card machine and hands it to her. Mayee inserts her gold Amex card and taps in her PIN. "Ooh, before I forget." The waiter snaps off her receipt and gives it to her. "An agent I know is looking for a British Nigerian ghostwriter to help write a short memoir for his client. Hope you don't mind, but I threw your name in the mix."

I shift in my chair and scratch the back of my ear. "Actually, I don't work at Bonsai anymore." And when Mayee's brows rise in question, I add, "I work part time now . . . shift work."

To my surprise, Mayee looks overjoyed.

"Oh, how about that? You have the time *and* the experience. I'll send you the job spec so you can take a look."

I don't have the time! I have half a novel to write! I want to yell.

"Money's good too."

Ah. "Sure," I say with a shrug. No harm in having a look.

She taps away at her phone. Within seconds, my own buzzes.

"Right. I'm off."

At the same time, we rise to our feet and give each other a hug.

Mayee bounds toward the exit as I flop back down, her heels clanking against the floor.

"Looking forward to reading," she calls over her shoulder.

I fake-smile.

As Mayee saunters past the window, tears teeter dangerously along my lash line. The second she vanishes, the dam breaks. Right in the middle of the restaurant, I have a meltdown. Shielding my face, I choke out a shuddering sob, tears sliding down my cheeks and in between my fingers. I'm too embarrassed to make a dash to the toilets. I feel like a failure.

Even though I knew there was a good chance that *Wildest Dreams* wouldn't get sold, I'd shoved the thought down, scared negative thinking would cause it to happen. What was the point? All this positive thinking malarkey is a load of bull. I think it's time I face up to the truth. Maybe I'm just not cut out to be an author. Maybe it's time to look for a proper job.

Wiping my tears with a crumpled napkin, I tap on my phone with an ombré nail. Mayee's email has come through.

> **Subject:** Freelance British Nigerian ghostwriter needed for celebrity memoir

I choke on air. Okay. Mayee did not mention anything about the client being a celebrity!

> **Urgent.** I am looking for a ghostwriter/editor of Nigerian heritage for my celebrity client. For confidentiality reasons, my client will remain anonymous until we hire for the position.

The ideal candidate will have:

- past experience working as a freelance ghostwriter/editor and/or book-writing and editing experience
- the ability to write effectively in the English language and capture my client's youthful voice
- access to a laptop with writing software (e.g. Microsoft Word)
- an interest in contemporary popular culture

My client's memoir will be published by Kingston Books and will be released next spring. However, due to publishing schedules, the ghostwriter would need to submit a first draft in six weeks. (Please note: the final manuscript will need to be roughly 65,000–75,000 words.) **This deadline is non-negotiable, so please take this into consideration before applying.**

Compensation: Between £15,000 to £20,000 depending on experience, plus food and travel expenses

Start date: ASAP

To apply, please reply to this email with your CV and an example of your work. Only short-listed candidates will be contacted.

Kind regards,
Greg Butcher
Talent Agent

I hiss. Nope. Defo not applying for that. Nope, nope, nope, nope. Sure, £15K would give my account a much-needed boost, but no way could I take on such a responsibility. And for a celebrity? What if I do a shoddy job and it gets terrible reviews? No, whoever this celeb is, they deserve to work with someone competent. Someone experienced. A safe pair of hands.

I'm about to archive the email when Patrick, my supervisor—well, the name I saved him as, Pat-dick—flashes across my screen. I groan. Why is he calling me on my day off?

"Hi, Patrick," I answer. *The Villa: The Reunion* is now finished and there's a program about pets showing on the TV.

"Where are you? You were supposed to be here over twenty minutes ago."

Patrick's tone gets my back up. "You do know today's my day off, right? I put it in the staff calendar—"

Patrick sighs as if I've been keeping him on the phone for a long time. "Temi, if you did, I wouldn't be calling, would I? You need to come in. Now."

"Are you serious?"

"You either come in within the next hour or don't bother coming back."

My blood boils. I've had such a shitty day; I don't need his attitude right now.

"Fine. I won't bother."

The words slip out so fast that, by the time I try to retract them, Patrick is telling me when I should expect my last paycheck.

He ends the call.

My eyes well.

Oh no. What did I just do?

3

The following day, I start my job search. It's already 2 p.m. and I have yet to start working on *Love Drive*. Instead, I'm in bed in the same knickers I wore yesterday, and all I've done is apply for a couple of part-time jobs.

Beside my laptop, my phone lights up. There's a WhatsApp message from my parents.

> **Mum:**
> Are we still on for our catch-up tomorrow?

I whimper.

I don't know how I'm going to tell them that I quit my job without another one lined up. After I told them I was going full tilt with writing, they couldn't have been more supportive. Knowing that I would be on a much lower salary, they said I could stay in their one-bed rental flat in Catford, as long as I covered the bills and kept the place clean. Conveniently, their tenants were moving out at the end of the month and their mortgage was pretty much paid off.

Now I have to tell them about what happened with my job *and* my novel. The thought is heart-wrenchingly unbearable. They haven't exactly been great with bad news.

When I told them that I'd been let go from Bonsai, there was such disappointment in their eyes, you would think I had failed my degree. Although being let go sucked, I didn't sink into a great depression; I didn't enjoy my job. The whole point of pursuing a career in publishing was to rub shoulders with editors in the hope that, someday, one would offer me a book deal—how naive I was. But competition was stiff, so a junior role at an understaffed, floundering ghostwriting company was the best I got. My manager was the type who would let out an audible sigh if you dared utter a question, so I struggled in silence, trying my best to meet deadlines, sometimes at the expense of quality. In some sense, being let go was a relief. It was telling my parents that gave me heart palpitations.

Thankfully, the day before I planned to tell them, I got a phone call from Mayee offering me representation. I was able to frame the news of my being let go as an opportunity rather than a failure.

I dread the idea of telling them I've left the call-center job too. I don't think I can bear their disappointment again.

The weight of my predicament has me feeling low and, naturally, my mind wanders to where it always does when I'm this down—Wale and our breakup. How I called in sick and spent the majority of my days eating crackers in bed. I am unable to stop poking at these memories. The good times: when we got matching fake cheeseburger tattoos at Blackheath funfair; when Wale made me laugh so hard that lemonade projected out of my nose. And also the not-so-good times: when he first told me he'd been scouted for the show and when he led me to believe he was going to drop out . . .

Five months ago . . . March

"Ooh, ooh, ooh! I love this part!" Lifting my head from Wale's shoulder, I wriggle around and nearly tip over the bowl of popcorn on his lap. We're in my flat watching what we recently discovered is our favorite romance movie: *The Best Man Holiday*.

On the TV screen, four Black men dressed as if they're in a nineties boy band—black leather jackets with trilby hats—perform a choreographed dance to New Edition's "Can You Stand the Rain" while the four women on the sofa holler and laugh.

Pretending that my fist is a mic, I sing along to the intro, shoving it under Wale's mouth so that he can join in too. We fail miserably to hit the high note. And then, suddenly, I'm being passed the bowl of popcorn. Wale jumps to his feet.

My boyfriend knows every move.

"Shut. Up!" I say, wide-mouthed as Wale spins around before seamlessly transitioning into a slide.

Impressively, he doesn't break character. With a cool, sultry expression, he clicks his fingers. He does a two-step while miming along to the lyrics. His gray hoodie and sweatpants are worlds apart from what the men on the TV are wearing.

I play my part by turning into a fan girl. I clap. I squeal. I pretend to throw my knickers at him. Wale carries on with his performance until the dance sequence comes to an end. I give him a standing ovation.

"And you watched that scene how many times?" I ask after he bows.

He slumps back on the sofa and gives a half shrug. "Only about twenty times."

I chortle.

He kisses me on the cheek. "You enjoyed my performance?"

"Hell yeah!" I cry.

"Good, 'cause I'll be taking donations at the door."

I make an act of patting my pockets. "Don't suppose you have change for 20p, do you?"

I duck as he tosses a popcorn kernel at me.

Shaking his head, he returns his attention to the screen, its soft glow highlighting his chiseled profile.

I can literally feel my heart swell. *How did I get so lucky?* Over the last few weeks, I had been trying to ignore the ways my body would respond to him—the tingling sensation blooming in my chest and how my breathing would randomly go shallow whenever he was close. It's happening now. My feelings are becoming too big to contain.

Wale, aware that I'm still staring at him, turns his head a little and laughs self-consciously. "Temi," he says, "the performance is over. You can stop watching me."

"I think I'm falling for you." The words tumble out of my mouth like a confession.

Wale's brows quirk. He shifts his body around to face me.

The silence that follows is horrible. My heart pounds violently.

Dammit. I shouldn't have said anything. Five months is too soon. Isn't it?

I open my mouth to say something to smooth over this now very uncomfortable moment. But then Wale picks up the remote control and pauses the film.

"Tems, I have something to tell you."

My belly clenches. Nothing good ever comes after that sentence.

I watch him intently as he scratches the side of his beard. I'm trying to dissect his every movement.

Finally, he lets out a resigned sigh. "I'm signed up for *The Villa*."

I release a breath. Then the meaning of his words hits me.

"What?!"

"Don't worry! I'm going to drop out. I was scouted for the show months before we even met."

Wordless, I turn and look straight ahead. I feel numb.

"I'm so sorry. I should have told you from the jump." He places a hand on my knee and stares at the side of my face.

My nostrils begin to twitch. *I'm so stupid. I'm so stupid.*

"I only signed up for a laugh," he's now saying. "C'mon, Tems, you know me. I don't care about clout or brand deals. Actually, lemme not lie, the bag was tempting, still."

If there were an award for the biggest side-eye . . .

"Aw, c'mon, babes." He shifts closer; I scoot away slightly. "I know

The Re-Write 17

it's no excuse, but I wasn't even looking for a relationship when we first started hanging out, remember? But me and you, we just . . . clicked. I couldn't fight our chemistry. But yeah, I should have told you as soon as we got serious. And for that"—he places a hand on his chest—"I'm truly, *truly* sorry."

I try to take everything in—I can't believe he's been sitting on this news the entire time. Whenever we hung out, whenever we kissed, whenever we made love—

He knew.

Wale gives me a moment before taking my palm into his.

"Temi, look at me. Please."

I tear my attention from the TV. His eyes, usually filled with mischief, are now laden with guilt. Then, as if he's about to make an oath, he dips his chin and fixes his gaze on mine.

"I don't want to do the show," he says. "I'd rather be with you."

. . .

Buzzzz. Buzzzz.

I return to the present and grab my phone. My pulse quickens.

"Hi, Mayee," I answer in my best attempt at a cheerful tone. *For the love of God, please don't ask me to send my manuscript.*

"Hi, Temi. Have you checked your email?"

"Errrrrr, not since . . ." My finger trembles as I click on Gmail. I spot Mayee's email at the top of my inbox. The subject heading: "Are you free this afternoon?"

"Well, you see, that job I was telling you about," she carries on, "Greg and his client want to have a video interview with you today."

"What?!" My laptop nearly topples off my bed as I scrabble to sit up. "I mean, I didn't even apply."

"I know," says Mayee airily. "But I recommended you. And you said you were interested, remember?"

I skim through the email. The interview is at 2:15. Basically in five minutes.

"But I haven't even prepared for it."

"Don't worry. It's just a quick, informal chat for you to meet the client and ask any questions. Between you and me, not many people have applied so this should be a walk in the park. Personally, I think you're a shoo-in."

I catch sight of my spooked face in the mirror opposite. I still have my hair bonnet on.

I guess it won't kill me to do the interview. At the very least, I can find out who this celebrity is.

"Temi, I'm going to have to push you for an answer."

Sod it. "I'm in."

"Brilliant! I'll let Greg know. Zoom link is in the email. All the best."

I jump out of bed, yanking off my hair bonnet and pajama top before flinging it in the vicinity of my laundry basket. With one Herculean pull, I wrench out my underwear drawer and rummage for a bra. Frantically, I reach for my nearest top—a slouchy gray sweater with the words MELANIN QUEEN emblazoned across it. Good enough. Next, my face. There's no way I'm going on camera without my eyebrows done. With unprecedented speed, I pencil brown feathery strokes before moving on to undo my six large plaits, ruffling my fingers through my natural roots until my hair at least slightly resembles a twist-out. I then scour my ridiculous glasses collection—basically, the entire top drawer underneath my desk—substituting Carla (one of my many home-wear frames) for Keke (my sophisticated "mama, you got this" glasses), rubbing the browline-frame lenses against my shirt to clean them. After I put them on, I throw my laptop onto my desk, flopping into the chair tucked underneath. I immediately locate Greg's email in the thread that Mayee forwarded and click on the link. I'm just about to do a quick relay sprint to grab my Vaseline—*man, my lips feel dry*—when a message pops up: "Do you wish to join the meeting with your mic and camera switched on?" I hit "Yes." I'm in. A square with my face joins two others on the screen.

And that's when my heart stops.

It's Wale.

My ex-boyfriend.

In a panic, I turn off the camera.

4

"Oh. Where did she go?" says Greg as I clutch my chest, which is pounding like a bass drum.

I'm struggling to breathe.

"Err, Temi? We can no longer see you," Greg says. "Your camera is switched off."

Pushing my chair back, I keel over. My breath is coming fast. *What kind of sick, twisted joke is this? What the heck is Wale doing here?* My brain is whizzing with possibilities.

Greg says, "Can you see the camera icon on the bottom left of your screen? You need to click on that."

Reluctantly, I turn my camera back on. My flustered face reappears on the screen. Behind me is my unmade bed. I should have used the background blur effect—too late now.

Well, this is embarrassing.

I clear my throat. "Sorry about that." I can barely look at Wale, who's doing a better job at keeping his cool. Closing his slightly parted lips, he resets his dark features before rolling the cuffs of his denim shirt to reveal a familiar arm of black ink.

The last time I saw Wale in the flesh we were at his friend's house party, arguing. It was the same night we broke up.

Annoyingly, I have a sudden urge to wee and yet I glug my glass of water. My neckline slides over my left shoulder and exposes my pink bra strap. I pull my top back up.

Will he admit that he knows me? Or is he just going to sit there and be fake? Should *I* say something? Flippin' heck. This is stressful.

I fluff the left side of my hair before realizing that everyone else can see me do it.

"Right, this interview won't take too long," says Greg, his eyes trailing to the time in the bottom right of his screen. He has sun-tanned skin and looks like a man who is forever in a hurry. Of course he is—Wale is hot property now. He's probably got some huge deals on the table. Although he was this season's villain, he practically carried the show.

"I'm Greg, as you know. And this is my client, Wale Bandele. Wale appeared on this year's season of *The Villa*. I'm sure you're familiar with it?"

I nod.

Then, like two kids forced to apologize, Wale and I drag our eyes to each other.

"Nice to meet you," we say, one after the other. But while my tone is miserable, Wale tries to sound jovial, as though he's meeting me for the first time.

So we are going to pretend that we're strangers.

"You're probably wondering what this project is all about," says Greg, pulling my attention. "Well, Wale was a real hit on the show. The only downside is he's got a bit of a ... bad-boy reputation. Is that fair to say, Wale?"

Wale lets out an audible huff. "Yeah, and not in a good way."

"We want to show the public a different side to him," Greg continues. "Kingston Books approached us with this opportunity, given Wale was such a strong character and had a knack for sharing anecdotes while he was on the show. Wale, what's that phrase you kept saying?"

Wale develops a small itch behind his ear. "Lemme tell you a story?"

"That's the one!" Greg grins. "They think his voice would translate well into a book and appeal especially to young Black Brits."

A scoff escapes me. I disguise it as a cough and reach for my water, which I had forgotten I'd finished.

This is absolutely ridiculous! The guy has only been famous for two minutes and now he thinks he's qualified to write a memoir?! Black Twitter will drag him through the mud! And rightfully so. And yes, Wale is charismatic, but does he even have enough life experience to fill an entire book?

I push out my lips. "It's quite soon for a memoir. Do you or the publisher have an angle?"

Greg considers my question. "It won't be out till next spring, which gives us plenty of time for an authentic rebrand. Besides, everyone loves a redemption story."

I arch a brow at Wale. He looks proper embarrassed.

"The working title is *Mister Understood*," Greg carries on, and I hold back a hoot of laughter. *Terrible.* "And we're looking for someone to help Wale write a coming-of-age type of memoir to show the different sides to him. Perhaps if the public had some insight into Wale's childhood and adolescent years, they'd understand some of his actions on the show. In terms of structure, we're happy for the ghostwriter to take the lead. Anyway, this interview is a chance for us all to get to know each other. To see if we're a good fit. Before we start, do you have any other questions?"

What would I say? *FYI, Wale is my dumb ex and I would like to end this interview?*

"Nope. I think you've covered everything." A delicious smile spreads across my face. "Thanks for answering my question. Looks like you have a great idea on your hands."

If Greg notices my sarcasm, he doesn't show it. It's hard to know what Wale is thinking; he's staring blankly at the screen.

"Right"—Greg looks up again—"as mentioned in the job ad, due to the publishing schedule, the first draft will need to be submitted in six weeks. Can you confirm whether you have any commitments that might prevent you from completing this task?"

I blink.

Gosh, he sounds as though he's reading me my rights.

"No, sir." Might as well reply as though I'm standing on trial. But then, I remember the novel I'm supposed to be working on, and I open my mouth only to close it again. *Temi, it's not like you would actually take this job.* He doesn't need to know all that.

"Excellent." Greg picks up his pen. "Tell me about your background. What genre or niche do you have experience writing in?"

I think back to my short but insanely busy stint at Bonsai. "All sorts," I reply because this is the truth. "Novellas, memoirs, self-help." I give a quick summary of my time at Bonsai, skipping out the part when I used to cry in the toilets.

"And what's the fastest you've written something of significant length?" Greg asks.

My eyes pan to Wale. "I wrote an 80,000-word novel in a month."

At this, Wale raises a brow.

Yeah, that's right, biatch.

"Impressive," says Greg, sounding far from impressed. "Mayee mentioned that you've moved on from Bonsai. Where do you work now?"

I no longer feel badass.

I reach for my water again. "Um, I write for a living."

"Oh, you freelance?"

"No, I write for myself."

"So, you're self-employed?"

"Not exactly."

Greg stares at me, tired of this game.

"I mean . . . I'm currently not in formal employment," I finally say.

"So, un-em-ploooyed." Greg enunciates each syllable as he ticks the relevant box.

Without meaning to, my eyes flicker to Wale. He looks sympathetic. I'm riled up.

"I mean, I recently quit my job to focus on my writing," I backtrack. "It's all I ever wanted to do."

Greg breezes through the interview. He asks me questions ranging from "What is your process for learning your client's voice?" to "Can you talk me through your working style?"

"Wale, feel free to jump in," he keeps saying. But Wale doesn't say anything.

"Finally, last question."

Thank God.

"When you were at Bonsai, did you work with any high-profile clients?"

I withhold a hiss of disbelief at the implication: Wale? High profile? Don't make me laugh.

"Err, let's see." I make a show of looking around my room as though I'm rifling through my extensive memory. Clearly, Greg hasn't bothered to check Bonsai's website, otherwise he would know that the only "celeb" they've worked with was a woman whose claim to fame was rapping badly on *Britain's Got Talent.*

"Ooh, funnily enough"—I click my fingers—"I actually worked on a memoir for one of the Teletubbies. Not an actual Teletubby, obviously. The person who did one of the voices."

Greg stares at me, not sure how to react. Wale scratches the side of his nose and stifles a smirk—he knows I'm taking the piss. Somehow, I maintain a straight face.

"Ah, I see," Greg says eventually. "Right, that's all from me. Temi, do you have any questions—"

"No. All good."

Greg glances over to the next square. "Wale?"

There's a taut silence. I can literally taste the tension. Is he going to reveal this for the farce that it is?

Wale strokes the tuft of his beard. "Temi." Hearing my name from his mouth is like a spear in my heart. "Did you"—he fidgets in his chair—"did you watch this season of *The Villa?*"

My nostrils flare.

What he's really asking is, did I see his foolish girl-jumping antics? Did I see him coupled up with Kelechi? Did I see all those times he had his tongue down her throat?

I roll my shoulders. "Not all of it. But enough."

Wale's Adam's apple juts up and down.

Another rigid silence follows. I allow him to see my pain.

"All right, well, we should really shoot off now," interjects Greg, his eyes back on the time again. "We have a few more interviews to do, but we're hoping to make a decision ASAP. I'll be in touch with Mayee as we're ideally looking to have someone start straight away. Thanks for your time."

"Likewise," I say.

Wale has the bloody nerve to say, "Good seeing you, Temi."

I click the button to leave the meeting.

Because it was not good seeing Wale. It was pure hell.

5

Immediately, I dial Shona's number. She doesn't pick up so I leave a voice note.

"I'll be at yours around seven," I say, finishing. I wince at the eight-minute time stamp.

My unexpected run-in with Wale has left me with no desire to continue job hunting, and I'm having an even harder time working on *Love Drive*. Eventually, after several glances at my phone, I give in to my urges and do the unthinkable.

700,000 followers!

Shit, that's a lot. Before Wale went on the show, he barely had 300. And that was only just over two months ago.

A weird feeling washes over me. The last time I checked his Instagram—which was just before he went on the show—he had deleted all but one of his photos, including the few images of us. Now his grid is filled with stills from his time on *The Villa* and photos of him promoting something: whitening toothpaste, safe sex, himself.

I click on a selfie he's taken in what looks like a hotel bathroom, which has already garnered thousands of likes. Below are a flurry of heart-eye emojis and thirsty comments:

jasminepilates Why are you so sexy, though? 😍

Wale's never been that much into social media; I wonder how he'll get on as an "influencer."

Ignoring my conscience, I continue to swipe through his photos.

He's having a fresh start. Building a new life.

A new life without me, I can't help but think.

My eyes sting but, like a horror movie, I can't stop looking.

Ten months ago... October

"How's the edits going, babe?" Shona pops her gum and glances over at my laptop, her long, blue braids swaying with each move.

I flick through my printed-out manuscript lying on the table. "Do you know what? I'm actually enjoying it."

We're sitting in a small café inside a bookshop in Camberwell. I stumbled across Anansi Books after I googled "cozy places to write in south London." Now that I'm on the brink of becoming a published author, I feel the need to act like one. Hence the Zadie Smith–inspired head wrap and Keisha (my most intellectual-looking glasses).

I continue to type. "How's your stuff going?"

Shona works as an event coordinator for a big company that puts on music festivals. But as her side hustle, she organizes parties, weddings, showers, you name it. We met at uni at an African and Caribbean Society cookout on one of the rare occasions I ventured outside of my room. (Obviously, she was the ACS social exec.) We instantly clicked, connecting over our love for manicures and our struggle to buy hair outside of London. Having attended a white-majority private school nearly all my life, it was nice to finally have a friend who looked like me.

I peer at her phone. She's supposed to be updating her business budget. Instead, she's watching a TikTok skin-care hack.

"What? A girl can't take a break?" She puts her earpods back in.

Mulling over Mayee's editorial notes, I turn to the window—the pavement a patchwork quilt of orange and yellow leaves matted together from yesterday's rain. A reflection catches my attention. I turn my head. An insanely hot guy has just walked in.

Wow.

Fresh trim, full beard, very fit bod. *And* he has thick eyebrows. God, I love a man with thick eyebrows. I also love what he's wearing: body-tight silver-gray Under Armour athleisure, which is doing an incredible job of highlighting all those muscles.

He makes a beeline to the till.

I type frantically—**HOT GUY ALERT!**—then give Shona a repeated nudge.

Shona pauses her video and leans over to glance at what I've written. She thins her lips as if to say, "Let me be the judge of that," and then, with no subtlety whatsoever, she stares right at him.

"He aight," she says eventually while I nearly combust in my chair. "Personally, he's not my type. Too much of a pretty boy."

She would say that.

Shona has been out of the dating game for some time now. After she found out that her boyfriend was sexting another girl, she has developed a major distrust for the male species. It happened three years ago, during our first year at uni. We're now both twenty-two. Since then, Shona has been a loyal member of the "I don't need a man" club. But I know her tentativeness toward men is also connected to her relationship—or lack thereof—with her dad. He left when she was thirteen and she hasn't seen him since.

I'm pretending to type when I brave another glance. Hot Guy has just bought himself a drink and is scanning the room for somewhere to sit—naturally, I have a look too. Every single table is occupied.

I genuinely want to cry.

Now he's making his way toward the exit, which is just beyond where Shona and I are sitting. As he approaches, my nose fills with the scent of luxurious-smelling oud. It takes everything I have not to look up at him as he passes, but I have to play it cool.

"Mind if I sit?"

My head snaps up. For a second I'm starstruck. Not only is he even better looking up close, but he's got a sexy, deep voice to match.

"Go for it," Shona says to him, saving me from looking like a mute. I scrabble our belongings out of the way.

"Thanks." The bass of his voice is a low rumble in my belly.

I catch sight of an abstract inked pattern just above his wrist when he slides his rucksack off and places it on the floor. He reaches for the chair opposite mine; I repeatedly hit my knee against Shona's under the table.

Still pretending to work, I watch him. He sets his hot drink down and leans over, pulling out his laptop. He places it on the table, flips it open—and promptly knocks his drink over, spilling it everywhere.

"Oh, shit! My bad!" He picks up the cup and grabs a stash of napkins, dabbing them over my manuscript, apologizing profusely.

"Don't worry, it's okay." Weirdly, he's even more endearing after that blunder.

With a wry smile, he takes out his Beats headphones. "Sorry about that," he says again as he's about to put them on.

Go on, Temi. Say something.

"Why's your latte green?"

I've never been great at thinking on the spot.

He lowers his headphones, glances down at the damp stains and then at me. "I take it you haven't tried pistachio hot chocolate before?"

He has a great south London accent, like he should have his own podcast. I like it. A lot.

"It's my first time hearing of it," I reply, stopping myself from full-on grinning. "To be honest, I'm not even sure if I remember what pistachios taste like."

Hot Guy's thick brows go up as if I've just told him I've never eaten cheese-and-onion crisps before. "You're taking the mickey, right?" he says.

I laugh. "Seriously. I find them odd to eat. All that cracking and peeling."

He guffaws—a rich, hearty sound. I feel a sense of achievement. "See," he says, his dark eyes flickering down to my hands, "it's those long nails of yours."

My cheeks warm. I can't look at his face. Instead, I glance down at my Halloween-inspired manicure: almond-shaped, pumpkin-orange shellacs with a different ghoulish expression on each.

"They're real, you know," I say with true enthusiasm. As if I'm wearing an engagement ring, I wiggle my fingers. Beside me, Shona looks up from her phone and glances between us.

"Oh, swear down?" he says, sounding genuinely impressed.

My skin fizzes with electricity as his fingers briefly touch mine.

"Yeahhh, you've got nice nails, still." There's a boyish glint in his eyes as they return to meet mine. "Lemme guess, collagen supplements, right?"

I jerk my head in mock offense. "Supplements? Not even. I have good genes. *Obviously.*"

"I need to make a call." Shona rises to her feet and takes off. Truthfully, I'm too engrossed in the moment to know whether she departed with a knowing look or has suddenly gotten the ick.

Hot Guy nods at his drink. "No, seriously, you should try it someday."

"How about you buy me one?" I surprise myself and him with my forwardness. "After all, you did spill your drink on my manuscript."

I admire his straight white teeth as he belts out his lovely laugh. Perfection. "Aw, c'mon, man. It was barely a tablespoon—"

"Mate, it was a whole pint glass!"

He tilts his head and gives me an "Are you for real?" look. "Let's meet in the middle," he says. "A ladle. And hold up, you said the word 'manuscript.' Are you writing a book?"

I flash him a full megawatt grin.

For the next ten minutes, I tell Hot Guy all about *Wildest Dreams* and how I'm on the verge of getting it published. I'm not sure if he is fascinated by me or the entire process but his eyes are sparkly and locked on my face.

"Then once I've finished with my edits," I say, cautious that I'm talking too much, "my agent will submit it to a number of publishers."

Hot Guy leans back in his chair as though mighty impressed, his top taut against his broad chest. "Wow. Good genes *and* smart."

I fight back a smile.

"And what are *you* up to?" I nod to his laptop while trying to keep my cool.

"Oh, me?" He bats a hand. "Nothing as exciting . . . Work," he finally says after I stare at him with raised eyebrows. "I know, I know. On a Saturday."

"Hmm. Let me guess, you work in the private sector, don't you?"

He hisses. "Far from."

"Yeah, you don't look like you have an office job." Sinking back in my chair, I squint at him. "Are you a content creator?"

"A charity worker," he relents eventually. "I work for a charity."

"Oh, cool," I say, nodding. "Which one?"

He rubs the back of his neck. "You won't have heard of it," he says. "It's local. They're called ACE. We provide support for carers."

I tilt my head in admiration. "Wow, that must be really rewarding."

He gives me an adorable shy smile.

"And your role there is . . . ?"

"Fundraising officer," he replies, more confidently this time. "I look for ways to make the charity money. Basically, I organize events and pester people. Don't worry, I'm not going to guilt trip you for a donation."

"You like it?"

He nods profusely. "I do, actually. Just wish they paid me more."

There's a comfortable silence as Hot Guy takes the lid off the cup. I notice his fingernails. Of course, they're neat.

"So, what made you think I was a content creator, then?" He blows over his drink only to set it back down again.

I shrug. "I dunno. Maybe 'cause you look like one."

He makes a sound of disbelief. Then his brows knead together in genuine curiosity—*hot*. "Elaborate," he says.

"C'mon, you've seen yourself in the mirror. I'm not going to sit here and stroke your ego."

"Nah, nah, nah. I'm not fishing for compliments, but thank you." If my eyes could reach the ceiling. "It's just"—he exhales—"I get that a lot."

"What? You looking like a social media influencer?"

He shakes his head. "Me always looking like *something*. If I'm not a bad boy then I'm an F-boy. And if I'm not an F-boy then I'm a party boy. *Sheeit*, I've even been told that I look like a cheater."

I open my mouth only to close it again. I need to be tactful with what I say next.

"It's your eyes," I say finally after staring at him. "They make you look pretty."

He barks a short laugh. "Wooow, so now I'm a pretty boy, yeah?"

"It's not a bad thing. Take the compliment."

"And wait, how does that make me a cheater?" he counters. "You're a pretty girl, no? Are you saying *you're* a cheater?"

I reach for my water bottle before my budding smile becomes gawky. I take a sip. "The rules are different for women."

He makes a *pfft* sound.

"It's true! I didn't make them. You have men to thank for that. And the way some girls think hot guys—I mean, pretty boys—are cheaters, is the same way some men assume that attractive women have no personality or are complete airheads."

A flurry of thrills runs down my spine as Hot Guy's chocolate eyes bore into mine. "Well, that shit doesn't hold because *you're* writing a book and you need brains for that."

I turn into a puddle.

"I'm Wale, by the way," he says, stretching out a toned arm.

"Temi." I almost forgot my name.

Wale's eyes light up. "Ayeee!" Then in a jovial Nigerian accent, he cries, "My fellow sista!" Then, "My friend, what is your full name?" he adds, committing to the act.

The Re-Write

I'm giggling. "Temiloluwa," I reply, smiling.

Wale jerks his head back with the same exaggeration of a stereotypical Nigerian uncle. "You mean, Tè-mi-lo-lú-wa," he corrects me, emphasizing each syllable as though he's playing a xylophone.

I roll my eyes. "Whatever, O-lu-wa-le." I attempt the same enunciation but I sound more like Hugh Grant.

"My full name is Adewale, actually. But nice try."

I'm about to ask him whether he has visited Nigeria before when I'm distracted by a loud male voice to my left.

"Aight, cool. Your loss," says a man walking right behind Shona, his eyes on her bum.

Shona holds on to her "urgh" face all the way to her seat.

"You all right?" I ask her, just as the man responsible for her disgust arrives at our table.

"Yo, you good, bro?" Wale half rises to his feet and greets him with a hug. His friend—by the looks of it—has big, frog-like eyes and he's stocky and broad as if he has an after-hours membership at his gym.

Shona mutters, "Great. They know each other."

I pacify her with a hand on her shoulder. "Wale, this is my friend, Shona."

Wale says, "Nice to meet you," then to me, "Temi, this is Kojo."

Kojo looks at me with an inscrutable expression, then claps Wale on the back. "Bruddah, you're always making friends wherever we go, man!"

So, he is a flirt.

Wale laughs. "I'm a positive guy. What can I say? I attract good energy." He smiles at me.

"Yo, Temi." My name sounds foreign coming out of Kojo's mouth. He nods to Shona. "You see your friend here. She's stush, y'know."

Shona flutters her eyes in annoyance.

"Or maybe you just have no game?" I say, tilting my head.

Wale covers his mouth and says, "Ooooh," as if I'm murdering Kojo in a rap battle.

Kojo just stares at me—if looks could kill—and then he turns his whole body toward Wale. "You good to go?"

Wale glances down at his laptop. He has barely started his work. "Bro! You said you'd be an hour!"

"I know, I know. But the gym was rammed, still." Kojo looks around. "Oi, where's your boy?"

"Fonzo's next door, picking a book—no, my bad. There he is."

Jazzy Jeff is the first thing that pops to mind as a tall, slim-built man walks over. He has the same high-top haircut. Same goatee. He's even wearing one of Jazzy Jeff's trademark patterned dashiki shirts. Wale does the introductions. Shona and I say hello.

"What did you get?" Wale nods to the paper bag in Fonzo's hand.

Fonzo pushes up his glasses and pulls out a book with a red cover. "*All About Love* by bell hooks." He grins. "It's been on my TBR for a while."

Kojo grabs the book and reads the back. "You're so moist, man," he hisses.

Fonzo snatches it back. "It's a classic. And for the record, my mum recommended it."

"Fonzo's mum owns the bookshop," says Wale, filling us in.

"Well, your mum has excellent taste." Shona gets in ahead of me. "It's a dope book."

"Oh, yeah?" Fonzo smiles warmly at Shona. Shona gives him a weak smile back.

"Right. Let's bounce." Wale flips his laptop closed, and I feel a pang of disappointment as he shoves it into his rucksack. I want to suggest that we exchange details, but we have an audience.

Instead, I say, "So, where are you guys off to?"

"Westfield Stratford," he replies, stuffing his headphones into his bag. He rises to his feet. To say I feel hopeless as I watch him sling his rucksack over his shoulder is an understatement.

"Ladies"—he pilot salutes—"thanks for kindly sharing your table. Temi..."

My pulse races.

"Good luck with the book, yeah."

My shoulders slacken as I watch him and his friends head toward the exit. *At least I got the name of his employer*, I tell myself. I could try to find him on LinkedIn.

I'm about to do just that when Wale turns and heads back toward me.

Hope rises in my chest and I realize I'm halfway out of my seat.

"Forgot my drink," he says, gesturing at it.

I drop back down.

For the second time, I watch him leave only for him to turn around again. "Actually, you have it." He beckons his cup at me.

"Really? You sure?"

"Yeah, saves me from having to lug it around. Don't worry, I haven't drunk from it yet—it was too hot earlier. But you're gonna have to tell me what you think, though." And with a smile I know I will remember when I look back on this day, he says, "What's your Insta?"

6

"I cannot believe you ran into Wale on that call. I would have *loved* to have seen your face." Using the back of her foot, Shona closes the door behind her, shutting out the loud sounds of her mum and sister speaking in Lingala in the living room. She hands me one of the two bowls of madesu—a popular Congolese dish made with cannellini beans, palm oil, and tomato sauce.

"Honestly, I'm still in shock."

Shona lifts the back of her long purple braids before lowering herself gently onto her bed. She pulls them over one shoulder. Her room is small but cozy. It's full of plants, candles, and wall memorabilia from the music events she's helped organize: crumpled-up tickets, wristbands, stickers, and photographs.

"Is it bad that I wish I was more made-up?" I take a big inhale of the madesu's different spices. "By the way, this smells divine."

"Can't take any credit," she says. "All Mumsy. And no. Every girl wants to see their ex when they're looking like a baddie. But you, my friend, are lucky. You have great skin." With a wink, she blows over her spoon and I give her a faint smile. "So, how you feeling?"

Words can't even describe.

"I feel . . ." I push air through pursed lips. "And I literally saw him on TV yesterday! You were right, Shon. He got roasted on the reunion. The women he played were not having it."

"And rightly so!" Shona cries. "Look, he deserves every smoke for ending things the way he did. You been on The Tea Lounge recently? He's catching heat there as well."

I pull out my phone and jump straight to The Tea Lounge: the go-to Instagram page for daily celebrity news—well, for many Black Brits. And I use the word "news" lightly here, as the page is basically just an accumulation of pictures, tweets, and Insta Stories that the bloggers behind the account repost with the aim of getting a reaction from as many people as humanly possible.

My eyes are instantly drawn to a still.

> **THE VILLA STAR WALE PARTNERS WITH CARERS CHARITY TO HOST GALA**

Okay, this was not the controversial post I was expecting.

Underneath the headline is Wale's cast member photo from *The Villa*. He's standing in front of a bubblegum-pink backdrop in blue beach shorts with his bottom lip sucked in—I think he was attempting a sexy smile. He's also topless . . . *Unhelpful.*

I swipe to the next pic—a screenshot taken from Wale's Instagram Story . . . posted three days ago, it seems. He has his arm draped over a friendly-looking, middle-aged woman with straw-blond hair and lots of gold rings.

> **ECSTATIC TO ANNOUNCE THAT I'LL BE PARTNERING WITH ACE TO ORGANIZE THEIR FIRST CHARITY FUNDRAISING GALA ON 21ST SEPTEMBER!**

I hiss. Seriously, this guy is doing anything to salvage his reputation! First his memoir, now this! I scroll down and skim the comments—a never-ending stream of people not afraid to express their opinions. There is clearly a divide between those who are outraged at his girl-hopping antics and those who see his character on the show as just pure entertainment.

davethedon This guy carried this year's season on his back!

pattycakestrina Boy, bye! You're clearly only doing this to save face! #WaleIsTrash #JusticeForKelechi

ruthiep The most iconic Love Villa contestant ever 🔥

lexijordan08 For charity?! LMAO 😂😂😂 Like "mental health," charity is the new buzzword (rolls eyes)

I scroll and scroll and scroll. Many are not buying his altruism, even though Wale has been affiliated with ACE charity since before he went on the show. It's weird seeing complete strangers tear apart the person you once loved. I wonder how his new fame is affecting his mental health, affecting his family. Despite everything, I really do hope he's doing okay.

"Quick question." Shona pulls me out of my thoughts. She scrapes her spoon into her bowl and pops it into her mouth. She makes a loud sucking sound. "Do you think it was purely coincidental? You bumping into Wale?"

"Go on."

She puts her bowl down and then tugs on one of the drawstrings of her leopard-print hoodie. "Think about it," she says. "Wale *knows* you write. He knows you have ghostwriting experience. He knows who your agent is."

"So, what are you trying to suggest? That he recommended me? Mayee said she put my name forward . . ."

She shrugs. "Yeah, but maybe he told his agent to approach your agent." She pinches her bottom lip with her fingers and then, after a short ponder, she says, "Do you think he's trying to reconnect?"

I belly laugh. She clearly doesn't know Wale as well as I do. "Wale wouldn't do that," I say with absolute certainty. "The man struggles to have conversations where he's forced to be direct about his feelings. Besides, he had no way of knowing that I would even go for it."

"True." Suddenly, Shona bursts into a fit of giggles. "Oh gosh. What if you *do* get the job? Would you take it? Twenty K is a lot of money."

I stare at her square in the eye. "I am *not* getting that job. I don't even have enough experience. And please, why would Wale want to work with me? The same person he said he couldn't trust?"

The memory of our breakup sends me into a quiet mull. Shona doesn't notice—she's pouring her glass of water into the soil of a peace lily. Shona is a dedicated plant mum.

"No offense, hun," she says, moving on to water what looks like a mini palm tree. "But you really know how to pick them. Between Seth and Wale, I don't know who's worse."

I met Seth when I was fourteen; he was seventeen. We dated for about a year. On the low.

When we moved to Orpington, a suburb in Greater London, my parents sent me to Jeffrey Moore—an independent private school. I was the only Black girl in my year group. And since I didn't want to be known as "that fat Black girl," I decided that every day I would wear a different pair of glasses. I wore thick ones, sparkly ones, multicolored ones, smart ones. I much preferred to be known as "that glasses girl."

And one day, it actually worked. I was waiting at the bus stop when a familiar-looking boy with a Jack-from-*Titanic*-inspired haircut tapped me on my shoulder.

"Oi, I know you," he said animatedly. "You're that girl who changes her glasses all the time. You go to Jeffrey Moore."

For the first time in a long time, I felt seen.

I don't know how Seth and I went from exchanging small smiles when we crossed each other in the corridors to hooking up in his tinted-window sports car after school, but things between us progressed quickly. Because of my age, Seth told me we had to keep our relationship a secret. As far as his parents were concerned, he was my math tutor. It was the only lie he could think of that would allow us to spend some time together at his house.

From very early on, I noticed that Seth's parents acted off around me. They gave me tight smiles and promptly fluffed their cushions anytime I got up. Whenever Seth offered me some biscuits, they watched me as if they were counting how many I took, and they were visibly surprised when they heard that I didn't attend Jeffrey Moore on scholarship.

Anytime one of these subtle incidents would happen, I would lock eyes with Seth, hoping he would do something about it—if not in front of his parents, at least in private. But he never spoke up. It was like he was completely oblivious.

Then one afternoon, as I walked round the back to come in, I overheard Seth and his parents in the garden. They were concerned about how many hours he was spending tutoring me—after all, I wasn't paying him.

"She's not your girlfriend, is she?" said his mum, as if the very possibility was horrific.

Seth couldn't reply fast enough. "What?! Hell no! Who do you take me for? Look, she doesn't have that many friends at school. I feel sorry for the girl, okay."

To this day, I wish I had burst through the gate. I wish I had told Seth and his parents what I really thought of them. That they were rude, snobby, fat-phobic *racists*—yeah, that would have really got them clutching their pearls.

Instead, I retreated from the gate and cried all the way home.

Later that evening, I dumped Seth over the phone. Apparently, he panicked when his parents came close to the truth. He was blindsided; he didn't know how to react or what to say. He apologized; said he was a knobhead but agreed that it was best we go our separate ways. After all, once summer was over, he would be off to uni.

For a long time after our breakup, I struggled to connect the Seth I thought I knew to the Seth in the garden. Did he really keep our relationship a secret because of my age or was it because of what I looked like? It's been roughly seven years, and still, I haven't gotten over the trauma.

"C'mon, Shona. Wale wasn't all bad." I shove my thoughts of Seth into a dusty corner. "Hey! You even said you liked the guy, remember? And he was thoughtful. Funny. Encouraging."

"Yeah, I guess he did support you loads with your writing. Oh—" Her face softens. "I'm so sorry about . . . you know."

The sudden reminder of *Wildest Dreams* brings up the gut-wrenching sting of rejection that I've been trying so hard not to relive, to the point where seeing Wale again was a welcome distraction. But Shona is looking at me kindly, and I can feel the tears start to well. Heart burning, I focus on shoveling food into my mouth, my eyes fixed firmly on my bowl. But the more spoonfuls I take, the more fragile I become. Eventually, I crumble.

"Ohhh, hun." Shona scooches closer and thrusts an arm over me.

"I'm sorry," I say between snuffles. "It's just . . . so shit. I worked bloody hard on that book."

"I know." She tilts her head against mine, rubs small circles on my back and tells me everything will be okay.

"And if worse comes to worst," she adds, her thumb brushing away a stray tear, "you can always send Mayee your other book."

I frown before realizing what she's talking about. "Now *that*," I say with a laugh, "would be *the* ultimate payback."

7

```
Love_Drive_Draft1.doc
Target word count: 1,000
Current word count: 1,265
Four weeks to go . . .
```

"This is sooo bad."

It's a new day and I can barely read over what I've spent the last five hours writing. Actually, three hours if you minus the time I've spent intermittently looking for a job, checking my emails to see whether I've received any updates on the applications I submitted yesterday (I have not), and reading the comments under Wale's Instagram photos (he has his fair share of haters, but people still thirst).

I've worked out that if I manage to write 1,000 words per day, in four weeks' time I should have racked up just under 30,000, which, hopefully, should be enough to appease Mayee. My plan is simple: write whatever comes to mind but with the speed of a coke addict. Lucky for me, I've never been one of those writers who are hell bent on having their story all mapped out before they can start. Neither have I been one of those writers who spend copious hours drafting up ten-page bios on every single bit-part character. No, when I write I'm a loose cannon. Anything is up for grabs. I become that manic shopper who enters Tesco minutes before it's about to close and hauls practically anything into their trolley. The goal is to reach the till and pay before the security guards get all huffy. The goal *here* is to Get. The. Story. Down.

But like most things you do in a frenzy, you end up having a few regrets. You realize, as you unpack, that although you conveniently picked up some butter, you did not pick up any toilet roll—the very thing that made you do a late dash in the first place. And although you have a month's supply of milk, you, unfortunately, do not have the fridge space for it. Gradually, as the adrenaline wears off, you think, *Hmm, maybe I should have thought this through.*

That is exactly what I'm experiencing as I read over my work. I actually feel like I'm on a comedown.

Thanks to giving the wacky side of my brain free rein, I've managed to write a chapter as outlandish as a fever dream, where anything and everything happens. In this chapter, there's a minor car accident, a limping turkey, and a young, handsome stunt driver who used to be a race car champion.

I rake my hair vigorously. I know my draft doesn't need to be perfect—after all, it is a draft—but I can't stomach the thought of Mayee reading it and thinking this is all I've got to show for the last several months.

Maybe Shona was onto something. Maybe I *should* send Mayee *The Ultimate Payback*.

I scour the many thumbnails on my desktop before finally locating the manuscript. I'm seconds from clicking the document open when I'm distracted by a PowerPoint thumbnail titled "Vision board." Gosh, I haven't looked at that in months.

This is going to hurt, but I can't help myself. I open the PowerPoint.

Pictures. Loads of them. There's an image of a Waterstones, a Barnes & Noble, Ocean Books' logo. There's a picture of my dream dress—the one I visualize myself wearing to my jam-packed book launch event. There's also a photo of my parents from my graduation day; the proudest I've seen them. And right at the very top of the page is an affirmation I wrote to myself: *My name is Temiloluwa Ojo and I'm an author.*

There's a gnawing ache in the pit of my stomach.

I only get one chance to be a debut, so if I'm going to publish a book, I want it to be about something that I'm passionate about, not a hastily written treatise about my ex. *The Ultimate Payback* was born out of anger. I want to spread love through my writing. Granted, I'm not crazy about *Love Drive* but who's to say that passion won't come in time? And, who knows, perhaps a story involving a car accident, a limping turkey, and a stunt driver slash former race car champion who later becomes my protagonist's love interest would turn out to make a genius novel? For now, I just have to sit in the discomfort of my word puke and celebrate having achieved my word-count target for today.

8

```
Love_Drive_Draft1.doc
Word count update: 2,532
```

I snatch my giant-size bag of Doritos and throw a handful into my mouth, my writing Spotify playlist still playing in the background.

Dad flashes on my phone.

I tut. I forgot we were catching up today.

With a grunt, I deposit the chips back into the bag and dust off my fingers.

"Hi, Mum. Hi, Dad." I raise my phone in front of my face.

They're sitting side by side on the sofa. Mum is wearing an understated designer shirt while Dad is neatening the collar of his polo as if he's at an interview. Judging by the angle, they've propped his phone up against something on the coffee table.

"So. How's things?" Dad says.

"Things are good," I shrill. "No complaints. How's things with you?"

Mum runs her own optician's—hence my insane collection—while Dad is a senior director at John Lewis—one of the UK's largest retailers. Given what they do for a living, they are never short on things to chat about, though Dad is more of a talker. For the first time ever, I'm grateful for this. In his usual elaborate manner, he tells me about his department's latest strategy—something about SEOs and algorithms. Honestly, it goes over my head. Mum is more interested in talking about the garden. She insists I try her zucchini the next time I visit.

I do my best to keep the conversation going. As soon as I sense their answer is drawing to an end, I follow it up with another question, a verbal tennis match. Unfortunately, Mum sees through my sudden interest in gardening.

"Temi, we didn't call to talk about ourselves," she says, cutting in. "How are *you*? Shifted any tissue this week? . . . Oh, I'm only playing," she adds after wrongly reading into my silence.

"Weren't you catching up with your agent?" Dad says.

"Ohhh. *That*." During our last catch-up, I had—reluctantly—told my parents about the meeting in an effort to show them that *something* was happening. I throw in a small laugh. "In the end, it was just a light check-in."

Guilt digs into my skin like fangs. I hate lying.

"Buuut," I carry on gingerly, "she also said that while we wait to hear back from publishers, it's better to concentrate my efforts on writing a second book."

"I've been telling you that, haven't I?" Dad can't get his words out fast enough. "You have your plan A and you have your plan B."

I snatch my glass in irritation. But somehow it slips out of my hand and water spills everywhere.

Fuck!

I turn my camera off and set it down on my desk.

"You come up with anything yet?" Mum says, not the least phased by my disappearance.

I want to cry. The water has seeped into my keys.

I reach for my towel and mop it against my laptop furiously. "Jeez, Mum. It's only been two days."

"All right. She was only asking."

Dad's right. "Sorry."

"But you're okay, otherwise?" Mum is eyeing me tentatively. "You're not stressing about it? You eating?"

My eyes pan to my bag of Doritos. "Yes."

The Re-Write

"On the topic of food," Dad says brightly, "keep Sunday the eighth of September free. We're hosting a celebration lunch."

"For what?"

"For Rosemary—Anu's daughter," Mum says. "She's now a doctor."

Rosemary is a childhood friend. She lived next door, way back when my parents and I used to live in a council estate in New Cross. We also went to the same primary school. Sadly, our friendship pretty much ended after we moved away—my parents were doing well enough in their respective careers to buy a big house and send me to private school. I can't remember when I last saw her—so this should be interesting.

"Anu asked if we could host the dinner at our place," says Dad, adjusting the camera. "Since we have more space."

Last year, my parents bought their dream home in Oxford. It has a massive kitchen, an even bigger garden, and a real fireplace.

"You'll come, won't you?" Mum says as if I have a choice.

"Yeah, course."

We speak a little more, mainly about the news. After my contribution tails off, they take the hint and end the call.

I return to my manuscript. I hope my laptop is okay. I begin to type... *Phew.* Wait. Hold on. The letter "L" isn't working.

A sickly whirlpool forms in my stomach as I test each key in turn. *Pleeease. I really can't afford a new laptop right now.*

I try the letter "N." It doesn't work. Nor does the letter "P."

I slam my laptop shut.

With my head resting in my hands, I stare at my bookshelf, my eyes growing more teary with every blink. I zone in on *The Alchemist* by Paulo Coelho. Like Santiago, I need an omen.

And then my phone buzzes.

I growl. "What do Mum and Dad want now?"

I'm about to let it ring out when I realize it's Mayee. My body rushes with adrenaline. *Deep breath.*

"Hi, Mayee."

"Temi. Sorry to call so late, but do you have a quick sec? I've got some good news for you."

I've been disappointed so many times, but hope rises anyway. *Does Ocean want to buy my book?!*

But then she says, "It's about the ghostwriting gig you interviewed for yesterday," and I deflate like a decompressed air bed. "You've got the job!"

With everything that has happened in the last forty-eight hours, I can barely take this information in. My mouth opens and closes. I don't know what to say.

"Temi, are you still there?"

Dumbstruck, I yank off Briony (my can't-be-arsed glasses). "Sorry. I'm just—*what*? Why me?"

Mayee laughs. "Apparently, Wale insisted you were the one."

My eyes widen. *Hold up, Wale picked me?* Now I'm even more confused.

Clearly unaware that I am in shock, Mayee explains the next steps, something about sending me a contract.

This is definitely the moment when I should tell her that Wale is my ex, but my tongue is stuck to the roof of my mouth.

"As Greg mentioned many times, I'm sure, this project has a tight turnaround, so you'll be starting as soon as the contract is signed—I'll send it over to you now. Wale wants to meet with you tomorrow. Sorry. I haven't even asked. Are you happy to accept?"

Wale is my ex! my inner voice prompts. But all that comes out of my mouth is a long "Ummm."

My eyes trail back to *The Alchemist* on my shelf. *Wait, is this my omen?* The timing seems more than coincidental. I sure as hell need the money, and now a new laptop. And honestly, I would rather not attend Dr. Rosemary's celebration dinner unemployed. Plus, telling my parents that I'm ghostwriting for a celebrity is bound to get a nod of approval—that's if I don't mention it's for a reality TV star, of course.

And so, surprising even myself, I lean back and say, "Yes."

9

It's the following day, and I'm en route to meet with Wale. Ironically, we're meeting at Anansi Books, the place where we first bumped into one another. As the bus crawls toward Camberwell Green, everyone else's life continues as normal.

Acidic gloop bubbles in my stomach as I realize I only have three stops to go, so I take out my phone and put it on selfie mode. Thankfully, the sweltering heat hasn't ruined my makeup (my red lippy still looks fresh) and, unlike last time, my hair is a proper twist-out. Today, I've gone for Giselle: boss-bitch, oversize sunglasses (I'm wearing contacts underneath) and a black ruffle playsuit to match.

Fiddling with my gold, chunky necklace, I try to regulate my breathing. The magnitude of my decision is beginning to dawn on me. For more than a month, I will be working with Wale. If I'm hyperventilating now, heaven knows how I'll survive the next few weeks. And how will I juggle ghostwriting alongside working on my second book? I really didn't think this through. My mind begins to churn . . .

Four months ago . . . April

"Do you really think this is a good idea?" I ask Shona as we clamber out of the Uber.

It's a Friday evening and we're on the way to a house party; the sky is still bright. I can hear the bass of a Kaytranada beat in the near distance, muffled slightly by the sounds of people having a good time. Now that we're here, I feel even more nauseous. I'm tempted to get back in the car.

"Well, technically, we were invited," Shona reminds me, linking her arm into mine. Coincidentally, we are both wearing green, except I have on a shirt dress while she's wearing a crop top and jeans.

"Yeah, but that was before everything blew up." The events from yesterday rush back. "He was so pissed off, Shona. He still is."

It all started when we went out bowling last Friday. At the till, Wale had pulled out his card to pay, as per usual.

"I'm sorry, sir, but the payment hasn't gone through," said the till assistant.

Thinking he had merely entered his PIN wrong, I said, "Your account has insufficient funds," in a robotic Siri voice.

Wale tried again.

The till assistant shook his head.

"What? You serious? That's strange. I just got paid. Hold on, lemme try swiping my card."

Conscious of the line forming behind us, I rummaged for my purse. "Babe, don't worry. I got it." But Wale had already swiped his card down the machine.

Card declined.

After I covered the bill, we were assigned to a bowling alley. En route, Wale apologized profusely and swore he'd pay me back.

"Stop saying sorry. It's cool," I told him with a light chuckle. "Besides, you pay for so much and I'm happy to cover it. I know you want to be a gentleman and all, but I do have a job."

When we reached our alley, I tapped on the screen to set up the game. Wale remained glued to his phone.

"What the—" he said suddenly. He glanced up like a deer caught in headlights. "They haven't paid me, y'know."

I joined him on the bench and put my hand on his shoulder. "You okay?" I kissed his cheek. He leaned into me, putting a hand on my lower back. "Don't worry," I said. "I'm sure it will come through before midnight. C'mon. Let's play."

I don't recall Wale being too hung up about what happened at the till. In fact, he beat my arse at bowling . . . roundly and without grace. Anytime he got a strike, he would do an Afrobeat dance or crouch into a Usain Bolt pose. He also took great pleasure in showing me how to bowl—pressing up behind me and holding the curve of my waist as he guided my swinging arm. He would nibble my ear and blow on my neck to distract me, which descended into some giggly kissing on the hard seats. Thank goodness the lanes were emptying out. But then, once the session ended, he fell quiet.

"You sure you're all right?" I asked again as we headed toward the exit. I hoped he wasn't still upset about what had happened at the till.

"Yeah, yeah. Just feeling mad tired, that's all. Mind if we give dinner a miss?"

The following day, Wale was still acting off. And the day after that. And the day after that. When I called him, his tone didn't sound right but he said he was fine. On Thursday, he made a transfer to my account. *At last, he got paid*, I thought. *We can go back to normal.* But when I called him later that evening, it still felt strange between us—uncomfortable when we were normally so easy with each other.

I became paranoid. I was unable to get the truth out of him so I had no choice but to take matters into my own hands. I couldn't show up at his house. Wale felt as though it was too soon for the whole meet-the-parents thing, even though we had been together for nearly six months. I was disappointed; I couldn't wait to introduce him to mine. But Wale reassured me that it had nothing to do with me. He didn't have a close relationship with his parents. And as someone who has a great relationship with my mum and dad, I could understand why he was hesitant, why the thought of meeting each other's parents made him feel uneasy. It was a massive step he didn't want to be rushed into taking.

And since going to his house was out of the question, I decided to rock up at his football game. He played every Thursday at Burgess Park.

The match was already in full swing: blues against reds, a soggy pitch, a mud-stained ball. Wale, in his usual T-shirt and shorts, was running into position.

"Go, Wale! Woo!" I cheered as I made my way toward the pitch.

He glanced in my direction, doing a double take. Then, with a less-than-enthused expression, he ran over.

"What you doing here?" he hissed, guiding me a few feet away. His tone threw me—it was cold. Harsh, even. It wasn't the first time I'd watched him play. Why did he react like that?

"I've actually come to check in on you," I replied.

He threw a glance over his shoulder. Opposite us, a young Black man linking arms with a frail, older woman was staring. For a fleeting second I wondered whether he was embarrassed—none of the other players' girlfriends were here. But he had introduced me to all of his teammates before; they knew me.

One hollered at him from the pitch.

Wale yelled back, "One sec!" He looked painfully uncomfortable and my patience was starting to thin. Enough was enough.

"Why have you been so off with me lately?"

"Temi, I'm in the middle of a game—"

"And I'm your girlfriend," I countered. "Why are you being so—so weird? Are you angry with me?"

He pursed his lips, mute.

"I knew it—you *are* pissed off. Look, Wale, I'm sorry. It was only a joke. A bad one—"

"A joke? What you chatting about?"

I glanced down and nibbled my lip. "When your card got declined," I began tentatively, "I said, 'Your account has insufficient funds,' in one of those stupid AI voices. That was really lame of me—and people were behind us."

"Oh, yeah," he scoffed. "That was kinda lame. But that's not why I'm pissed off—"

"What, then?!" I was so frustrated my voice hitched up an octave.

Wale swiveled his head to the young man and older woman again. But I didn't care who was watching; I wanted answers.

When he turned back, his face was drawn, his jaw square. It was as though he could no longer recognize the person standing right in front of him, and that hurt. After all, it was only last Monday when he told me he was working late, and I ordered him a large barbecue chicken pizza—his favorite. He told me that I was thoughtful, that he appreciated me, that I would win the award for the best girlfriend ever. And now he was looking at me as if I were a complete stranger.

My throat stung as he peered at me intensely, his eyes unwavering, as if by just staring long enough he could coax a confession.

"Don't you have something you wanna tell me?" he finally said.

I lost it.

"Wale, I'm not going to stand here and play mind games with you, so you might as well just open your damn mouth and tell me."

His expression didn't flicker one bit, but there was something about the way his head drew back a little that made me regret my choice of words instantly.

"C'mon, Wale! We need you!" a teammate called out.

He looked over before dragging his gaze back to me.

"I need to go," he said brusquely, and with that, he ran back to the pitch, leaving me standing there alone.

Over the next few hours, I obsessively replayed our bowling date in my head. Besides the stupid joke, I couldn't come up with anything I had done to hurt him, and when I tried calling him, I kept getting his voicemail. I felt helpless, desperate, but at the same time, I was majorly pissed off. How could I apologize for something I didn't even know I'd done?

And that was how both Shona and I ended up here—inside a bass-filled semidetached house on Clapham Common. Going by Fonzo's Insta Stories, they're definitely around somewhere.

Shona grabs my hand and leads me down the hallway packed with clammy bodies. The place reeks of alcohol and sweat. We poke our heads into each room: in one, people are dancing and chilling; in another, there's a mountain of jackets and bags on a bed. We head upstairs, my mind running through so many possible scenarios that I'm no longer thinking in complete sentences. Shona's walking so fast we nearly pass the door.

"He's there!" I whisper loudly, tugging her back. I can hear Kojo speaking on the other side of the wall. He's telling Wale to stop sulking, that they should go downstairs and chat to some girls—of course he is.

My fingers twitch in Shona's hand. I'm so angry I don't know what to do.

"He's still with Temi," Fonzo says sternly.

I hear a tut.

"Did you not hear him?" It's Kojo again. "The man said, 'He's done.'"

Done? My mouth falls open, my chest tight. *What does he mean by done?* My twitch turns into a violent tremble. Shona squeezes my hand.

"Wale. Talk to her," Fonzo is now saying. "Who knows? Maybe you jumped to conclusions."

Conclusions about what? Suddenly, my heart is jumping out of my chest.

Kojo kisses his teeth. "What's there to talk about? He gave her a chance to say the truth and she blew it. Well, good thing you didn't drop out of *The Villa*, innit."

Shona and I turn to each other, eyes wide. She pulls free from my grasp and enters the room. I have no choice but to follow her.

"What the fuck?!" Shona walks right up to Wale but I hang back by the doorway.

Our appearance takes Wale by surprise and he sits bolt upright at the foot of the bed.

Kojo smirks. "Y'right, Temi?" He gives me a slow nod.

"Wale, is it true?" I ask, my voice breaking. "You're still signed up for the show?"

Two men playing FIFA look over their shoulders before returning to the game.

I wait—the bass of the music reverberates under my feet. Wale can barely meet my gaze. My stomach drops with ice-cold certainty and suddenly I can't bear to be here anymore, in this loud, anonymous party.

Tears building, I run down the corridor toward the stairs. Wale and Shona are calling my name. Somehow, Wale manages to overtake me and he stretches his arms out and blocks the end of the stairwell, his face the picture of fear. This is too much—I can't believe he wants to do this here, of all places.

"Move!" Shona takes my hand.

"Please, Temi. Let me explain." His words tumble out, fast. "I swear on my life, I was gonna drop out—"

"What? When? When you were on the damn show?!" I cry.

Our loud exchange has caused the music to stop. People are openly staring. A few begin to raise their phones, unashamedly recording us. But I'm too heated to care.

"How can you pick a stupid dating show over me?!"

This gets a reaction from the crowd: chuckles, mutterings, more raised phones. Wale pleads with me again. "Please, Temi. Let's talk outside." Oh, *now* he wants a private conversation?

The gravel on the driveway crunches under my sandals as Shona and I power walk away from the house. Wale is jogging to keep up, Fonzo in tow.

"Please, Temi," he says.

My head is scorching hot; I feel as though it's about to explode.

"There's nothing to explain," Shona says in a scathing tone over her shoulder.

I desperately want to get away from him but I also need answers. I tell Shona to give us a minute and Fonzo guides her to the other side of the road. Wale and I are standing just a short distance from the house so the loud music will make it difficult for anyone to overhear us. This is about as private as it will get.

"You lied to me!" I nearly spit at him, I'm so mad.

My heart feels like it's been ripped out of my chest, and yet it is Wale who stands in front of me looking crestfallen and broken. Anguish and guilt ripple across his face.

"Well, go on, then. What do you have to say for yourself?"

"I was going to drop out—"

"Yeah, you've said that already. But you told me that weeks ago. Why didn't you actually do it?"

Wale's silence is loud; his eyes flick to the ground and then past my ear. "I was waiting," he says finally, so low I can barely catch it.

"Waiting for what?"

Wale peers up at the sky, blows air out of his cheeks, then glances back at me again. "I just . . ." He grunts. "I just wanted to see if this thing we have is real. If I could trust you."

A mirthless laugh escapes me. I feel unhinged. "You were waiting to see whether you could trust me? Wow, what is this now? A test?"

Wale doesn't say anything. "Are you *sure* there's nothing you wanna tell—"

"Oh, for goodness' sake, Wale! I'm not doing this again!"

He pushes out his lips and nods slowly as though to say, *Cool*. And then, looking me dead in the eyes, he says, "Why didn't you tell me Seth got in touch?"

Suddenly, everything falls into place and breaks into pieces at the same time. His words knock the air out of my chest. As though I'm reading it from a teleprompter, I recall Seth's message:

> **Seth:**
> So sorry, can we do six instead? Looking forward to seeing you next Monday! X

So, this is what he was angry about.

A few months into our relationship, I opened up to Wale about my ex, hoping he would then open up about his. But in the end, it turned into a therapy session; me spilling my guts into Wale's chest as I curled into him on my sofa. I told him how stupid I felt for secretly dating Seth for as long as I did, and how guilt-ridden I still feel sometimes for not standing up to him and his parents on that day. Wale was perfect. He told me not to beat myself up, that I was so young when it happened, and at least I would never have to see Seth again.

But I did.

A few weeks ago, I bumped into Seth at Waitrose.

I stare back at Wale, speechless. Wale is spiking his brows up as if to say, *So?*

"I can explain." I wince at my lame choice of words, a bubble of panic rising up. Then something hits me. "Wait, how did you—"

"*Know?*" he finishes. "No, I didn't go through your phone if that's what you're thinking. Last Friday, when we went bowling, remember when you told me to take your picture? Well, his message flashed up then. I believe the two of you had made plans to meet, no?"

"It's not what you think." Oh, for flip sake. Not again. "It was a professional meeting. To discuss a job opportunity."

Wale says, "Job opportunity," as if to say, *Sure*.

"And I didn't even go!" I cry in a desperate attempt to redeem myself. "I canceled the meeting. That's why I didn't bother telling you."

Yes, initially, I was torn on whether or not to meet up with Seth, but after talking it through with Shona, I had decided that the "opportunity" wasn't something I could comfortably sacrifice my integrity for. So, in the end, I canceled and told him to delete my number.

The text message! Of course!

I rummage for my phone. "Look"—I tap the screen—"I even have the text to prove it." But I'm in such a hurry, I type the wrong PIN twice.

"You were dishonest, Temi."

I stare up at him. The gall.

"And you weren't?"

Wale cuts his eyes as he glances away. "Well," he says with a sniff, "maybe we're just bad for each other."

My heart thuds. "What do you mean?"

Wale can barely look at me. The pause before he speaks feels life threatening. "I'm not sure how we can come back from this, Temi. I don't trust you."

. . .

For a good week after our breakup, I cried and cried; could barely eat the takeaway that Shona would bring over. In bed, I tossed and turned, and in the morning, I'd wake up feeling like death.

Then the anger came. I felt like a defendant thrown into prison without receiving a fair trial. I didn't know how to cope, to *live*, with this all-consuming, raw emotion.

Until, one night, I woke up, jolted by a crystal-clear thought. Heart hammering, I grabbed my laptop and opened a new document, my fingers fizzing. Without second-guessing myself at all, I typed the title:

```
The Ultimate Payback
By Temiloluwa Ojo
```

From that day on, I channeled my anger into writing.

10

I'm knocked out of my thoughts by a loud whooshing sound. I spring to my feet.

"Driver! Hold the door! Hold the door!"

Off the bus, I retrace my steps from memory, passing by a few local shops before finally reaching Anansi Books. Taking a deep breath, I prop my sunglasses on my head and step inside.

It's as if I've walked into a time machine. Everything is the same—the smell, the floor-to-ceiling pine bookshelves, the giant poster of Anansi the Spider in the children's section. Behind the till, a light-skinned, older woman with voluminous hair flashes me a warm smile. I follow the scent of freshly brewed coffee until I get to the café.

He's there. In the left-hand corner. Sitting with his back toward me—*Thank God*. I take a deep, yogic inhale—*you can do this*—and then, pretending that I'm wearing heels and not flats, I sashay toward him.

"Temi," Wale says, standing.

I pull out the chair opposite and sit down.

We will never again be on hugging terms.

Wale slowly lowers himself back to his seat.

As though we're in court, we stare at each other; my heart breaks with every passing second as I relive our breakup again. Wale thins his lips. He looks . . . sorry. Annoyingly, my brain registers how much hotter he looks. His skin is still tanned and dewy despite being back in the UK for over a month now, and his beard would make even the likes of Drake proud. And how the heck can I still see his muscles through his black shirt?

I hate you, my inner voice says.

And yet, I'm here.

Wale clears his throat. "You look well."

I blink at him pointedly. He's going to have to do better than that.

He shifts. "I got you . . ." He pushes a plastic cup toward me. I catch a whiff of the familiar scent rising from the lid.

Pistachios.

"I wasn't sure if you wanted something to eat—"

"Wale, cut the crap. What the hell are you playing at?"

Wale stares at me, stunned, as if I've physically struck him.

"Why am I here?" I demand. "Is this some sort of sick joke to you?"

His eyes widen. "No, Temi. Course not. Honestly, I'm surprised you took the job."

I suck in a sharp, irritated breath. I, too, can't quite believe it.

"Tems, I'm sorry." He puts out a flat hand in the middle of the table. On his forearm is a tattoo of a jeweled crown and the word "King" scribed underneath it. The sight of it nearly pushes tears to my eyes. I used to love trailing my fingers along each letter. I steel my shoulders and drag my eyes back toward his face. "I'm sorry," he says again, "for how things ended. For not being honest with you. Temi, I feel so bad. We should talk. Whatever you want to say, I'm all ears."

He goes to hold my hand and then stops himself, his eyes and expression an apology letter. For a heart-aching second, I feel myself soften, and then I harden again.

I was ready to have this conversation before we broke up. Before he made a decision about *our* relationship for me. Now that he has made a fool of himself on national TV, he wants to come back with his tail between his legs. Does he not know how painful it was, him leaving like that? How painful it will be for me to relive it? Back then everything was on his terms; now it will be on mine.

"No," I tell him calmly.

Wale looks confused. "No?"

"No," I repeat. "I do not want to talk about it. I don't want to talk about us, not now, not in a few weeks' time, not ever."

Wale blinks. He looks even more confused. "But we're working together—"

"Yeah."

"So, what? We're just going to pretend that we're strangers?"

"No, Wale. We're going to be professional because you hired me."

Wale chews his bottom lip as though he's thinking very carefully about what to say next. It takes more effort than I expect to keep my eyes trained on his.

"Okay," he says simply, taking a sip of his drink. "Whatever you say, boss."

I reach into my bag and pull out my laptop and bottle of water. A coffee machine whirs in the background. After I log in, I open up the document Mayee sent me when she emailed me my contract.

"I've read over your book proposal," I say, cutting straight to it. "The brief is a bit broad, but we can work on that. It says here that the memoir will be told through the voice of a young, attractive Black British man"—I stop myself from rolling my eyes—"and how, throughout his childhood, adult life, and now his appearance on TV, he has been misunderstood. Does this sound right to you?" I glance up at him.

Wale is stroking his beard. "Did it really say I'm attractive?"

Now I can't help myself; I give him the biggest eye roll.

"Oh, come on, Tems." I bristle at the use of my pet name. "I'm just tryna break the ice. We're gonna be working together for six whole weeks. We don't have to be all serious, y'know."

"Well, *I'm* taking this seriously. And it's Temi," I fire back, grabbing the hot drink before hastily putting it down again. "Going back to your memoir . . ." I take a sip from my bottle of water instead. "Do you have a structure in mind? Have you looked at any other celebrity memoirs?"

Wale pulls a grimacing face.

"What?"

"I hate that word," he says. "I definitely don't want it to read like a celebrity memoir." He chuckles to himself. "It's not like I got a long credit sheet, anyway. And I don't want it to be in chronological order either. I want it to be relatable. Introspective."

"So, a reflection on your key experiences?"

Wale's lips curve up slightly. "Yeah, something like that."

"Okay, for ease, how about we start with a simple structure? We divide your memoir into three parts—childhood, adult years, and your appearance on TV—and you tell me in what ways you've been misunderstood, followed by your truth. We can always play around with the order later."

"Sounds good to me."

"Now"—I open a new document and lean back in my seat—"what misconceptions do people have about you?"

Wale looks to one side. "That I like sausages," he says finally, and because I'm not expecting this, I snort loudly.

"It's true!" he cries, laughing. "Okay, when have you seen me eat one before?"

Despite myself, I ponder. He normally had an omelet for breakfast anytime he stayed at mine.

"See," he says after a short while. "Man looks like he eats sausage, innit? Wait—that came out wrong."

I swallow my rising laugh. I forgot how funny he can be without even trying. "Okay, that's good to know but it's not exactly what I'm looking for. C'mon, expand your thinking. What labels have people put on you? This is your opportunity to set the record straight. I know. Let's start with the easiest section first—your appearance on TV."

Wale's face goes serious. "That I'm a bad boy. An F-boy."

A flash of déjà vu. He said this when we first met. Back then, I felt for him. But now, I feel appropriately avenged.

"Anything else?" I say, typing his answer.

"That I'm cold. That I can easily detach my feelings."

I maintain a neutral expression as scenes of the week leading up to our breakup replay like a show reel in my head. Wale, however, is telepathic.

"You think I'm cold, don't you?" he says.

I focus on typing. "We're not speaking about our past, remember?" And then I tut.

"Wassup?"

"Nothing. It's just that I spilled water on my laptop yesterday. Keys are being temperamental. Anything else?"

Wale comes up with a list of misconceptions people have had about him during his childhood and adult years. I'm surprised at how open he's being. I thought working with him would be like pulling teeth. Well, I guess things are different now. His reputation is on the line and since he cannot wipe all the things said about him on the internet, he wants to replace them with something else. After a few minutes, I read what we have.

"Number three: people assume that I'm the popular kid. Number four: that I don't have a sensitive side. Five: we've agreed to include something about your career. Anything else people assume about you?"

"That I'm scared to love."

His words suck the air out of my lungs. I stare back at him with parted lips, my heart unusually fast.

I will never forget that evening at my flat when I told him I was falling for him. He never did say it back. And even though he told me he's a man of action and that he prefers to show someone how much he cares about them, there's nothing quite like hearing the guy you're head over heels for say he's falling too. Is Wale now trying to insinuate that he loved me? If he is, it's too late; and it didn't look as though he was thinking of me while he was on the show.

"Okay, I think I have enough to start with," I say, breaking eye contact, my mouth suddenly dry. We've barely scratched the surface but my brain can't think straight.

I'm jotting down some notes to myself when Wale asks, "So, what's new with you? How's the book going?"

I avoid looking at him by typing nonsense words.

Pants. Garbage.

"Same ol'," I say. I press the backspace button. "And how's life as an influencer? You're getting dragged on The Tea Lounge, you know?"

Suddenly, Wale goes from looking pretty normal to looking sullen and vulnerable. He rubs his lips and holds his drink between his palms. I feel a tinge of guilt. I could have been more sensitive.

"My therapist advised me to stay away from the blogs."

My brows arch up. "Wait, you're doing therapy?"

Wale nods. "Part of the show's aftercare. Mandatory." Then he gives me a boyish smile and says, "Serves me right for going on a reality show." He lets out a laugh, but I can see the hurt underneath.

I'm about to ask him whether therapy is helping, when Wale says, "So, what's next?"

I regain focus. "Well, I'm going to need some supporting material from you. So, videos, journals, voice notes—anything that you think will be helpful for me to get in your head. I know you're a busy man now, but we'll also need to have regular catch-ups. And by regular, I mean like every day. It can either be in-person or over the phone."

"Cool, cool. No problem."

"Oh, and of course, I'll need to interview a few people. The ones who know the real you. Do you have any names in mind?"

The first person who rolls off his tongue is his former manager, Kathy McGiffin, CEO of ACE.

"She's Mother Teresa," he says.

Next, he mentions his childhood friend, Fonzo. And then, Aunty Shirley and Uncle Les (Fonzo's mum and dad). They are practically his second parents.

"How about your family?" I ask tentatively. "Your mum? Your dad? Ayo?"

I sense a discomfort from Wale as he glances away. "My dad wasn't too happy with me going on the show. My mum's got too much on her plate," he replies in a matter-of-fact tone. "Ayo's in Australia, so finding a time would be difficult but you can try. However, I warn you. My younger brother is notoriously hard to get hold of. Too busy living his best life." He chuckles. "Obviously, you'd want to interview Kojo," he says, taking a sip.

My entire body stiffens.

"If there's time," I say flatly.

Wale looks at me as if to say, *C'mon, he's not that bad.*

No, he's worse, I want to say. One day, he'll find out on his own.

I glance at the time—gosh, has it been an hour already? "Okay, I think we have enough for now. Please send me their details." And because I'm mindful that I need to work on *Love Drive*, I add, "I have to get going."

I'm packing my things away when Wale says, "I didn't answer your question earlier."

"What question?" I ask, frowning.

"Why you're here," he says. "Don't you want to know why I chose you?"

Shona's theory comes to mind. *Do you think he's trying to reconnect?* I shove it away.

"Go on, then," I say with a sniff.

Wale continues to stare at me, his eyes steady and assertive. Something close to what feels like a shiver runs down my spine.

"It was a no-brainer," he eventually says. "One, you're talented. Two, you already know me, so that's half the job done. Three, as much as you may think I'm a dickhead, I know you'll give this project one hundred percent. And I need that, that passion. Because despite what Greg said, this book is not just about me. It's bigger than that. Temi, my dad thinks I've brought shame to the family." My heart cracks. "Not to mention, there's all the shitty stuff they've written about me on the internet," he carries on bitterly. "You think I want my future kids to read that?" He sighs deeply. "Temi, it's hard enough being a Black man but the last thing I need is to be a stereotype. So, to put it simply, I chose you because I need you."

The passion in his voice melts me. I can barely get my mouth to move.

He chose you because he needs you, my inner voice reprimands me. *Not because he wants you. Focus on the job, Temi.*

I clear my throat. "I'll do my best." And despite myself, I add, "Promise."

11

```
Love_Drive_Draft1.doc
Target word count: 3,000
Current word count: 2,911
```

After our meeting, Wale introduces me to Aunty Shirley. She was the woman who smiled at me from behind the till when I arrived. I connect the dots—she's *Fonzo's* mum. I remember Wale telling me she owned Anansi Books when we first met. Aunty Shirley suggests that I interview both her and her husband the following day in the staff room of his barbershop.

Later that evening, I write a list of questions for Aunty Shirley and Uncle Les. Given Wale grew up with them, it makes sense for me to ask them about his childhood. I order a few memoirs by young, popular influencers for inspiration too. Then, before I get too tired, I set a timer on my phone for two hours. I work on *Love Drive*, forcing myself to string sentences onto the page, no matter how terrible they are. I'm a bundle of emotions; my mind is unsettled. I feel panicky knowing how much work I have to do. And I feel physically sick whenever I remember that I'm also writing Wale's memoir on top. I get so hot that my body breaks out in beads of sweat and I have to stick my head out of the window to gulp some fresh air. I'm so annoyed at myself. This could have been avoided if I'd started working on *Love Drive* months ago. And I can't stop replaying my meeting with Wale in my head. The way he looked at me when he said, "*That I'm scared to love*," made me feel as if I were being cut open, exposed. I wish I had broken eye contact sooner. I wish I never held it in the first place. I also wish he was less attractive than he is. He is frustratingly distracting.

The following day, I make my way to Camberwell Green—I have a feeling I'll be here a lot. I'm following the blue dot on Google Maps until I reach a shop called Crown, its front window plastered with posters of Black male celebrities such as Denzel Washington and Jamie Foxx. The door is open. I can hear lively chatter over the backdrop of the buzzing clippers and a football match playing on the TV.

I step inside.

I'm met with stares.

"Yuh all right, darling?" says an older man, holding down a customer's ear as he shaves the hair above it. He has black skin tags under his eyes and a flat cap.

I'm about to tell him that I'm looking for Wale when the man himself appears from behind a door marked "Toilet." His athleisure is so tight, he might as well be Black Panther.

"Ayee! Temi!" he says, striding toward me. He stretches out his arms. I stretch out a hand.

"Thanks so much for inviting me." I offer him a handshake with a look that says, *We're not there*.

The barber I spoke to turns to me. "Ahh, so you must be the ghostwriter."

Wale introduces me to Uncle Les, who then tells another barber to take over cutting his customer's hair.

"Shirl's at the back," he says, brushing his hands clean. "Come, come."

When we enter the staff room—a tiny kitchen with a round table and a few chairs—Aunty Shirley is browsing on her phone, her glasses on the end of her nose.

She greets me with a hug. "Hello, sweetheart. I see you found the place okay."

While Uncle Les puts the kettle to boil, I pull out my laptop and phone, reiterating what Wale's memoir is about. Uncle Les places four cups of tea on the table. We all take a seat.

"I still don't know why you went on that stupid show," says Aunty Shirley to Wale, who slumps his head down as though he's being scolded.

Uncle Les smirks. "Shirl, leave the boy. He's young. He wanted to find himself a girlfriend."

"What, by going on TV?" Aunty Shirley sounds incredulous. "Wale, mi tell you plenty of times there's plenty of nice girls at my church." This gets another head loll from Wale. "And weren't you seeing a girl before you left?"

Wale and I trade glances, then quickly look away.

"Err, was I?" He deliberately scratches his head and laughs.

I resist the urge to say something snarky like, "She dodged a bullet."

Aunty Shirley, clearly not one for BS, sits forward and glares at him over her glasses. "Wale, I may look young but I wasn't born yesterday! Mi know a spring inna man's step when mi see it."

"Ahh, now that explains the weekly haircuts." Uncle Les laughs. "So, wah happen wit the girl, hmm? It never work out?"

Wale jumps to his feet as though his pants suddenly caught on fire. "Right. Anyone here want anything from the shop? No? Cool." He claps. "Temi, I'mma leave you to it."

He rushes out the door.

Aunty Shirley sips her tea. "The boy lie."

. . .

It's been nearly an hour since we started the interview, and I've only made it to question one: tell me about your relationship with Wale. Let's just say, Aunty Shirley and Uncle Les are good talkers. They have known Wale since he was a kid—he has been best friends with their son, Fonzo, since nursery. After school, Wale and his brother would hang out and do their homework at the bookshop. Uncle Les and Aunty

Shirley shared funny anecdotes, such as how they would often get into Nigeria versus Jamaica debates. The one on how to pronounce plantain (or plan*tin* as they call it) is still ongoing.

"And what was Wale like as a kid?" I ask, sipping the last cold dregs of my tea.

To my surprise, Uncle Les says, "Shy. Quiet."

Really? Wale?

"He found it hard to stand up for himself," says Aunty Shirley, twiddling with her crucifix necklace. "Fonzo would often have to jump to his defense. He was a sensitive boy."

A loud bell rings in my head. *People think I don't have a sensitive side.* Maybe I can connect the two?

"In what ways was he sensitive?" I ask, typing a note to myself.

Uncle Les and Aunty Shirley look at each other for confirmation on who should speak first.

"His eyes would well up quick." Uncle Les takes off his cap and rubs his balding head. "Anytime someone teased him or made a joke, the tears come. Then over time, he'd get so . . . what's the word mi looking for, Shirl?"

"A kettle that would boil and boil without boiling over," she finishes. "You could tell he wanted to cry, but he just wouldn't allow himself to. We'd ask him, 'What's wrong? Why you upset?' but he would shake his head so fiercely and *insist* he was fine."

"That was his favorite word," Uncle Les says. "*Fine.*"

I think back to how distant Wale was in the days leading to our breakup. Not much has changed.

"So, we said to him"—Aunty Shirley twists her mug—"whenever you say you're fine but don't feel it, write whatever is troubling you down—keep a journal. You don't have to share it with us or tell anyone. It's for your eyes only. The most important thing is to get it down. It's not good for a young boy to be so pent up."

I nod and make a note to ask Wale whether he still has this journal.

"And what about now?" I ask, looking back up. "Would you say Wale's still sensitive?"

Uncle Les and Aunty Shirley stare at the ceiling in thought.

"Well, he a grown man now," says Uncle Les with a small chuckle. "Obviously he'll express his emotion different. But I think what he went through, it toughened him up."

"What he went through?" I raise a brow.

"You know. At home," he continues, but then Aunty Shirley puts a hand over his and says, "Les, she doesn't know."

There's an awkward silence.

Aunty Shirley purses her lips. "Temi, it's not our business—"

"Of course. I understand." Whatever it is, it must be serious.

I make a point of skimming through my list of questions—coincidentally, Aunty Shirley and Uncle Les have managed to answer a good number of them—when there's a chorus of laughter down the corridor.

"Yo, yo, yo. Look who I bumped into." Wale bounds into the room, holding Fonzo by the shoulders from behind.

As usual, Fonzo is dressed Glastonbury ready: straw hat, pink shirt, thick white socks rolled up to his calves under denim shorts. Funny. You'd think Wale with all his muscles and tattoos was the protective one. It's true. You really can't judge a book by its cover.

Fonzo hugs his parents. I'm not sure whether to remain seated or stand. Sadly, our friendship came to a natural end once Wale and I broke up.

"Temi! Good to see you." Fonzo looks genuinely pleased to see me. My body relaxes as he gives me a warm embrace.

"You guys know each other?" Uncle Les looks between us.

"Mutual friend," I quickly answer. Then to Fonzo: "You look well."

"Thanks. You too. How's things? How's Shona?"

I suppress a smirk at the mention of my best friend's name.

"She's good." The voice in my head cannot resist adding: *Still single.*

Wale plonks a bag of satsumas on the table. Then he heaves himself on to the counter, promptly jumping off after Aunty Shirley throws him a pointed look.

"So"—he looks around the table—"what did you guys talk about?"

"Don't you worry, my dear. All good things," Aunty Shirley says.

Uncle Les looks at me. "Temi, we okay to wrap up now? Mi need to head back." He's about to rise to his feet when Aunty Shirley says, "So, Wale, how's prep for the gala going?" She turns to me. "Wale is organizing a fundraising gala for the charity he worked for."

I bend over to reach for my bag. "Yeah, I heard about that."

"So, you're following me on Insta. Noted."

My head snaps up.

Wale's lips are twitching, a smirk teasing his lips. *Actually, I saw the post on The Tea Lounge*, I want to say. But then I remember what he said about his mental health and staying away from gossip blogs. "All part of the research," I say instead. "And your page is public."

"Well, you're invited to the gala," he says. And then he carries on looking at me as if he wants me to verbally accept his invitation. This time I look away, but I can feel his gaze still lingering on the side of my face. "I think you should come," he says finally. "You can mention it in my memoir."

I take off my glasses and rub my lenses. "Okay."

"So?" Aunty Shirley slices through our exchange. "How is it all going?"

"My bad," Wale says, shaking his head. He scratches his ear. "Yeah. Fine."

In unison, Aunty Shirley and Uncle Les turn to me as if to say, *Told you.*

"You got catering sorted?" she presses. "DJ?"

Wale slides a hand down the back of his neck. He's wearing his guilty face. "Well, um, not yet," he says. "Soon, though." He smiles. "Still waiting on a couple of quotes from suppliers."

Aunty Shirley's eyes widen as if she's about to choke. "Good Lord, you haven't got long, child. The gala is in a few weeks! Let me sort out catering. That's my good deed for the month. I'll talk to a few people this Sunday."

Uncle Les leans sideways. "Not Sister Diane, though." And in a hushed voice, he adds, "Her curry goat too dry."

Aunty Shirley winces. "Yes, you're right. Okay, that's catering sorted." She claps her thighs. "What else?"

"DJ." Uncle Les puts his cap back on and, with a wide grin, waits expectantly.

Aunty Shirley shakes her head slightly. "Don't," she mouths to Wale. "Obviously, Fonzo can help take photos," she says, swiftly carrying on.

"Already on it," Fonzo says. "A couple of students in my class have volunteered to help out too."

Wale pinches his nose and pretends to get choked up. "You see, this is why I love you, guys." He goes over and stoops down to give Aunty Shirley a kiss on the cheek before patting Uncle Les on the shoulder. He stops abruptly when he gets to Fonzo. "Not sure about you, mate."

Fonzo kisses his teeth. "Cha, man! Come here."

I watch them laugh and hug like brothers, trying to memorize every detail. What Wale has is beautiful; it's clear he sees these people as family. I wonder what he went through growing up? Maybe it would explain why he's not so close to his parents, why he doesn't like to talk about them as much. I'm so deep in thought that I don't even realize that I'm openly staring at Wale until he catches me looking at him. I glance away too quickly and instantly regret it.

"Anyone know a good—Sorry. One sec." Wale pulls out his buzzing phone. "Hey, Greg. Wassup?" His expression changes. "Yup . . . Sorry. Will do that now." He ends the call. "Guys, let's take a photo real quick," he announces suddenly. "My agent said I should post a pic on the gram."

Fonzo gives him a slant smile. "Falling behind on the algorithms again?" he says. "Okay, let's do it in the barbershop."

Aunty Shirley, Uncle Les, and Fonzo head out the door. Wale waits for me, his chest broad as he stands with his hands in his pockets. "Useful?" he says.

"Very," I reply, trying not to look at his pecs. "Debrief later this evening if you're free? Over the phone, I mean."

Wale pushes out his lips in thought. Again. Distracting. "Hmm," he says. "It depends on what time. I got a club appearance, you see."

"Hah! And you say you're not a celebrity." I shake my head. "And jeez, I didn't mean *that* late."

Wale laughs. "Gosh, remember when we used to do that in the early days? How did we even function the next day?"

He says this innocently but my gut feels like it's been sucker punched with the force of a cannonball. I remember we used to speak on the phone nearly every night. We would talk until the sun came up, mainly about randomish and hypothetical scenarios—*"Would you drink toilet water for a million pounds?"* (Apparently, Wale would.) I miss those days. I miss us.

"My bad," Wale says, studying me tentatively.

I remember myself and brace a smile. "Shall we go?"

And with that, I walk ahead of him out the door.

12

```
Love_Drive_Draft1.doc
Target word count: 4,000
Current word count: 3,302
```

The interview with Uncle Les and Aunty Shirley is still fresh in my head, so I start planning as soon as I get home. I use an app to transcribe what I recorded, and then I experiment with a few chapter headings—something that isn't necessary now but tends to help give me focus. I try to infuse Wale's humor.

> **People assume that I don't have a sensitive side**
> **The truth is, I'm as soft as fudge (well, I can be)**

After reading the interview transcript a couple of times, I work with what I've got—Wale would fill in the gaps. I'm so engrossed in the process of ghostwriting again that I have to drag myself away to begin my next task: *Love Drive*. And still, I don't start straight away—I make dinner first (Pot Noodle) and give myself a generous break because I deserve it. Then the critical step before I can write: choosing the perfect Spotify playlist to listen to.

By the time I open the document, it's nearly midnight.

Regardless, I commit to the task of writing, reminding myself after every few words that it does not need to be perfect. But unlike yesterday, I struggle to push through. My fingers itch to work on Wale's memoir. Weirdly, writing about your ex is kind of fun. Eventually, after hours of trying to force myself to get some words down, my unmade bed begins to look very appealing. Sod it. I give in.

There's always tomorrow, I tell myself as my head hits the pillow.

. . .

I wake to a panicked 7 a.m. phone call from Shona: she has a kids' party starting in five hours and her sister has come down with a bug—"Help!"

So much for hitting my word count today.

Now I find myself in the large garden of a detached house in Bromley, minding the candy station so that none of the children get a sugar overdose. Honestly, I don't know how I'm going to find the energy to write *and* work on Wale's memoir when I get home. Maybe I should fuel up on sweets.

I reach for a bag of Haribo and scan the garden that Shona and I have transformed into a five-year-old's dream: propped up on the grass are a bouncy castle, a dinosaur-themed peep board, and a ten-foot balloon arch, which is routinely being used by the parents for photos. Shona is still face painting, so I get out my phone and FaceTime Wale. We didn't manage to catch up yesterday evening in the end.

"Oi, oi, tiger," he says when he sees me.

I scowl before remembering that Shona had painted whiskers on my face. When we were together, Wale and I used to video call each other all the time. I should have just called him.

"I'm actually supposed to be a Siberian cat," I deadpan. "I'm at a children's party."

"Ahh, sorry. My mistake. There was me thinking you had a new kink or something. Anyways, how can I be of help?"

What happened to us agreeing to be professional? I want to say. But I have no leg to stand on when I have actual paint on my face.

"I'm just calling to—wait, are you still in bed? Dude! It's like one in the afternoon."

Wale brings up his free hand from under the duvet and places it behind his head. He's wearing a vest, so I now have a front-row seat to both his muscle bulge and the tuft of hair underneath his armpit.

"I was out late last night," he says as I strain to keep my focus on his silk durag. "Remember, I told you 'bout that nightclub appearance."

"Oh, yeah. How was it?"

"Honestly?" he says with a lazy smile. "I kinda just wanted to be at home, drinking herbal tea with my durag on."

I laugh so loudly that a few children turn their heads. "What are you? Twenty-five going on eighty?"

He chuckles. "Thankfully, I only had to show face for two hours. And at least I got a good check out of it."

I'm still struggling to believe that this—being a public personality—is now Wale's profession. Not only is it so far removed from what he was doing before but he was never one to crave the spotlight or post heavily on social media. He always preferred to live in the moment, not worrying about capturing the perfect photo.

"Don't worry, I won't keep you." I cast a glance at Shona. She's currently transforming a five-year-old into Spider-Man. "I've emailed you a draft of what I've done so far to get your thoughts on the voice."

"Gosh, already," he says. "Speedy Gonzales."

A growing smile spreads across my face before I can stop it. "It would be good to go over it. You free tomorrow?"

We agree to meet at ten at Anansi Books.

"Ooh, one last thing," I say, remembering. "Aunty Shirley mentioned that you kept a journal when you were a kid?"

"Oh. Yeah. What about it?"

I bite the inside of my cheek. "Now, only if you feel comfortable, but it would be really helpful if I could read it. Even if it's just a few pages," I add quickly.

Wale blows air out of his cheeks. "To be honest, Temi, I'm not even sure if I still have it."

"Are you able to have a look?"

"Yeah, sure. Can't make any promises, though."

I'm in the middle of telling Wale to send me a few childhood photos when Shona makes a beeline toward me. As though I have been caught skiving on the job, I tell Wale that I have to go.

"Is there anything else you need doing?" I ask when she arrives. She's wearing loosely fitted black clothes with chunky New Balance trainers.

Shona walks around the candy station and leans her body weight on the back of the chair beside me. With the sun in her eyes, she scans the garden. "Nah, I think we're good. At least for now. Honestly, babe." She pushes back the chair and with a loud exhale collapses on to it. "I owe you one."

"In that case, what are you doing on Sunday the eighth of September?"

She now looks dubious. "Um, nothing. Why?"

"Fancy free food and a trip to Oxford?"

I tell Shona about my childhood friend, Rosemary, and how my parents are throwing her a celebration lunch.

"I'll be your date, don't worry," she says, and I feel an instant sense of relief. "Anyways, how's the new job going?" she adds, reaching for a handful of jelly beans. "What's it like working with your ex-boyf? Still keeping things profesh, yeah?"

"Always, girl! You know me."

She hisses. "I take it he doesn't know about your revenge novel, then?"

I push out my lips. "I've been meaning to talk to you about this. Does he need to know? It's not like I have any plans to publish it. Writing *The Ultimate Payback* was basically therapy for me. Cathartic. However"—I rummage through my packet for a gummy bear—"I am in two minds about telling him about—"

"Kojo?" Shona finishes.

I can barely get my head to nod. The memory is like a burning coal in my skull.

Shona sits up and turns her full body toward me. "You didn't do anything wrong," she says. "What's holding you back from telling him?"

My eyes drop to my lap. I, too, have asked myself this very question.

"Look, I know they've only known each other for a few years." I sigh. "But at the end of the day, Kojo's still Wale's friend. It's not going to be a comfortable conversation. Plus, I don't know how Wale is going to react. I'm not saying he'll get physical with him—Wale isn't like that. But he may go within himself. Withdraw. And I can't afford for him to be distant with me right now. Not when I have his memoir to write."

Shona chews her lip. "Hmm. I see where you're coming from. But whatever you decide, just make sure you're choosing yourself first. Because the longer you leave it, hun, the longer you're protecting Kojo. And we don't enable dickheads, do we?"

"No, you're right. We don't."

She scans the garden again, stopping to wave over a sulky boy nearby who's eyeing the candy. With a finger in his mouth, the boy repeatedly twists his body, and then, as though he has just seen a ghost, he promptly runs away.

"Oh yeah," I say, remembering. And with a knowing smile, I add, "Fonzo says hi by the way."

Shona doesn't even look up from her phone. "Yeah? How is he?" She's swiping through Instagram. "What is he up to these days? Is he still doing his master's in photography?"

"Um, yeah. I think so," I reply. "So, what do you think of him?" At the exact same time she holds up her phone to my face.

"Err, what's this?" she says.

My mouth falls open.

On her screen is the picture that Wale and I took yesterday. Along with the photos he took with Aunty Shirley and Uncle Les. I really didn't want to get in the picture but Aunty Shirley kept insisting.

"What the hell?" I whip out my own phone and open Instagram. I have so many notifications. I tut. Why did Wale tag me?

I breeze through the comments, not quite sure what I'm looking for. To my relief, the comments are pretty typical. Well, as typical as one would expect for a reality star.

razzle_dazzle It's the eyes for me 😍😍😍
unicorn63 I'm melting 🫠🫠🫠👿👿👿
tataloves I would do anything to run my fingers through his beard 😍😍😍

But it's a particular one that catches my attention.

kelechi_iwobi Love this for you! 🐼

My lips part.

It's her.

She's blue ticked and her comment has already garnered over two hundred likes.

And then I notice there's a reply.

From Wale.

walebandele 🙈🙈🙈

I'm still staring when Shona says, "Babe, you okay?"

"Yeah, yeah. Fine." I wince. I just pulled a Wale.

The last time I saw Kelechi was on *The Villa: The Reunion*. She was going off at Wale, saying he made her look like a right mug. I don't get it. What has changed since then? The reunion aired on TV not too long ago, but maybe it was filmed earlier.

Knowing I will regret it, I click on Kelechi's handle—something I have not done since her first appearance on the show. In a little over a month, she's already gained nearly one million followers. I work my way through her perfect photos.

Swipe. Swipe. Swipe.

There's no question Kelechi is stunning. She has big Bambi eyes and lips women would pay thousands for. And she's got a banging body: slim thick. Perky boobs. Abs. It's no wonder Black Twitter was rooting for her and Wale. Together, they look like a power couple.

I think back to when Wale and I dated and the reception we got. There were a few occasions when women would openly stare at him, no doubt assuming that I was just his friend. And there were other times I would receive shifty looks when we linked arms. *How in the hell did you bag him?* their eyes said. Which is hilarious because I actually think that I'm hot too—not hot for a plus-size girl but hot. Period.

I always thought I was good looking growing up. And I found it frustrating that people would automatically put me in the less-attractive box just because I carry a bit of extra meat on my bones. Why does being "fat" need to be something derogatory? Is it not a descriptor like the words "thin" or "tall" or "pale"? Sadly, not everyone thinks this way. For some, if you're overweight, you're by default unworthy, less than. It's partly why I stopped watching the show. Kelechi was a visible reminder of the type of person the public felt Wale should be with.

Ignoring my better judgment, I click on Kelechi's Insta Story. She's at a nightclub with a few of her fellow castmates. They are taking shots, singing the lyrics to a Burna Boy song. I tap the screen to view the next story. This time, she's with Wale. He has one hand over her shoulder, while the other is holding a drink. She's posing like a true influencer—tongue sticking out between two fingers.

I can't quite say why but a weird sensation stirs inside of me.

"What's the deal between Wale and Kelechi?" I ask Shona this as if she could possibly know. "Are they cool now?"

"Huh?" Shona is serving the boy who ran off earlier a bowl of sweets.

I wait for her to finish and then thrust my phone in her face. "Is it just me or do they seem pally to you? And look—" I go back to Kelechi's comment under Wale's photo and point to it. "'Love this for you.' What in the world does that mean?"

Shona studies the screen for a few seconds, then hands me my phone back. "Who knows? And why you so bothered anyway?"

Her tone isn't accusatory, and yet I reply with a defiant "I'm not!" I blow out a breath. "Sorry, I just wanted to get your opinion, that's all." I look straight ahead and pop a Haribo heart into my mouth. I can feel her still watching me.

"You're not jealous, are you?"

My head snaps back to her so fast, I practically give myself whiplash. "Shona, for me to be jealous would mean that I'm catching feelings for Wale again."

"And are you?" she says.

The feelings never really went away.

"No," I say boldly. "I'm not. Me and Wale are done."

13

```
Love_Drive_Draft1.doc
Target word count: 5,000
Current word count: 4,002
Just over three weeks to
go . . .
```

The next day, I decide I need a new plan. For the second day in a row, I failed to meet my word count, and if I carry on like this, I will have nothing to show Mayee in a few weeks. My excuse this time? Exhaustion. Who knew sitting in the sunshine blowing balloons and scoffing sweets could be so tiring? So, my new plan is to spend the day working on Wale's memoir—after all, ghostwriting *is* my day job—then spend the late afternoons and evenings working on *Love Drive*. It's just gone 9:30 a.m., and I've arrived at the café in Anansi Books, which is where I agreed to meet with Wale to discuss the writing sample I'd sent him. I'm off to a promising start.

Rolling my neck until it clicks, I power on my laptop. The café is nice and quiet. I'm sitting at the same table where I reunited with Wale a few days ago. I open up my emails. There are two that catch my attention. The first one is from Mum. She's booked me my train tickets to Oxford next month. Wow. I wonder if she thought I would try and get out of attending Rosemary's celebration lunch.

Trying not to read my mother's kind gesture as a hint about my low-paying job, I send her a quick WhatsApp reply—

> **Temi:**
> Aww, you shouldn't have. Thanks

—and then I add a kiss at the end so that I don't seem too passive-aggressive.

I tap on the second email. It's from ACE's CEO, Kathy McGiffin—Wale's former manager. She has responded to my request to interview her at her office and is available this Wednesday. Perfect.

I'm taking a sip of my coffee when Wale walks through the entrance. He's wearing a white Daily Paper T-shirt, a thick silver chain on top. I'm transported back to that very first day I laid my eyes on him. Why is he so annoyingly hot?

"You're early." I glance at the time as he slides into the chair opposite. I wasn't expecting him for another half an hour.

"Yeah, bad news," he says as he tucks himself under the table. Suddenly, he's distracted. "Hold up. Are you wearing Sasha?" I touch the side of my cat-eye frames. I wore Sasha with a little black dress to one of our dates and, since then, she has been Wale's favorite glasses. I deliberately wore her today to remind him what he's missing.

"Oh, I didn't clock," I say airily. "So, what's the bad news?"

Wale's eyes are still flickering as he admires my face. I feel a sense of achievement but now my cheeks are starting to flush.

"Wale?" I say.

"Sorry. Yeah, I can't stay for too long," he says, finishing his train of thought. "Got a radio interview at eleven."

"Celebrity," I mouth.

"Contractual obligation," he corrects me.

I roll my eyes. "Let me guess. You'd rather have an herbal-tea-and-durag day?"

Wale tosses his head back and laughs. It reminds me of the old times.

The Re-Write 85

"Nah, don't watch that," he says. "I'd rather be here working with you, innit."

There's nothing about his tone that suggests he means it in a flirtatious way, and yet my face feels as though it's on a frying pan.

I pretend to do something on my laptop and then I clear my throat. "Who's the interview with?" I say casually.

Wale says, "You know Gary at BBC 1Xtra?"

"Oh, I love his shows. Well, if we need more time, we can always catch up on the phone later this evening if you're free. That's if you don't have any nightclub appearances, of course."

Wale reclines in his chair and squints. "Sarcasm. It suits you."

With a smile, I pick up my coffee and toast to myself.

"Anyways, how's things with you?" he says, lifting his chin a little.

I should tell him we should get cracking given he'll be off soon, but for some reason his Insta Story replays in my head. I can't unsee him and Kelechi.

"Things are good." I take off my glasses and clean them on my top before putting them back on. "So, this interview, will you be doing it with any other castmates?"

"Nah, just me."

I nod slowly and move my laptop cursor absent-mindedly. For goodness' sake, I'm supposed to be getting his thoughts on my bloody sample pages. Why can't I let it go?

"And how are you feeling about it, this interview?" I ask, ignoring my better judgment. "You know you're going to be asked about Kelechi, right? In fact, how are things between you two?"

I was so desperate to know their status that I completely forgot we haven't had our postbreakup talk yet.

Wale goes somber. "Look, Temi. Me and Kelechi, it's nothing like what we had . . ."

A lump forms in my throat at the word "had." A reminder that we exist in the past tense.

"Tems . . ." His voice trails again. He looks truly heartbroken.

For a fleeting, chest-aching second, I'm tempted to allow him to grovel, to explain himself, to beg for my forgiveness. But then I immediately ask myself why? So that we can have a better working relationship? Or do I still want to leave the door open just a crack? And I think this is what I'm scared of—my readiness to let him back into my heart despite him breaking it when he went on the show. I loved Wale, and if I'm to be one hundred percent truthful with myself, I still do. But getting back with Wale wouldn't resolve our earlier relationship issues. I was always more vocal about how I felt about him, more open, more vulnerable. And as much as Wale was a great boyfriend, I would need him to step up to balance the scales. That's not to say I'm perfect. Transparency is something I need to work on.

"Temi, I care about you."

Wale's deep voice pulls me out of my escalating thoughts. I quickly shake my head before he can get his next words out.

"It's fine," I say, bracing a smile. "I know you're sorry and I'm sorry too. Can we just . . . ?" I gesture at my laptop.

In a low voice, Wale says, "Sure."

I catch what looks like a hint of disappointment in his face but I do not read into it, afraid that I'll change my mind. So, instead, I lighten the mood. "Oh, thanks for sending me those photos of you when you were a kid. So cute."

Yesterday, Wale had WhatsApped me a couple of his childhood photos from his family's old albums. And let's just say, he was a late bloomer. His teeth weren't as straight as they are now and his thick, dark brows met in the middle. I still think I would have had a crush on him.

"Cute?!" Wale jerks his head. "Did you not see my teeth? No wonder they called me Willy Wonky." He snorts. And then, in his usual effusive, charismatic manner, he shares with me a few anecdotes. I think back to what Uncle Les said about Wale being picked on.

"Urgh. Kids can be so mean." I shake my head. "We need to include a few of these stories in your memoir. Dammit. I should have recorded it. Can you voice note it to me later?"

"Course."

"And anyway, the joke's on them. You have great teeth now."

From the slow way a smile spreads across his face, you'd think I'd told Wale he's packing or something. "Appreciate it," he says coyly, and he flashes me his teeth. I giggle. "You too."

"Thanks." My voice comes out too high. I clear my throat. "Oh, yeah. Did you manage to find that journal?"

Wale shakes his head. "Sorry. No luck. Think I chucked it away."

Noticing the time, I pull up the sample pages on my laptop. "I know you haven't had long but did you manage to read over what I sent you? What did you think of the voice?"

Wale has on a "my dog ate my homework" face.

"Don't worry. I've got it here," I say with a smile. I whip my laptop around and push it closer to him, and when he sits forward, I catch a lungful of his spicy oud cologne. His dark pupils skim across the page as he reads. I don't know where else to look.

"Soft like fudge. Love it," he says.

I take a sip of my drink to hide my glee.

He resumes reading. My gaze trails from his eyes down to his lips. I snap them back up to his eyes again—but that doesn't help. They're rich and chocolatey and incredibly magnetic. Every now and again, Wale chuckles to himself or says something like "Oh yeah. I remember that," or his iconic line, "Lemme tell you a story," before following it up with one. But then, as he gets toward the end, he becomes less animated, more subdued.

"So, as you can see, I was a crybaby," he says with a small, rueful smile, which doesn't quite reach his eyes.

I stare at him head-on. "No, Wale. You were a kid," I correct him gently. "You were *just* a kid. And there's nothing wrong with being sensitive," I add when he says nothing in response.

His face is a picture of disbelief. He makes a *pfft* sound and shifts in his chair. "The rules are different for boys. And you know it. Would you want to date a guy who cries all the time?"

His question throws me. And I nearly say, *I wish you would have shown me more of your sensitive side.* Instead, I turn my laptop back around and tap record on my phone. "I think now would be a good time to hear your story, if that's okay?"

Wale shrugs.

"You said people assume you don't have a sensitive side. Do you?"

He seems transfixed by my phone. He fiddles with his beard. "I do," he says eventually, briefly glancing up. "But it's not something I like to show."

I know.

"Why?" I ask softly, my voice laced with genuine concern. I'm no longer Temi the ghostwriter. This is Temi his ex.

Wale lets out a short, mirthless laugh. "C'mon, Temi. I'm a man. Men can't show their feelings. It's just the way it is."

"That's a load of crap," I say passionately. "Why shouldn't men show their feelings?"

Wale looks away in silence. He glances at his fingernails, rubs one thumb on the other. I'm starting to feel like he thinks my question is rhetorical but I'm genuinely curious to hear his thoughts.

The silence lingers, so I decide to change tack. What Uncle Les said—or rather, didn't say—floats to mind. I wonder if it's linked to that.

"Let's go back a bit," I say, dropping my tone in the way that I learned when I did my interview training at Bonsai. "How was life at home when you were a kid? Paint me a picture. Be as descriptive as you want. Your parents, they're Nigerian. What was that like? Were they quite traditional? Did they have strong views on what it means to be a man and a woman?"

"What is this now? Therapy?" Wale says this through a strangled laugh but there's a sharpness in his tone.

I blink. "Wale, I'm writing your memoir; I'm supposed to ask you questions."

His expression softens. "Sorry. It's just . . ." He drags a hand over his mouth. "I just thought I was more mentally prepared for what this process would involve, that's all. There was me thinking me being in therapy was enough." He lets out a short laugh. "Is it okay if we work toward the deep stuff?"

"Yeah, of course. Sorry."

"Nah, no need to apologize. You're doing a great job, trust me. It's . . . me. Like I said, this process, completely opening up—it's still new territory. But I'll get there. *We'll* get there."

It's then I realize the magnitude of Wale's commitment. *He's writing an actual memoir.* Wale doesn't do vulnerability. He's good at disguising his feelings with humor. But in order for me to do his memoir justice, he needs to be all in. He needs to not only cut himself open and bleed onto the page but do so in front of his ex-girlfriend—the very person he believes broke his heart. He needs to learn how to trust me again.

14

We spend the rest of the meeting focusing on his school years. Wale has a lot of stories. He was far from a popular kid. He wanted to be the popular kid.

"I have to give it to you," he says, after taking a quick glance at his watch. "You're a sick writer. You write like how I would write if I could write. If you know what I mean?"

I'm in the middle of packing away my belongings so that I can nip out for a quick walk when Aunty Shirley enters the café with the most gigantic smile.

"Good meeting?" she says as she looks between us, standing over our table.

Wale and I exchange a glance.

"Yes, I'd say so," I reply.

"Well, if you ever need anything"—she puts a hand on my shoulder—"you know where to find me." I give her an appreciative smile. "Oh, and the other day, forgive me. I was too busy chatting away that I didn't even ask you about your line of work. You been a ghostwriter long?"

I stall for two seconds. "Um, I'm actually still fairly new to it . . ." I stop myself from saying more.

"She's written a novel, you know," says Wale as if he's disclosing an epic secret. I stare at him. He gives me a toothy grin in return.

"A novel!" Aunty Shirley's eyes turn into saucers. "My Lawd, look at you. What's it called? Maybe we sell it here."

"It's actually not published yet," I say, feeling sheepish.

Wale jumps in once again. "Only a matter of time, though. Aunty

Shirley, you're looking at the next Malorie Blackman. Make a note of the title: *Wildest Dreams*. It's a rom-com. Think love triangle but with a paranormal twist. I'm telling you, it's sick, Aunty Shirl. Ended up reading it in two days!"

I snatch my bag and pretend to rummage for something, my forehead heating up from the sudden spotlight. I appreciate Wale's enthusiasm, I do. But I really don't want to get into the specifics right now.

"Well, you have to let me know when it comes out." Aunty Shirley beams down at me. "You can even launch your book here—"

"I'm so sorry but I just remembered I've got another meeting." I reach my tipping point with more force than I expect. My chair scrapes the floor as I rise to my feet. Aunty Shirley stares at me, stunned. Wale looks confused.

"Wale, I'll catch up with you later." I'm speaking so fast my words blend into each other. I turn to Aunty Shirley. "Nice seeing you again."

I power walk out of the café feeling equally flustered and embarrassed, and when I reach outside, the sun stings my eyes. Holding my bag tightly, I head in the direction I came from, maneuvering around slow-moving pedestrians that are in my way.

And then I hear Wale call my name. I groan. A hand catches me by the shoulder. I turn around.

"What's wrong? Why did you leave like that?" he says.

"I told you. I've got another meeting." Even I don't think I sound convincing. "And don't you have a radio interview to get to?"

Wale stares at me. "C'mon, Temi. I know that face. Speak to me. Wassup? Did I say something wrong? We used to manifest about you becoming an author all the time."

He dips his head so that he can look me straight in the eye. It was what he did whenever he wanted me to tell him what was troubling me. I avoid his gaze and glance at a nearby dustbin. Eventually, I succumb. As always. "*Wildest Dreams*," I croak. "It got rejected again."

Wale closes his eyes briefly as he absorbs the news. He looks utterly devastated. "Man. Temi," he says. "I didn't know. I'm so sorry." He places a hand on my forearm and I flinch.

"It's okay. I'll be all right," I say shakily, scared that I'll burst into tears. "Besides, we're still waiting on one editor at Ocean. So, who knows? They may be the one." My attempt to sound optimistic is let down by my quivering voice. I swallow. "Anyway, I've started working on another novel. So, we'll see what happens with that." I smile; my lip wobbles.

Wale is still staring at me—his dark, piercing eyes searching mine.

And then, he tugs me closer to him and wraps his strong arms around my shoulders. I hold still, defiant, but the pressure of my emotions is too much.

"Shh, shh, shh. It's okay," he says in hushed tones as I choke back a throaty sob. He strokes my hair, squeezes me tighter.

I don't want to give in so easily but I feel so overwhelmed. I find myself hugging him back.

"I feel like such a failure," I whisper, and in a smooth, low tone, Wale says, "You're not."

I sniff. "Sometimes I just want to pack it all in," I carry on. "I mean, what's the point? I'm only going to get rejected anyway. Even with your memoir, now I'm starting to think, *Can I even do it?* I'm the same girl who got fired, remember! Honestly, Wale. I wouldn't be offended if you decided to hire somebody else."

Wale lets go of me quickly. He places his hands on my shoulders then looks at me as if to say, *No, we're not doing that.* His gaze is so earnest, so strong, that I have to turn away.

"Temi, look at me. Look at me."

With tears running down my face, I slide my eyes back to his. People nearby are probably staring. But I don't care.

With a familiar, calm conviction, he says, "You. Temiloluwa. Ojo. Are. A. Writer." Each word pushes fresh tears to my eyes. He gives me a moment to absorb them. "Listen, as long as you're writing, you're a writer. And nothing, and I mean *nothing*, can ever take that away from you, yeah? I meant what I said the other day—you're fucking talented, Tems. I chose you as my ghostwriter 'cause I believe in you. But whatever you do, please, *please* don't ever stop believing in yourself."

A single tear falls.

Around us, the street noise dissolves into a liquefied blur. Wale continues to stare back. My heart aches with every beat. This is the Wale I fell in love with. This man right here. The Wale who was always a shoulder to cry on whenever I got a rejection email. The Wale who encouraged me when I couldn't motivate myself. The Wale who affirmed me. The Wale who was the type of prince who would hand me his own sword to help me slay my dragons. The Wale who saw me. Who trusted me.

"Do you want another hug?" he says after a quiet moment.

This time I don't hesitate. I nod.

15

Despite my protests that he will be late for his interview, Wale insists on walking me to the bus stop. After my public meltdown, I just want to go home.

En route, he catches a bit of attention. A couple of passersby do a double take and one guy even heckles his catchphrase. I find it rather hilarious, but Wale looks as though he wants the ground to swallow him whole.

At home, with a soulful house mix playing in the background, I continue working on Wale's memoir, his reassuring words replaying in my ears. I decide to start a new chapter.

> **People assume that I was the popular kid**
> **The truth is they called me Willy Wonky**

I enter flow state quickly, even though it's frustrating having to repeatedly press the keys that are not working properly. But once I get them to work, the words keep on coming. Which is why, after I glance at the time, I'm surprised to see it's nearly three.

And then I remember:

Shit! Wale's radio interview!

I type BBC 1Xtra into the search engine. Thankfully, there's an audio recording of the interview. I put my earphones in and press play.

Ten minutes in and Wale is a complete natural. He's talking about how he got on the show and then he addresses the fact that he's not a "clout chaser."

This is all useful research, I think to myself. One of the sections we agreed to cover was the misconceptions people have about him based on his appearance on TV. I write down the time stamps and jot a few notes.

"Now, Wale," says Gary, the presenter, in a conspiratorial tone, "it's not uncommon for cast members to say that they got a bad edit after they leave the show. What are your thoughts on this and your whole heartbreaker narrative?"

Wale makes a sound as though he's laughing through his nose. "We need to remember, yeah, *The Villa* is a reality TV show. It's all about ratings. It *has* to be entertaining. Now, if I'm a producer, how am I gonna do that? I'm going to repackage things, innit? I'm gonna chop and move footage around, show scenes without context. And play the most overdramatic music. Ever."

I chuckle.

"It's true!" Wale says over Gary's laughs. "I'm telling you, *The Villa* is more over the top than any Nollywood movie. Trust me. Not sure if you seen any but at some point during the film, an aunty is going to throw herself on the ground—guaranteed. She'll then start shaking her body like this." Gary begins to crack up as Wale, I assume, demonstrates by jiggling in his seat. Gosh, I wish there were visuals.

"Now, going back to what I was saying? What was I saying? Oh, yeah. I'm not suggesting what the viewers saw didn't happen. I take full accountability for everything; I mean, it's all captured on camera. It just didn't happen like *that*, if you know what I mean? In one scene I watched when I came back, they showed me flirting with Taleesha straight after I ended things with Sally, with just a quick toilet break in between!"

Gary says, "Yeah, that didn't do you any favors."

"First of all, the producers told me to go and chat to Taleesha. And second of all, the conversation happened later on during the day—not right after. They didn't bother to show how much I tried to amend my friendship with Sally and how she even admitted that we weren't a right fit. So now, I just look like a complete dick who cracked it on with the new bombshell right after taking a piss."

"Yeah, man, you were trending on Twitter that week," Gary says good-naturedly. "Thanks for clearing that up. Now, talk to me about Kelechi. Where do the two of you stand?"

If I was connected to a heart rate monitor, there'd be all spikes. I tell myself to calm down but, I swear, I can sense a smile on Wale's face before he even speaks.

"Kelechi and I are cool, y'know," he says in that easy-breezy way of his. "To be honest, I'm cool with all my castmates, including all the girls. I know it didn't look that way on the reunion but you have to remember, it's prerecorded. I was also able to have a sit-down with them. Away from all the cameras."

"Oh yeah? When was this?"

"Not long after the reunion. I'm not going to air all my business by sharing what was said. But to put it short, I had a lot going on in my personal life before I went on the show. I wasn't in the right state of mind. At all. And so, I guess, what people saw on TV was me ... overcompensating. You know, to mask how I was truly feeling."

"So, what I'm hearing, Wale, is that you shouldn't have gone on the show?"

"Yeah," he says. "I shouldn't have gone on the damn show."

Wale's admission stirs something in me. I knew he was apologetic but to hear he's regretful makes me feel less alone. Did he also miss me? Is that why he chose me to write his memoir? And what else did he have on, besides our breakup? I wish Wale would have let me in more on what was going on at home. Whatever it is, or was, I would have been there for him.

"When I met up with Kelechi," Wale is now saying, "I gave her more context about what I was going through. Bless her, she understood."

"Did you apologize?"

"Apologize? Gary, I was practically on my knees! Nah, in all seriousness, I apologized for not handling our situation with grace, for wasting her time. At the end of the day, if I had a sister or a daughter, I wouldn't want her to be messed about like that. Especially not on TV."

The presenter praises Wale for his introspection. Therapy is definitely helping.

"So"—Gary claps—"put us out of our misery, then. Should we hold our breaths for a Walechi rekindling?"

My heart speeds up again. Argh, this is fucking annoying! Why can't I be like Shona and have tougher skin?

Wale laughs. "We're just friends," he says finally.

I release a pent-up breath I didn't know I was holding. Gosh, what is wrong with me? It must be because the breakup is still fresh.

"Ladies and gentlemen, there you have it," Gary says. "They're just friends. Time to carry on with our lives now."

And that applies to you, Temi, I can't help but think.

They move on to a different segment: Gary asks Wale a list of questions emailed in from the listeners. They range from light-hearted—"Who was the loudest snorer in the villa?"—to pot stirring—"Who was the biggest game player?" A listener even asks Wale whether he'll ever consider writing a book. ("Never say never." Wale laughs.) But when Gary says, "Ho, ho, ho. This is a good one," I do not expect him to follow it up with, "Have you ever been in love before?"

I freeze.

I was not ready for this question.

People assume that I'm scared to love.

I'm back at the café again, Wale on the other side of the table.

And he never did say it back, a voice reminds me.

But what if he didn't know how to? another counters.

I can hear myself breathing as I wait for Wale to speak, see my chest rising, feel it.

Finally, in a low voice, Wale says to Gary, "Yeah. About two years ago. I was madly in love with my ex-girlfriend."

He does not elaborate.

He does not need to.

Because before there was me, there was Cammie.

16

```
Love_Drive_Draft1.doc
Target word count: 7,000
Current word count: 6,102
A little under three weeks to go . . .
```

Over the next couple of days, I only have phone catch-ups with Wale. My old feelings for him are resurfacing and, if I'm not careful, things could get messy. I need some alone time, to shake off whatever this is. More importantly, I need some time to write. I have a little under three weeks before I have to submit *Love Drive* to Mayee, and the thought of my looming deadline is making my chest tight. All I want to do is curl up in bed and hide away from the world.

Sticking to my plan, I work on Wale's memoir during the day, shifting my focus to *Love Drive* in the evening. I glance at the time. Two hours and only two hundred words! I groan. I've been struggling to enter flow state, writing and rewriting sentences over and over and over again. I'm mentally and physically exhausted. I'm absolutely shattered.

I'm trying to get the letter "P" to work, when my phone flashes.

I sigh.

It's my parents.

I pick up their video call and tell them that I'm busy.

"We just have a quick question," Mum says briskly.

Ten minutes later, I'm still on the call.

"I dunno, pick whatever," I say, glancing at the time again.

They have been going back and forth on which celebration cake they should get for Rosemary, only for them to return to their original choice.

"Bad day at work?" Dad says.

I go quiet.

I've been so preoccupied with writing and trying to understand my confusing feelings for Wale that I totally forgot that I haven't yet shared my news with my parents.

"I've got a new job!" I blurt out.

I watch as the news settles on their faces.

"Darling, congratulations!" Mum cries. "Why didn't you mention it earlier? And we've been sitting here nattering about cake."

Dad beams. "That's great news, Temi. What's the role? What's the company?"

I feed off their excitement by telling them about how my agent put me forward for the gig and that I didn't even need to apply.

"Oh, so it's another ghostwriting job." Mum sounds slightly concerned.

"Don't worry, Mum. I'm in a much better place now. Plus, I'm freelancing, so I'm essentially my own boss."

Dad smirks. "So, aren't you going to tell us who it is?"

"Huh?" I say automatically.

"Your client." Mum tuts. "The one you're writing for."

I freeze. I can't tell them I'm writing for my ex, let alone a former *Villa* cast member. Dad thinks reality shows are trash.

"It's for a young TV star," I say, playing it safe. Yes, keep it nice and broad.

Mum nudges Dad. "She thinks we won't know who it is. Try us!"

They begin to throw out names: Steve Bartlett, Rochelle Humes.

"I know! I know! Stormzy!" Mum says.

"Stormzy is a music artist not a TV star," I tell Mum, who's looking all too pleased with herself. I decide to put a pin in it. "And I can't say who it is for confidentiality reasons." This is true. "Anyway, I should get back to writing."

Mum and Dad wish me luck.

. . .

The next morning, I wake up feeling groggy. I glance at the time. I only have a few hours left before Kathy from ACE will be expecting me. Dragging my laptop into bed, I down a glass of water and prepare questions for the meeting.

Now I'm on my way to ACE's office. Despite using Google Maps, I still walk right past it. There isn't a big, jazzy sign or an eye-catching window display. Instead, the charity's name is listed under an intercom beside a weathered red door sandwiched between a launderette and a coffee shop.

I'm buzzed in. I wait in the tiny reception area, where I stare at the peeling posters: ARE YOU LOOKING AFTER A LOVED ONE? WE CAN HELP.

I'm trying to imagine Wale working in this building when my attention is snagged by a loud creaking sound. A familiar-looking older woman with fine, straw-like hair appears from behind the door.

It takes me a moment to register where I've seen her before—Wale's gala announcement on The Tea Lounge.

"Temi, yeah?" she says.

I rise to my feet. "Kathy. So nice to meet you."

We shake hands.

On the way to her office, Kathy apologizes for the mess. In the corridor is a bucket collecting water from the leaky roof. She ushers me inside and then goes to make us both a cup of tea. Her office is very . . . busy. The room is tiny and stuffy and mostly overtaken by her overflowing desk, which is covered with receipts and printouts and multicolored folders. I gaze at the tired-looking cabinet. On the shelves are awards dating back to twenty years ago.

"The good ol' days," she says, closing the door behind her. She places an Arsenal cup in front of me and then collapses behind her desk with an audible exhale. Although she has a friendly, crooked smile, there's a weariness in her eyes. "So"—she wraps her hands around her mug—"how can I be of help today?"

I thank Kathy for her time and do my whole spiel: introduction, permission to record, interview format. She is already clued up on what Wale's memoir is about.

"We're thinking of dedicating a chapter to Wale's career," I explain as I hit the record button on my phone. "We haven't nailed the angle yet but I'm hoping something will come from this interview. I also know Wale is keen to raise awareness of ACE."

She smiles at this.

"Before we talk about Wale, can you tell me about the charity? I saw on your website that you set it up."

Kathy tells me about her experience of taking care of her parents from when she was a young girl. Her mum had multiple sclerosis and then her dad got cancer. After their passing, she founded ACE (Action for Carers Everyday).

"Do you know what, Temi?" she says, lifting her chin. "Back then, it never once crossed my mind that I was a carer."

"No?" I ask.

She shakes her head. "There was no internet or social media. No wide support for people like us. We were just busy being a daughter, a mum, an uncle, whatever, while looking after a loved one. It's difficult, though. Caring. You're always on duty. Twenty-four seven."

Kathy tells me about ACE in its heyday, when it was the go-to place for local information and support. They provided services such as short respites, food banks, and emergency funds. They were never short of volunteers and were even based in a much bigger office. But, sadly, over time, things had changed.

"We've had to downsize massively." Kathy twists one of her many gold rings. "We've been hit hard by the cuts. Donations are at an all-time low.

We rely on the goodwill of a small group of volunteers. God, it kills me whenever we have to tell a carer that we can't help. It's like we're turning them away."

Kathy's eyes begin to well. My heart aches with sympathy.

"Wale's brilliant," she carries on, rubbing a finger under her nose. She reaches for a tissue. "In the time he was here, he drummed up quite a bit of money. He secured a few grants and organized small fundraising events. We even toyed with the idea of something big like a fete or a gala."

So, that's where the idea came from. The gala has absolutely nothing to do with his rebrand. I feel a tinge of guilt that I even contemplated the thought.

"Temi, what I'm about to tell you is confidential."

I'm snatched back to the room again. A grave expression is carved on Kathy's face. I lean forward and pause the audio recording.

Kathy wets her lips and then, closing her eyes briefly, she says, "ACE is on the verge of going under. It will be a miracle if we make it to the end of the year." She dabs her tissue under her nose. She looks truly, utterly devastated. The news is soul crushing. ACE is her life.

"Oh no. That's awful," I say, a sharp pang in my chest. "I'm so sorry, Kathy."

Her eyes shimmer but she manages to hold it together. "We're hanging on by a thread, Temi." Her voice wobbles. "It's got so bad that we struggle to pay our staff on time."

Now it makes sense why Wale couldn't pay for bowling. He hadn't got paid because there was so little money to go around.

"We don't even have the money to recruit a new fundraising officer," Kathy carries on. She sniffs again. "Not that anyone would come close to Wale. Bless him. When I told him the news, he offered to work for free, but I wouldn't let him give up that much time. So, now he's organizing the gala pro bono. Told me I can't stop him." She laughs to herself. "I don't know how he's going to pull it off. But I know he will."

My heart melts hearing Kathy speak of Wale so fondly.

I smile. "Do you want to tell me more about your golden boy, then?"

Kathy is full of praise; she showers Wale with compliments. She tells me how organized he was—he loves a good spreadsheet—and how he would light up any room he walked into. She tells me how overambitious he could sometimes be and his habit of working on the weekends. I can't help but feel proud of him. Why didn't he tell me how great he was at his job? I guess he's too modest to say it outright.

"Sorry, I can go on a bit," Kathy says, interrupting herself. "I'm not sure if any of this is useful—"

"Yes. Absolutely. It is."

She gives me a teary smile and then she rummages under her desk rubble for her phone. "Apologies, I'm just conscious of the time." She looks at the screen and her eyes widen. "Gosh, has it been an hour already? I'm so sorry, Temi, but I've got another meeting."

"No worries. I really appreciate you talking to me."

Kathy knocks down the rest of her tea and gathers her notebook and pen. "I'm sure Wale can tell you more about his involvement with ACE. I think it would make such an inspiring story."

"Oh yeah? In what way?"

"I just find it lovely"—Kathy places a hand on her chest—"when one of your own pays it forward. Wale benefited from our services and now he wants to help young carers just like him. It will make a nice full-circle story, don't you think?"

17

It all makes sense.

Wale's reluctance to talk about his family.

His shift in energy anytime I bring them up.

Wale was a carer.

And perhaps he still is. Maybe this is what Uncle Les and Aunty Shirley didn't want to talk about. But I don't understand. Why would Wale not share this information with me? There's nothing wrong with looking after a loved one.

On the way back to reception, Kathy introduces me to a handful of people crammed into a small room, and then she ushers me into a crummy kitchen where we dump our mugs in an even crummier-looking sink.

She gives me a warm hug goodbye. "If you need anything else, you know where to find me."

Outside, the weather is the epitome of British summer: breezy with a hint of sun to fool people that it's warm when it really isn't. I'm wearing a sleeveless tank top. Damn. I wish I'd brought a sweater.

I brush my hands up and down my arms, then fetch out my phone. There's a WhatsApp message from Wale.

> **Wale:**
> Hey, how did the interview with Kathy go?
> Free to meet up for a debrief if you are x

I register the kiss at the end. *Interesting.* Then his status: online. I can't suddenly avoid him, no matter how perplexing my feelings are, so

I tell him that I'm available now, and after a few back-and-forths we agree to meet at a nearby park. Wale lives close by.

Ten minutes later, he approaches the entrance. For once, his athletic silhouette isn't the first thing I notice. Today he's wearing a black face mask.

"Hay fever," he says after he catches my questioning expression.

He stretches out his arms. I give him the quickest of hugs and yet my heart skitters as if it's being physically shaken.

"We can go somewhere else if the pollen is too much."

"Nah, nah. It's cool. I took one of those tablets."

We find a secluded spot on the grass with more sun than shade. I cross my legs and lean back, the dry grass prickling my palms. Since leaving Kathy's office, I've been drawing up different scenarios: Wale looking after his mum; Wale looking after his dad. Both of them are faceless because I've never met them before. Even as Wale plucks a daisy and twiddles the stem between his fingers, I can't help but see the teenage boy he used to be.

"So . . . your meeting with Kathy. How did it go?"

A gust of breeze cuts through my top. Wale was smart to wear a sweater.

"Really good," I reply. "You're right. The woman is . . ." I shake my head, breathless.

"Yeah, she's phenomenal, right? What did you guys talk about?" He pulls off his face mask and shoves it away. It's hard to tell if he's genuinely curious or trying to work out if I know more than I'm letting on. Kathy had innocently assumed that because I'm his ghostwriter, I had already been informed about his caring experience. It doesn't feel right telling him that she revealed it. This seems like something that should come from him.

"She said you were a slacker," I reply matter-of-factly. Wale chucks the daisy at my head and misses. We both laugh, and for a fleeting moment it feels like we've never stopped dating. "No, seriously, she gave me some really good insights. She also told me"—I exhale—"that ACE is struggling to stay afloat. That's why you're organizing the gala, isn't it? Wale, I owe you an apology. I'm not going to lie. I thought it was all just part of your rebrand."

Wale shakes his head. "It sucks, man," he says, completely bypassing my admission. "I mean, what's gonna happen to all those carers? And it's not like they get loads from the government, and yet they help keep this country running." He breathes sharply and then, looking directly at me, says, "Temi, any money I get from this book, I'm giving it all to ACE."

"Wow, Wale. That's very noble of you," I say. I hold back from telling him he won't see any royalties until his book outearns his advance—if it does at all. Then, tilting my head at an angle, I ask, "How come I'm only seeing this side of you now?"

A crease deepens between his brows. "What do you mean?" he says, swatting away a fly on his nose.

"When we were dating," I carry on, "you never told me that your job meant this much to you."

Wale's gaze flickers to his trainers. He pulls at one of the tongues.

Suddenly, I feel guilty. I wasn't expecting him to tell me about his caring experience now, and so I'm taken aback when he says, "Remember my ex, Cammie?"

His radio interview comes to mind. "Yeah, what about her?" I say.

He rubs his brow and avoids making eye contact. "When we were together, she tried to get me to leave ACE, y'know."

"Seriously?!"

Wale's impression says, *I know*. "Basically, she tried to steer me toward something more corporate."

I can't help it. I let out a loud scoff and wince. "Sorry, how long were you guys together?"

"For about three years."

"So, what I'm hearing is"—I fold my arms—"your ex-girlfriend forgot you have your own life."

"But we were building a life together," Wale says. "A lifestyle she didn't think I was earning enough to maintain. Basically, she was embarrassed about my job. Told her family and friends that I worked in 'sales.'"

I stare at him, shell shocked. "Gosh, Wale. No offense but she sounds awful. What the heck did you see in her?"

And with a twisty smile, Wale says, "She had a big bum."

I kiss my teeth and give him the biggest eye roll.

"Nah, in all seriousness," he says, laughing, "Cammie was like a goddess to me. She was crazy smart, ambitious, not to mention stunning as hell. In my head, she was out of my league. So, I guess I saw it as a privilege to be with her."

I scrunch my brows. How Wale can think any girl is out of his league is beyond me.

"So, when I met *you* . . ." He sets his eyes on me and what feels like a light shiver runs down my arms. *It's the wind*, I tell myself. *Definitely the wind.* "And you're those things too: smart, ambitious, beautiful"—he lingers on the word—"my guard went up."

I feel a tinge of heat. Thank God for my melanin, otherwise I'm sure my cheeks would be the color of beets right now. I shift my focus to a dog in the distance, chasing after a ball. Wale's compliments will always do something to me. After a beat, he carries on.

"I know you and Cammie are two different people," he says, "but like her, your parents are loaded—"

"They didn't always have money," I tell him.

"I know," he says softly. "And let me be clear, coming from a rich family is not an issue. But it does make me a bit insecure about mine. Cammie has one of those sitcom families. You know, the type that have dinner around the table and go on holidays abroad. Growing up, my brother and I ate in our bedroom. And the last time we went on a family holiday, I was practically a baby. I just wish I had what you have, y'know?"

He looks at me for an extra second before shifting his attention to the running dog. I see the great sadness in his eyes as he turns away. A pang of guilt hits me in the throat. I wish I had not put so much emphasis on the whole meet-the-parents thing. Because the more I learn about Wale, the more I realize that things with him are not black and white. Perhaps him keeping parts of his life to himself is his coping mechanism. Perhaps he gets the same insecurity I feel whenever I open up about Seth.

I try to think of something to say but I don't know what. No words feel as if they'll be enough.

He doesn't move; I don't rush to fill in the silence. Eventually, he turns to me with a wide grin. "Gosh. Therapy got man all vulnerable and that." He lets out a dry laugh.

"I like vulnerable Wale," I say softly.

18

A loud barking breaks the silence.

I adjust my sitting position and glance at the time. "Do you still want to do the interview?" I ask slowly, tentatively.

"Yeah, let's do it."

I put my phone on record, sit it on the grass, and begin to ask Wale about his time at ACE. He shares everything from the highs to the lows. Everything except being a carer himself.

"We still need an angle for this chapter," I tell him, chewing my bottom lip. "What helps me is coming up with different chapter headings. So, how about . . . 'People assumed that my charity job was just a nine to five, but the truth is so much deeper than that'?"

Wale stretches across the grass to give me a high five. "You see"—he wags his finger—"this is why you're the writer and I'm the client."

With a laugh, I reach for my phone. I type the chapter heading into my notes app and set it down again. "Speaking of jobs," I add, doing martial arts with a persistent wasp, "how *are* you getting on with being an influencer? Is it something you see yourself doing for a long time?"

"Hmmm." Wale strokes his beard. The *mmm* sound seems to go on forever. My eyes flick to his lips again. *Temi!*

"It's defo new territory," he finally says as I hastily search through my bag for my bottle of water. I down it. "Putting myself out there to complete strangers—it's a lot, y'know. It's something that I'm still getting used to. But I'm enjoying the financial rewards and choosing what brands I wanna tie myself to. Though all these VIP events are kinda long, still."

"It's 'cause you're a grandad," I say matter-of-factly.

Wale flutters his eyes. "So, yeah. Things are going okay at the moment. It's just been mad difficult trying to commit to it fully alongside organizing the gala."

"What you need is a Shona," I tell him jokingly. Then I consider it more seriously. "Hey, maybe I can ask her to help."

Wale doesn't say anything. His attention is stolen by something behind my shoulder. I turn around. Two Black girls about our age have perched themselves on the grass a few meters away. One of the girls cries to the other, "Pur-lease, he ain't shit." I tilt my head in an effort to meet Wale's gaze.

"Sorry, what was that?" he says to me, his forehead creased.

"Shona," I say again. "I can ask her to help if you want? Trust me, that girl would love nothing more than planning a high-profile event."

Wale seems distracted. His eyes keep flickering back and forth from the girls to me, his brows still slightly furrowed. Then my words hit him. He looks incredulous. "Shona?" he hisses. "That girl hates me."

"Not completely. And this is for a good cause. So, what do you need help with?"

The girls are now laughing.

Wale searches for something in his pockets. "Entertainment, prizes for the auction . . ."

I make a *psshh* sound. "Yeah, she can do all that with her eyes closed."

I wait for him to respond. But Wale is too busy rummaging.

"What are you looking for?" I ask.

The silence is broken by the girls laughing their heads off again.

"Can we go somewhere else?" he says, already clambering to his feet and starting to walk away.

I stagger to mine and hurry a little to catch up with him.

"Are you okay?" I ask slowly.

Wale continues to take long strides. He stares straight ahead. "Yeah, fine," he mutters. "Hay fever was playing up, couldn't find my mask." I take a sidelong glance at him; his jaw is tight.

A few months ago, I would have grabbed his hand and pleaded with him to share what was on his mind. But today, I give him space. I walk in silence and observe my surroundings instead. In the distance, a group of men are playing football.

"Sorry," he says after a long minute.

His voice pulls my attention toward his profile again. The tightness around his mouth has gone but I can tell he's still pissed off.

He slows his pace to a languorous stroll. "I was just"—he sighs—"paranoid. Those two girls, they were chattin' about me."

"Really? What did they say?" I wish that I had eavesdropped.

"I didn't catch the specifics," Wale replies. "But they were staring at me and laughing a lot."

"Wale, not to sound insensitive, but you were on *The Villa*—the biggest dating show on the planet. Of course people are going to recognize you."

Wale stops in his tracks.

I take a breath. "You don't really have hay fever, do you?"

He glances past my ear. "My therapist says it's normal," he says, not quite looking at me, "for my senses to be heightened, to feel as though everybody is watching me. Yeah, I'm not super famous—thank God—but I'm always mentally preparing myself to get looked at wherever I go. Can't really complain, though, can I?"

Right before me, he changes from a charming reality star to a sensitive young boy.

Before I realize what I'm doing, I wrap my arms around his waist and rest my head on his chest, just below his neck. Wale sinks his cotton-soft chin into my hair, and I feel him physically relax.

Our hug is a silent exchange.

Thank you: he squeezes me tight.

I've got you: I give him one back.

We're isolated in our own little bubble.

And then he brushes his hands up and down my arms, his soft palms transferring heat. "You're cold," he says in a near whisper.

With one swift yank, he pulls his sweater off over his head. I catch a flash of brown skin as his vest rises.

He drapes his sweater over my shoulders before promptly returning his hands to either side of my arms. Then he lowers his head toward mine, his heavy-lidded, dark gaze dancing over my face. Without my control, my eyes drop to his lips, a soundless gasp escaping me as his hand reaches toward my hair. I wait for him to pull me in. Instead, he lowers his hand toward my nose.

"Pollen," he says with a tinge of humor. He twiddles the fuzzy ball between his pinched fingers before blowing it away.

To say I feel embarrassed is an understatement. I might as well be wearing a red clown nose. Still, I try to see the funny side.

"Hay fever, my ass." I laugh.

Wale doesn't laugh. He stares at me through squinted eyes.

Suddenly, I feel self-conscious. "What?" I say.

"You wanted me to kiss you, didn't you?"

This boy! "What?!" I cry, mortified. "Hell no! I did not want you to kiss me, Wale!"

Wale smirks. "So, why were you looking at my lips?"

I kiss my teeth.

He laughs.

"Can we just carry on walking, please?" I say, already turning to leave.

Wale doesn't move. He stands with his arms crossed, a twinkle in his eye.

Cheeky bastard.

"One sec," he says. "I forgot something." He pats down his pockets.

And then he gives me a quick peck followed by the cheekiest grin known to man.

It happens so fast, I can barely move, let alone speak.

"Come on," he says, already walking ahead of me. "Let's get something to eat."

19

It takes me a bit of arm twisting, but I manage to persuade Shona to help Wale with organizing the gala.

"I'm not asking you to do this for him. Or even for me. Do it for the carers."

She huffs. "Like it's not weird enough you working with your ex. You want me tied to him as well."

"Wale and I are in a good place!" I contemplate whether or not to tell her about the kiss. Does it even mean anything? After all, it wasn't a real kiss. And Wale is such a tease, it's hard to take him seriously sometimes.

"Hello? Are you still there?" she says.

"Sorry, what did you say?"

"You didn't catch what I said? I said, 'Fine. As long as Wale introduces me to his celeb friends, I'll help him.' Might as well get something out of it."

After we end the call, I resume drafting the work chapter.

People assumed my charity job was just a nine to five
The truth is so much deeper than that

I channel Kathy's and Wale's passion. At some point, Wale is going to have to tell me about his caring experience—right now, I'm only writing half the story. Every now and then, *Love Drive* pops to mind but, like a gambler, I can't stop.

The following morning, I pay for my actions. I wake up at 11:36 a.m.

Shit! My plan was to get up early to work on *Love Drive*.

I'm about to jump out of bed when my phone chirps.

Wale!

I scrabble for it underneath my pillow, embarrassed by how weak-willed I've become. Gosh, what's wrong with me? I glance at the screen. It *is* a text from Wale.

> **Wale:**
> Tems! How's your day going? You free to interview Fonzo later? Was thinking I'll book a table for the three of us

I still myself. Should I wait an hour before I respond? The guy already thinks I want to kiss him; I don't want to come across eager. But then again, this is a work matter. Sod it. I draft a reply:

> **Temi:**
> Morning. Not long woke up. I am free. How about six?

Less than a minute, my phone chirps again. Someone's keen.

> **Wale:**
> Just started your day?! Tems, it's nearly twelve! Let me guess, you're still in bed?

I'm still drafting a reply when my phone pings with a new message.

> **Wale:**
> *in bed drinking herbal tea, wearing a hair bonnet

The Re-Write

I crack up. Nice try. I delete the message I was typing.

> **Temi:**
> I'll have you know I was burning the midnight oil working on your memoir!

And then I follow it up with another text.

> **Temi:**
> PS I'm wearing my pink bonnet

Within seconds, my phone chimes.

> **Wale:**
> The one that says Diva on the back with studs?

I curl back under the covers, holding my phone over my face.

> **Temi:**
> Yup

I hit the send button too quickly. I send another.

> **Temi:**
> Although, it currently says Div. I didn't follow the washing instructions. Put it in the dryer

My phone pings in quick succession.

> **Wale:**
> LMAO!

> **Wale:**
> Divvy move lol

> **Wale:**
> I'm not calling you a div

I reply:

> **Temi:**
> You better not be!

And then he replies:

> **Wale:**
> This evening, how about we go Jam Delish?

I stare at his message in thought. Jam Delish is a Black-owned Caribbean vegan restaurant in Angel. It also happens to be high on the list of places Wale and I were keen to check out while we were together. Yesterday, after he found a restaurant for us to eat at, I deliberately moved us to takeaway—too close to date vibes. I wonder why he picked Jam Delish? To make me feel nostalgic? But if he wanted me to feel nostalgic he would pick a restaurant we went to all the time, like Chuku's. Anyway, Fonzo will be there. It's just a work meeting. Plus, it's a popular spot . . . Hmm. I wonder if Wale has thought this through. I draft a reply.

> **Temi:**
> Sure, but will you be OK? There's likely to be a lot of people. I don't want you feeling paranoid. I don't mind us meeting at Anansi Books if easier?

Wale's reply comes in after three minutes. But it felt like three hours.

> **Wale:**
> Thanks. That's very sweet of you. I'll be all right. My therapist says it's part of exposure therapy:)

Sweet. I analyze the word as though I'm studying for my GCSE exams. My phone pings.

> **Wale:**
> Sorry, gotta go. Have a good one

And again:

> **Wale:**
> X

I stare at the kiss.

In that moment, my decision on whether or not to send Wale a kiss back seems momentous, life or death. If I choose not to, I'll be making a statement. No, I didn't want to kiss you in the park, actually. And no, there's zero chance of us getting back together. Zilch. But if I reply, I'm indirectly saying that I'm open.

> **Temi:**
> Cool. See you soon X

After I shower and have breakfast (well, lunch), I sit my bum at my desk and put on some Amapiano music. Right, I'm going to work on *Love Drive*.

I only manage to write roughly eight hundred words. It feels like I'm wading through a muddy swamp. I keep on starting and stopping and starting again. No matter how hard I try, I can't enter into a flow state. I had blitzed a novel not too long ago. Why can't I produce the same magic again? I even have deadline pressure this time. Maybe this is just part of the process for this book. I have to push through.

. . .

Later that evening, I blast some feel-good music. I put on a chic top, a leather skirt, and Sasha again. I'm nearing Jam Delish when I stop and put my phone on selfie mode. Quickly, I give my hair a fluff, rub and then pop my glossed lips. Perfect.

I open the door to a hit of succulent smells: barbecue jerk laced with curry and spices. There's a buzz of chatter over a reggae beat. I was right. The place is heaving.

A waiter greets me. I tell her I have a reservation. She grabs a menu and leads me past rows of tables, brass pendant lights hanging over the top.

And then my legs come to an abrupt stop. My heart leaps to my throat.

This evening, I expected a party of three but it appears we're a party of four.

"Y'right, Temi," says Kojo, lifting his chin a little to greet me. "Long time."

20

Several weeks ago . . . July

Voice-over: *Wale and Kelechi are getting cozy by the fire pit. Things are heating up. Excuse the pun.*

"You have insane eyes, y'know that?" Wale says dreamily.

Kelechi giggles and covers her face. "Shut-uuup," she says in her Brummie accent. "My eyes are literally dark brown, like yours."

Wale laughs. "Nah, man. It's not just the color. It's the shape too. The way they pinch at the corner and turn into a squint when you laugh."

Kelechi pretends to go shy. She covers her face again.

"C'mon, let's have a staring contest," he says.

She swings her knees toward him. Wale drops his head between his palms. They stare at each other for a good minute, their eyes locked in a starry gaze.

Until Wale blows out his cheeks like a puffer fish.

Kelechi bursts out laughing. "You're such a goofball. Come here."

She kisses him.

Dramatic music plays.

. . .

Right, that's enough!

I hit the pause button, tears stinging the backs of my eyes. *My God, Temi, why are you punishing yourself?* I stopped watching *The Villa* three days ago but then I saw a thumbnail of Wale and Kelechi on YouTube and silly me just had to click on it, didn't I?

I tilt my head back to prevent tears from falling. I will not cry in the middle of a Starbucks.

Fingers quivering, I reach for my bottle of water. It's practically empty; still, I bring it to my lips. I turn my focus back to my laptop.

Channel your anger into your story.

Gritting my teeth, I resume typing. I'm up to the chapter where Sophie has just released her exposé book about her ex and it's gone viral. Wayne is receiving a lot of backlash on social media.

```
The man deserves to be canceled
```

I type.

```
#CancelWale
```

I'm getting back into my writing groove when a familiar voice calls my name.

Kojo.

"I thought it was you," he says with a wolfish grin, a plastic cup in hand. As always, Kojo is dressed as if he's on his way to the gym, his cap back to front. He struts toward me and, to my disgust, he plops himself onto the spare chair.

"What you saying, T?" he says. "How's it going?"

I haven't seen Kojo since the night Wale and I broke up. If my memory is correct, he was bigging up Wale for not dropping out of *The Villa*. Even before I'd overheard him, I'd never been a fan—his excessive thirst for women makes me uncomfortable.

Folding my arms, I stare at him pointedly. But Kojo's too busy moving my phone so that he can make room for his drink.

"Oh, snap!" He notices the frozen still on my screen: Wale and Kelechi kissing. "You're watching yesterday's episode?"

A rush of prickly heat creeps up my neck as I snatch my phone from the table. Since Wale's appearance on *The Villa*, I feel as though I'm walking around with a sign that says, "I'm Wale's stupid ex-girlfriend." A couple of weeks ago, I bumped into an old friend from school—and even she knew.

"I'm sorry things didn't work out with Wale," she said with a pitying expression.

I stared at her, shocked. We hadn't seen each other in over a decade.

"I follow you on Instagram," she explained tentatively. "You took down your pictures . . ."

It's as though everyone knows.

Everyone.

"You all right?" I hear Kojo say as my eyes begin to well up again.

It all gets too much. I lurch to my feet and run to the ladies' bathroom, where I lock myself in the cubicle, push up my glasses, and cry.

I hate this, I hate this, I hate this.

I hate the impact this breakup is having on me. How the very mention of Wale's name makes me cry at the drop of a hat. I hate how fragile I've become. I never used to be this emotional. No, I'm going through a rough time; it's okay to cry. Still, I hate how Wale has quickly moved on while I'm locked away in the toilets bawling like a baby.

I hate him.

And I hate that I love him.

I take my time blowing my nose and wiping my glasses before drawing in a big lungful of air. I'm hoping Kojo has enough emotional intelligence to know that he needs to leave me in peace.

I return to the café and tut. Kojo's still here and—*What the hell!* Why is he looking at my laptop?!

"What are you doing?" I slam the lid shut.

"Rah, man!" Kojo scoffs. "Is that how you say thank you? I was keeping an eye on it for you."

I roll my eyes and slump back in my chair. I begin to pack away my belongings.

"Check you writing a revenge book," I hear him say. *"The Ultimate Payback.* Catchy title."

I shove my Vaseline into my bag, making an act of ignoring him.

"Lemme guess," he continues anyway. "You're Sophie. Wale's Wayne?"

I stare at him, speechless, for a beat too long. "You're out of order," I say finally.

Kojo holds up his two hands in front of his chest. "You're right. My bad, my bad. I shouldn't have read your work." Then, in a mutter, he says, "Didn't deny it, though."

My mouth feels as though it's been injected with anesthesia. It's not working as sharply as I would like it to.

"It's not about us," I say curtly.

Kojo smirks. He looks unconvinced. "Oh, yeah? So, why did you call Wayne Wale, then?"

My patience grows thin. "What are you talking about?"

Kojo motions toward my laptop. "Go on. Have a look for yourself," he says very calmly.

I know better than to let Kojo under my skin, and yet I open my laptop.

Kojo leans forward toward the screen. "There annnd . . . there," he says with a slanted smile. "Hashtag CancelWale." He laughs. "Rah, man. Are you that savage?"

A surge of blood rushes to my cheeks as I snap my laptop shut again and shove it into my bag. "It must have been a typo," I say, my voice breaking. "I must have got confused when I was watching . . ."

"Aww, Temi, I was only playing, man."

But it's too late.

Hot tears steamroll down my face.

"Aww, Temi, don't cry." Kojo puts a hand on my back.

I flinch at his touch and rise to my feet. Hurling my bag onto my shoulder, I make a dash out of the door. To my dismay, Kojo follows me.

"I said I'm fine," I say again as I stomp down the busy pavement, Kojo calling me.

He catches my wrist and tugs me back, forcing me to a standstill.

"You're a mess," he says softly. "I'm driving you home."

I try to object. He insists.

"Fine," I relent. I have no desire for a public back-and-forth.

In stony silence, I follow Kojo to his car—a silver hatchback Audi parked just a street away. Quickly, he steps ahead of me to open the passenger door.

I'm doing up my seat belt when Kojo reaches toward the back seat. He pulls out a can of Red Bull from his gym bag. "You want one?" he says.

I'm so thirsty, I nod.

"Thanks," I say after he opens the can and hands it to me. I down a large mouthful and place it in the cup holder.

Kojo smiles. "See, Wale isn't the only sweet boy." He starts the engine.

The drive to my flat is excruciating. Kojo bombards me with first-date-type questions.

"So, what you up to these days? You got any holidays coming up? How tall are you again?" (I never told him my height in the first place.)

I keep my answers short and to the point, every so often compulsively checking the GPS to see how close we are to home. Finally, we arrive. I unbuckle my seat belt.

"His loss," he says as I brace myself to get out.

He was just talking about Wale and how I shouldn't bother watching *The Villa*.

I actually snort. "Mate, you're not serious. *You* were the one egging him on!"

Kojo jerks his head as though he has amnesia. "Nah, man," he says. "I was just *testing* him. I wouldn't have failed."

He says this so quickly, my head swivels toward him in surprise.

Kojo looks me up and down with lust in his eyes.

My body burns with discomfort. I reach for the door handle.

"So, what? Man doesn't get a hug, now?"

With a strained smile, I turn around. "Thanks for the ride," I say, leaning over to give him a quick hug. But as I draw back, I feel a resistance. Kojo is holding me tight. He won't let go.

"Fancy doing something naughty?" he says, his voice a low rasp in my ear.

Shock sears through my chest; I recoil in disgust. Kojo, jumping at the opportunity, smears his lips on to mine. I want to gag. His tongue is like a slug in my mouth. A wet, rubbery thing.

"What are you doing?!" My cry comes out muffled. I keep shoving against him but Kojo won't loosen his grip. He's strong.

"C'mon, man. You wanna get back at Wale, don't you?"

We continue to struggle; I whack him again and again but it's like slapping feathers against a slab of cement. Useless. My hand makes a low, thudding sound against his body and over my cries. And then I remember the can of Red Bull. I grab it quickly and toss the contents at him.

"Argh! You bitch!"

Kojo finally releases me and fumbles at his wet trousers.

Heart thundering, I stumble out of his car and run to my flat.

21

I'm so taken aback by Kojo's presence at the restaurant that my body doesn't even react when Wale's hand lingers on the small of my back. He pulls out my chair and I collapse on to it, my legs no longer able to stand.

Fonzo gives me a tiny "Hey." Although he has on a bright mustard shirt, his face looks as though he would rather be at home. Something tells me he didn't know that Kojo was going to be here either.

"Kojo was in the area," Wale says, correctly reading my expression.

Kojo's wearing a fisherman beanie and a green bomber jacket, a silver chain over his top. He doesn't even have the decency to look embarrassed.

Fucking bastard.

The waiter returns and takes our order. I fire Shona a quick text:

And then I lock my phone and place it back on the table. She was right. I should have told Wale.

"Well, this is weird as fuck." Kojo leans forward, his frog-like eyes flitting between Wale and me. He then looks around the table in an exaggerated manner. "Yo, am I the only one here that thinks this is weird?"

Wale smiles. "Call it serendipity." He throws me a furtive side glance, clearly checking for my reaction.

No, I'm not okay, my eyes tell him.

He searches my face for a moment. And then, in what seems like a genuine effort to redirect the energy away from us, he says, "Oh yeah, thanks for putting me in touch with Shona. You're right. That girl does not play—"

"What's this about Shona?" Fonzo sits up.

"She's helping me with the gala." Wale fiddles with his beard. "She's got a background in event planning."

"Oh, that's great!" Fonzo brightens. "Well, if she needs any help . . ."

Fonzo is so into Shona.

"Oi, Temi."

Kojo's scratching voice slices my brief sanity. I drag my eyes to where he's slouched. He gives me another one of his chin nods.

"Apparently, you have a few questions for me and Fonzo."

. . .

I'm stabbing a cassava dumpling with my fork while trying to recall whether I've even asked a single question during this meal. Despite me saying, "I don't think this is the time and place," Kojo has been talking nonstop. He's been telling me—well, the whole restaurant, going by the volume of his voice—about his and Wale's history. They met spontaneously, roughly two years ago, at the gym, and since then they have been each other's right-hand man, regularly attending parties together. Numerous times, Kojo brought up the hot girls they had seen or approached on the night—perhaps to see whether he'd get a reaction out of me—to which Wale would respond with a rueful laugh and tease his friend for his photographic memory. Throughout Kojo's monologue, Fonzo, who has only interrupted once to state how much he loathes clubbing, remained heavily engrossed in his food (he's now finished) and kept checking his phone. I keep zoning in and out. I want to get this dinner over and done with so I can talk to Wale.

"Yo, Temi, you see this bruddah, here"—I catch an unfortunate glimpse of minced ackee in Kojo's mouth and scrunch my nose—"he wasn't always this hench, y'know," he finishes. He reaches over and pats Wale on the shoulder. "My man was *skin-ny*! Even skinnier than Fonzo."

Fonzo glances up from his phone irritably. "God, Kojo, you exaggerate everything."

"So, what happened, then?" I ask flatly.

"He met me, innit!"

The lady behind Kojo hisses as she looks over at him practically shouting.

"I basically became his PT," he carries on as he chomps another mouthful of food. "Gave him my regimen, showed him the ropes."

"Bet you regret it, though?" Fonzo says.

"Regret what?"

"Giving Wale his glow-up," Fonzo says. "Now girls aren't checking you. Though I doubt they were checking you in the first place. Isn't that why you tag along with Wale?"

Wale laughs. Whether or not Kojo means to, his eyes flicker in my direction, suddenly self-conscious. I'm tempted to lean over the table and give Fonzo a high five.

"Bruv, who even asked you?" Kojo says, his bravado returning. "You don't even know how to chat to gyal, let alone get one." He kisses his teeth. "So, yeah. As I was saying."

The monologue continues.

Kojo is now dissecting the social hierarchy of masculinity—apparently, he's an alpha. I ask the waiter for the bill. This is getting way too much. Wale tells everyone dinner's on him.

"Oh, yeah. I forgot you're Mr. Big Shot," says Kojo, slouching further in his chair. "And, bruv, what you saying about this podcast, man?"

"What podcast?" Fonzo and I speak at the same time.

"The one he keeps umming and ahhing about." Kojo throws Wale a pointed look.

"C'mon, man. You know I've been busy."

Kojo huffs and shakes his head.

"Sorry, what exactly will you be discussing on this podcast?" Fonzo says to Wale as a young couple walking by exchange in hushed tones, "Wait, isn't that Wale?"

Wale gives the couple a bashful smile.

"Oh, you know. The usual mandem stuff," Kojo says, rolling up his sleeves. "Football. Sex. Bitches."

Wale nearly chokes on his drink. "Bruv, c'mon, man!" He tilts his head at me.

"My bad, my bad. Girls."

I give him a side-eye. Honestly, he's insufferable.

"So, when do you plan to launch this podcast?" says Fonzo, still directing his questions solely at Wale. He sounds concerned. Like me, he must think this is a bad idea.

"It's still early days," Wale says, slipping his card into the leather bill holder. "We haven't even got a name yet."

"That's because you keep stalling, bro!"

"Bruddah, re-laaax." Wale tries to placate his friend. "Don't worry, Kojo. We'll talk, yeah."

It takes us a minute to leave the restaurant—one of the waiters wants a selfie with Wale, and then they all seem to want one. After we spill onto the pavement, we exchange quick goodbyes as it starts to rain.

Wale and Kojo clap each other on the back.

Fonzo gives me a hug. "We'll talk separately," he says into my ear.

Kojo turns to me. "Temi."

I give him a cold look.

We watch Fonzo and Kojo go their separate ways. Then, at the same time, we turn and gaze at each other. Light raindrops speckle Wale's skin.

"Let me give you a lift home," he says.

I'm glad he offered. We need to talk.

22

I've still not had the chance to speak to Wale. On the way to my flat, he received a call from Breezy Brett—a young, charismatic comedian who is currently taking social media by storm. Wale had somehow roped him into being the MC at the gala, so he was ringing to discuss details.

"Sorry about that," he says after he ends the call. We're now parked up outside my flat.

"Breezy Brett, yeah?" I nudge him in the arm and accidentally cop a feel of his muscles. "Look at you!"

Wale bats a hand as if it's not a big deal. It *is* a big deal.

"I'm proud of you," I say, filling in the silence.

Wale snorts. "Thanks, Temi, but all I did was send him a DM."

"I guess being blue-tick certified does help. Hey, reckon you can get Zendaya to get back to me?"

Wale stares at me, aghast. "Tell me you did not slide into Zendaya's DMs."

"What?" I shrug. "I'm a fan. And I like her box braids."

Wale snorts again. "Yeah, mate, you're definitely staying unread."

I laugh, and for a moment I remember how normal this was—to just sit in his car and chill. The vibe between us is so nice, it's tempting to ignore the Kojo situation. I open my mouth but Wale gets in first.

"Sorry, Tems," he says. "Mind if I use your bathroom real quick?"

While Wale is in the toilet, I pace my kitchen, rehearsing in my head what to say. My breathing is faster than usual. I did not expect to be this nervous.

"Thanks," I hear him say from behind me. I whip around. Wale is standing by the entrance, his hands in his pockets. After a beat, he says, "I guess I should get going."

"Are you sure you want to do the podcast?" My words tumble out in a flurry. "I mean, you already have a lot on."

Wale blows air out of his cheeks. Something tells me he is still uncertain.

"It's a sticky situation," he says eventually. "On the one hand, I want to support my boy—it's all he ever talks about and he wants to get into media. But on the other . . . I dunno. Maybe I'll revisit it after the gala."

"I don't think you should do it." My words shoot out like an arrow.

A frown appears between Wale's brows. He folds his arms and looks at me. "Why? Because you don't like Kojo?"

"Wale, the man is sexist. He called women bitches!"

"Fair enough," he says. "He shouldn't have said that. I'm sorry."

"And he talks too much. You wouldn't be able to get a word in edgewise. Wale, I hate to be the one who tells you this, but I don't think Kojo even likes you. He's just using you for what you can do for him."

My words must have cut deep because Wale breathes out heavily through his nose. "You don't know him, Temi," he says defensively.

"No, *you* don't know him. He—"

"Look, I know the guy is far from perfect but he's been there for me at my lowest—"

"What? He showed you how to lift weights. Wooow."

Wale looks hurt.

"Sorry, I . . ." This is not the way I planned to tell him. I lick my lips and try to recompose myself. And just as I take a breath, my phone buzzes.

I glance down at the counter. A notification has popped up on the screen. I have an email from Mayee. My heart pounds faster.

"I'm so sorry but it's my agent. I have to read this." With a trembling hand, I pick up my phone.

The Re-Write 133

Hi Temi,

Hope the ghostwriting job is going well. I can't believe Greg's celeb client is Wale Bandele!

Quick update—a new editor called Dionne Watts has recently joined Ocean Books. I know Dionne personally and she is a ferocious romcom reader. We met up earlier today and I pitched *Love Drive*. She absolutely loves the premise and is desperate to see an early draft ASAP! Can you send me what you've done either tomorrow or first thing Monday? In the meantime, she'll read *Wildest Dreams*—I can't guarantee she'll go for it but who knows?

I hope this news is encouraging and a massive well done for pulling yourself up by the bootstraps. I know these last several months haven't been easy. It's working with determined authors like you that makes my job even more delightful.

Fervently awaiting your manuscript!

Best wishes,
Mayee

"Holy crap," I say to myself.

"Temi, you okay? You look like you've just seen a ghost."

My legs turn into jelly. I make a grab for the counter, one hand on my chest.

Wale rushes to my side and holds me by my shoulder. All of a sudden, the kitchen is sweltering hot, and I can physically feel my cortisol levels rising.

"Temi, speak to me. What happened?"

I struggle for air. "I just got an email from Mayee."

"Yeah, you mentioned. What did she say?"

I manage to stand upright, my hand still clutching my cramped chest as if to slow my breath. I can't believe this is happening.

"Remember when I told you that Mayee said I should work on a new novel?"

"Yeah."

"Well, she actually set me this assignment nearly nine months ago."

"Okay."

"We caught up recently . . . and I kind of lied to her about how much I'd done."

Wale goes silent. "How much did you tell her?"

I bite the inside of my cheek. "About half a novel."

A flash of shock passes over Wale's face before he neutralizes it. "And how much have you *actually* done?"

Closing my eyes briefly, I tilt my chin toward the ceiling. "Nowhere close to that . . . about ten percent. And ten is being very generous."

"Shit," Wale says. "Sorry, do you mind if I have a look?" He motions for my phone.

I pass it over to him and then place my hands on my head. I feel faint.

"Oh, that's promising. She's also pitched *Wildest Dreams*."

"I appreciate your optimism, Wale, but what about *Love Drive*?"

Wale hands me my phone back with a long, deep inhale. "The way I see it," he says, "you have two options. You can either tell Mayee the truth. Or make up the other forty percent."

"I can't tell Mayee the truth!" The very thought is causing my brain to spin and send my anxiety into high gear. "I lied to her, Wale! She's going to be so pissed off! Trust me, Mayee is not the type of person you mess around with. What if she dumps me?"

"I'm sure she won't let you go—"

"But you don't know that! Her reputation is on the line too." I shake my head. "Do you know what she said when she signed me? She said she doesn't work with time wasters. She said, and I'm not even paraphrasing, that she won't hesitate to send them packing and has done before. And what will she tell Dionne? You read her email. She thinks I'm this role-model author."

"Then you send her what you can," Wale says calmly.

Everything is unfolding like a bad dream. I can't see a way out. Why, why, why did I get myself into this mess? Tears welling, I cover my face.

"Hey, hey, hey. Look at me." Wale gently prizes my hands away and then places his palms on either side of my cheeks. As though he's my human lifeboat, I cling on to his wrists.

"It's happening again." I start to cry. "I keep getting rejected." *Bonsai*, publishers . . . *you*.

The nightmare is now playing out like a prophetic vision. Mayee is on the other end of the call. "*Temi, I think it's best if you find another agent.*"

I choke on a bubble of tears and I begin to cry hysterically. I'm crying so much, I take in loud, ragged breaths.

"Hey, breathe, breathe." Wale demonstrates by taking a deep inhale before slowly exhaling again. He repeats this several times, his calm, even breaths cooling my clammy skin. Eventually, I fall in sync, and just like that, my breathing steadies. In the chaos, he still finds a way to be my anchor.

"You can do this," he says with that familiar conviction he'd used whenever I doubted my writing. He moves his head back so he can look me dead in the eye, his gaze locking on mine. "Send Mayee what you can and talk to her. She'll understand. You can do it, Temi. I know you can." He wipes my wet cheeks with his palms. "Don't forget—you've blitzed a novel before."

My body goes cardboard stiff. Does he know about *The Ultimate Payback*?

He smiles at my confusion. "You mentioned it in your interview," he says. "Or were you just trolling Greg?"

My shoulders sag with relief.

"Oh. That." I sniff. "Yeah, that was a long time ago."

"But you still did it, didn't you?" He tries to get a smile out of me. "Which meeeans"—he wipes another tear—"you, Miss Temi Ojo, have it in you to do it again. Look, let's cool off working on the memoir for the next few days. What can I do to help? I can be your Uber Eats."

I let out a throaty laugh. "I'm so glad you're here," I whisper, sinking into him.

Wale holds me tightly and presses a soft kiss to the side of my head. "Everything will be okay. I promise."

23

```
Love_Drive_Draft1.doc
Current word count: 7,104
28,000 words to go
Three days to go . . .
```

Wale leaves so I can get started. I run to my bedroom and power on my laptop. I grab a jug of water and an entire packet of digestives. It's going to be a long night. When I return, I collapse behind my desk. With shaky fingers, I shoot Mayee an email:

> Hi Mayee,
>
> That's such exciting news! I'm so pleased Dionne loves *Love Drive* and is reading *Wildest Dreams* too. I still need to tie up a few loose ends, so I'll send you my draft on Monday.
>
> Have a great weekend.
>
> Temi x

And then I open my manuscript and write.

I write as if my life is on the line, throwing everything on the page, hoping it works. Adrenaline rushes through my fingers as they clatter noisily against the keys. My mind is spinning. I can taste bile in my throat. It's as if I'm running a marathon I haven't trained for. I also feel majorly angry at myself. This situation could have been avoided.

An hour into writing, my phone buzzes. It's Shona—no doubt calling me for details on my run-in with Kojo. But I can't speak right now. I need to write. I *have* to.

And so, I write through the night. Pushing myself on even when my eyelids grow heavy and when I have brain fog and when my keys occasionally decide THEY NO LONGER WANT TO WORK! *For fuck's sake.* I write until the sun comes up, finally collapsing into bed, mentally and physically exhausted. When I'm woken by three sharp knocks, I mutter curses under my breath and drag myself up. I grab my phone en route—gosh, it's already gone 10 a.m.—while trying to recollect if I've ordered anything recently. I'm sure all the memoirs I bought for research have arrived by now.

As I swing open the door, I'm grateful that I'm still wearing yesterday's clothes and not my pajamas. I'm expecting to see a delivery man but, instead, it's Wale.

"I won't stay for long, mind if I come in?" he says.

I'd been standing there, staring. "Sure."

I watch Wale head toward the kitchen, a Tesco shopping bag in each hand, and then, when I realize I'm not dreaming, I follow.

"I got you brunch," he says as he opens the fridge and begins to unpack. "I wasn't sure if you'd want your pancakes sweet or savory, so I got you strawberries, sausages, and bacon." He smiles proudly and produces a plastic Tupperware out of the bag. "They're fresh. Well, they were. I fried them this morning. Ooh, I also got you some maple syrup and tons of healthy smoothies that claim to give an energy boost."

I stare at him in awe.

"Wale, you're a godsend," I say, giving him the biggest hug. This reminds me of that time when I got my fourth rejection. Wale had thrown me an actual "fuck 'em" party. He came over with banoffee pie ice cream and lemon drizzle cake. I felt much better after that. I feel a lot better now.

"And one last thing," he says, bending to reach into the massive Tesco bag for life. He pulls out a rectangular box.

I gasp.

No, he didn't.

"I got you a new laptop!" Wale holds up the MacBook Pro with a megawatt grin.

"Wale, this is too much!" I cannot bring myself to touch it. *And* it's rose gold. "How did you know I needed a new one?"

"Because you mentioned you were having problems with your current one, remember? Besides"—he shrugs—"every writer needs a good-quality laptop. One with keys that work."

My hands fly up to my mouth. *He remembered*.

"Thank you, Wale," I say breathlessly. "But this must have cost over a grand—"

"You need it, Temi. So, please accept it."

"Thank you."

"Oh, and I also got you a three-year warranty. In case of any, you know, future spillage."

I shove him. He laughs.

"Sorry, may I remind you that's how we met."

Wale says, "True. Gosh, who would have thought our clumsiness would lead to such blessings, eh?"

I can't stop smiling. He didn't have to do this but he did. He went out of his way for me. "Thank you, Wale," I say again. "I really appreciate the gift. More than you know."

For a hushed moment, we stare at each other like shy teenagers on a first date. I want to pull him in by the nape of his neck, rest in his arms, and kiss his beautiful lips. But I also don't want to make the first move. And I don't like the feeling of a kiss being attached to something—like, I'm only kissing him because he bought me a gift. Perhaps that's why he hasn't made a move.

"You know when we were together," he says, slowly now, "I always wanted to do something big and special for you, but I didn't have the means. I know receiving gifts is your love language."

"Actually, I said all five were my love languages. But I was only teasing."

"Still." He sets the laptop box on the counter. "Do you know, I used to imagine what I would do for you, if I could actually treat you the way I wanted . . . sorry, I'm bringing up old stuff again. I should go. You need to write."

Nooo.

With the most tender expression on his face, Wale plants a soft kiss on my forehead and says, "Good luck."

I hug myself as I watch him head toward the door.

"Wale!" I say.

He turns around.

I sigh. "Look, I don't know the ins and outs of your relationship with Cammie, but there isn't a salary requirement to be a good boyfriend. I know there's a lot of pressure for men to be earning an insane amount but try not to be influenced by the noise. Just do you, Wale. Be you. The right person will value you for *who* you are, not *what* you are."

A stretch of silence. Wale looks thoughtful as he takes in what I'm saying.

"Yeah, you're right," he says eventually. He clears his throat. And then he hisses. "Gosh, not me being introspective when you've got a whole novel to write—"

"Half, Wale! Half!"

"My bad, my bad. Half. Anyway, I really should get going. I've got a mad busy day. A charity photo shoot in Vauxhall and then a meeting with Spotify later. Crazily enough, the shoot is opposite the building where you used to work."

"Spotify, yeah? Check you!" I give him a playful look up and down.

Wale opens the door. "You need to get back to work." Then he stops and smiles. "Smash it."

24

```
Love_Drive_Draft1.doc
Word count update: 9,402
```

Right after Wale leaves, I set up my new laptop, feeling more determined to finish my draft. But I don't have the single-minded focus of the night before. Were Wale and I slowly finding our way back together? And do I even want us to get back together? Is it too soon? And I still can't believe that I haven't told him about Kojo. I am a knot of emotions as I attempt to write.

One hour and three clunky pages later, my phone flashes with a number I do not recognize. I set aside my half-eaten plate of sausage, bacon, and pancakes drizzled with maple syrup.

"Hello?" I answer with caution. Having worked at a call center, I'm skeptical of cold calls.

"Hi, Temi. It's Fonzo."

"Oh. Hey, Fonzo." He must have got my number from Wale. "How's it going?" I ask.

"Yeah, good. Sorry you didn't get around to interviewing me yesterday."

I'm wincing over a sentence I've just read. It takes me a second to reply. "Oh, um, you don't have to apologize. The restaurant was too noisy to do an interview anyway. Are you calling for us to arrange another time?" *Because I'm kind of in the middle of a crisis!*

"Actually, no," he says, to my relief. "But I can message you the days I'm free. Quick question—have you spoken to Wale today at all?"

"Yeah, he came by about an hour ago. Why?"

"Did he mention his meeting with Spotify?"

"Yeah. But he didn't tell me much about it other than it's later on today. Why? What's up?"

Fonzo lets out an audible breath that tells me he's concerned. "Okay, I'm not sure if I'm jumping the gun here," he says. "But he posted on his Instagram that he's excited about this meeting. And then, Kojo reposted it on *his* stories with the caption, 'These streets are not ready for us.' Do you think . . . ?"

There's a knot of dread in the pit of my stomach. In the past, a few contestants from *The Villa* have been offered Spotify deals. Deals that included creating their own podcast.

"But I spoke to Wale last night and he didn't exactly seem enthusiastic about it," I say.

"Maybe Kojo managed to persuade him," Fonzo says. "Or maybe it's something else and Kojo is getting ahead of himself."

I let out an irritated sigh. The timing of this news is inconvenient.

"It's probably nothing," Fonzo is now saying. "But I just thought I'd call you because you seemed to also think a podcast with Kojo is a terrible idea, and I haven't been able to get through to him."

"He's at a photo shoot," I say, remembering.

And then something hits me.

I know where Wale is. He mentioned the shoot is in Vauxhall, opposite Bonsai's office. I used to walk past the studio every day on my way to work.

Maybe this is a sign that I should go speak to him. If Wale goes ahead with this podcast, it can set him back—who knows what toxic masculinity BS will come out of Kojo's mouth. And he needs to know what type of person Kojo is before it's too late.

"Fonzo, hold on a sec." Bringing my phone away from my ear, I glance at the time. It's only been about an hour since Wale left. He is probably still at the shoot—hair and makeup take ages. He looked out for me this morning. He didn't have to. He didn't have to come by with brunch, make me pancakes. And he certainly didn't have to buy me a new laptop.

But he did.

Because he cares.

I might be about to make a stupid decision or I could be about to make a very brave one.

I return my phone to my ear. "Fonzo, leave it with me."

25

Taking a deep breath, I push open the glass door. Thanks to Uber, I was able to reach the studio in record time. On the way, I kept calling Wale, but he didn't pick up.

As I pace down the lobby, I have a gut-twisting feeling that I have reacted too quickly. I don't even know what I'm going to say. Too late, I'm here now.

"Hi, I'm here for the charity shoot," I tell the nose-ring-wearing receptionist. "I'm one of Wale Bandele's stylist's assistants," I add.

I'm in luck, the receptionist buys it. She hands me a clipboard and tells me to sign in.

"Room is on the third floor to your left," she says as she points me toward the lift.

On the third floor, I can hear the beep and flash of a professional camera, as well as an exuberant voice that keeps saying, "Nice!" and "Hold that pose!" I follow the sounds to an open, airy room, complete with a small kitchen and wide windows.

I stop dead in my tracks.

Wale is naked.

Like, actually naked.

Well, not nuts-out naked. He's posing with a football, which he has placed right in front of his crotch.

I don't know who is more surprised—me or him—but when our eyes meet, he almost drops the ball.

"Temi!" he exclaims.

I shield my eyes as if I've never seen Wale in the nude before.

"Sorry, may I help you?" says an achingly fashionable woman who, sure enough, looks to be the *actual* assistant to Wale's stylist, with her floaty, bohemian dress and wide, floppy hat.

Although, would a naked model need a stylist?

Just as I'm about to introduce myself as Wale's PA, Wale says aloud, "Don't worry, she's with me. Mind if we take five?" He grabs a towel nearby and literally side skips around the backdrop before reappearing again looking like a god of a man on the way to the sauna. *Damn, I've missed those abs.* With his towel now wrapped dangerously low around his hips, he strides toward me with an inscrutable expression.

"Let's go in there," he says.

We enter a dressing room with a vanity table covered with a refreshment spread, a full-body mirror, and a railing with swimming trunks on hangers. Wale shuts the door behind him. Thanks to the vanity's intense light bulbs and the baby oil I now realize he's slathered in, I can see the man in his full glory. The black ink along his defined arms shimmers like obsidian in the sunshine.

"You're naked." My thoughts practically fall out of my mouth. I'm so flustered by his lack of clothes.

Wale peers down at himself as if he's just realized this too. "Charity calendar," he says with a coy smile. "To raise awareness of prostate cancer. What you doing here? Is everything okay?" He puts a hand on my shoulder.

I'm hyperaware of his touch. *Focus, Temi.*

"Don't worry. I'm fine. I'm actually here for you."

His brows converge in confusion as he waits for me to explain.

"This Spotify meeting that you mentioned earlier, is it to discuss the podcast?" I'm speaking so fast, desperate to get it all out.

His frown deepens. "It's to discuss sponsorship for the gala, Temi. Shona set it up."

All my pent-up worries flood out of me, and I keel over, feeling both exasperated and relieved. I can't believe I abandoned my writing with the deadline imminent. I clutch my chest and stand. "Have you seen Kojo's Insta Story?" I ask.

Wale stares at me, irritation filling his eyes. "Did you seriously gatecrash my photo shoot?" he says. I open my mouth but he carries on sharply. "Do you not trust me to know what's right for me? I get it. You don't like Kojo."

"He kissed me!"

The words shoot out before I can soften them.

There's a deafening silence. My pulse is racing.

"It happened while you were on the show," I say quietly, rubbing my elbow. "We bumped into each other at Starbucks in Lewisham. We got talking about you and suddenly everything hit me and I got incredibly upset. I should have listened to my gut and turned down his offer to drive me home, but he insisted. Then, just as I was about to leave, he made a pass at me. I kept telling him to stop. I tried to shove him off. But he wouldn't let go. So, I threw my drink at him and ran."

Wale is rooted to the spot. He doesn't say anything. Instead, he's looking past my head toward the wall, quietly enraged.

He's fuming. I can tell. His nostrils are twitching and the light in his eyes has gone. I wish I didn't have to tell him like this. But I had to. I had no other choice.

"He assaulted you," he says finally, his piercing, hot gaze scorching holes into the wall.

The word "assault" triggers a memory—me hitting Kojo's arms, telling him to get off. Even though I know what Kojo did to me counts as sexual assault, I never gave it a name. It was this ugly thing that I didn't want to give power to. I also didn't want to identify as a victim. No one ever does.

Wale goes silent again, but I can tell that his mind is racing from the way he keeps shaking his head.

"You tried to warn me," he says, more to himself. "That fucking prick. And he had the audacity to sit across the table from you." He's getting riled up now. He pinches the bridge of his nose and inhales a ragged breath. Finally, he looks at me, guilt pooling in his eyes. "I'm so sorry, Temi."

I stare at him, a burning lump at the back of my throat. Remorse grips his face. He looks distraught.

I now understand why people keep secrets from the ones they love. They do it to protect them; they don't want to see them hurt. Because once the truth is out, not only are things not the same and relationships irreparable, but a part of them dies inside too. Maybe that's why I held back from telling Wale sooner? Trust means everything to him and, when broken, he completely withdraws—after all, doing therapy doesn't necessarily get rid of coping mechanisms. Perhaps I held back the truth because I was scared about him retreating within himself, going backward. I was scared the truth would reset his healing.

"Are you okay?" he says softly. He places a hand on my shoulder, concern laced in the creases around his eyes.

I nod. "I've had time to process what happened. Are *you* okay?"

"Don't worry about me. This is about you."

"Kojo disrespected you—"

"And Kojo violated you. Did you report it?"

"To the police?" I make a sound of disbelief. "You know how it is with these types of cases, Wale. They rarely go anywhere. It's hard to get justice. Besides, I very much believe in the power of my ancestors. Kojo will get what's coming for him."

Briefly, Wale closes his eyes, drawing air into his nostrils.

"I will be having words, though. I may not be confrontational but, bruv, don't ever take me for a dickhead. And then—" His jaw tics before he says, "He's dead to me."

A swell of emotion rises. I respect Wale for taking the high ground. I also appreciate him believing my story without poking it with questions or asking me to go into more detail.

"I'm sorry," he says again, pulling me into a baby-oil-scented hug. He wraps his strong arms around me, his mouth muffled in my hair. His body is warm and comforting like a snug winter jacket. I feel protected. Safe.

"It's not your fault," I whisper.

He responds by tightening his grip around my shoulders. I splay my hands on the contours of his back.

Then he releases me. "You should get going. You have half a book to write."

My belly clenches at the sudden reminder.

I watch Wale walk toward the door, his shoulders lower than usual. He goes to open it, stops, turns around. "How do you feel," he says, "now that you've got all that off your chest?"

"Um, free," I reply. "Relieved. Lighter."

Wale gives a slow nod. I can tell he's mulling something over.

"Well, maybe tell Mayee the truth too?"

26

I stare at my phone, then at my laptop. It's been nearly an hour since I got home and I'm still torn on what to do about Mayee. And I haven't managed to write anything of note either. I'm too churned up. Wale's suggestion is ringing in my head. Should I just tell her the truth? I'm starting to think I should.

But is it too much of a risk?

I put my phone down and let out an agitated breath. Okay, I need to make a decision. I need to know if *Love Drive* is worth fighting for. And I'll only know if I read back what I've written. Up until now, I've refrained from reading over my manuscript, worried I'd be vacuumed into the self-destructive, endless task of editing.

But right now, I have no choice.

. . .

I remain motionless in my seat. The silence in my room is profound.

I cannot send Mayee *Love Drive*.

And it's not even because the writing is rough, or the plot is both nonsensical and inconsistent. This story lacks one main ingredient: heart. While *Wildest Dreams* was born out of love, and *The Ultimate Payback* was born out of hate, *Love Drive* was born out of fear.

Before I can convince myself not to, I grab my phone and ring Mayee, steeling my spine to feel more confident. For a fleeting second, I think, *I've got this.*

Until Mayee picks up.

"Hi. Temi. What can I do for you?"

A surge of panic runs through my veins. I physically shake.

"Hi, Mayee. Um, do you have a minute?"

"For you? Of course."

All of a sudden, my mouth goes dry. I wish that I'd written some notes. Mentally prepared.

The silence that follows grows longer. It's loud in my ears.

"I've got something to tell you," I say finally.

There's a brief pause before Mayee says, "What's up, Temi?" She's gathered something is off from my tone.

I feel as though I'm about to parachute off a plane. I close my eyes and jump.

"I'm so sorry but I won't be able to send you my manuscript by Monday." I'm speaking in such a rush that my words run into each other. I feel the weight of Mayee's lack of response compressing my lungs. My body tenses.

"Oh, " she says finally. "Is everything okay?"

The concern in her voice is making things twice as hard. For a quick, passing second, I consider telling her that I've got a family emergency but I've told enough lies.

"The truth is . . . I haven't been working on *Love Drive* over the last nine months. For the last couple of weeks, I've been playing catch-up but it just isn't working."

There's a fraught silence. My heart thuds uncontrollably.

"I'm so sorry I lied," I croak, my voice a near whisper.

The wait before Mayee speaks again is excruciating. My blood pressure must be going through the roof.

"I have to say, Temi, I'm disappointed." Shame hits me in my core. "I didn't expect this from you, especially the lying. You've wasted both of our time."

Mayee's words are like a knife to the chest. I've never heard her sound like this. Ever. So, when she says, "I think we need to have a separate conversation about our working relationship," I panic.

"No, the reason why I can't send you my manuscript is because I've actually been working on another book!" I cry. "Sorry, I wasn't clear earlier. I *do* have a draft to send you; it's just not *Love Drive*."

"I see. What is this book called?"

And with my eyes squeezed shut, I say, *"The Ultimate Payback."*

27

Mayee loves the concept of *The Ultimate Payback*. She sounds much less annoyed.

"With dating shows like *The Villa* becoming so popular, it's very current."

I wince.

"So, what sparked the idea, then?" she asks.

And with a rueful laugh, I reply, "My ex."

After the call, I email Mayee the manuscript.

Overwhelmed with guilt, I curl myself in bed into the fetal position and sob. How did I get here? How could I be so stupid?

Then there's Wale.

Wale who has been so sweet and supportive. Wale who has been nothing but encouraging and even bought me a new laptop. Wale who's currently in therapy and becoming a better man. How could I betray his trust knowing he's still working on trusting me again?

I'm a terrible person. I don't deserve a second chance.

I phone Shona and tell her what happened. She listens, tries to reassure me.

"Try not to worry, hun," she says after I list out every worst-case scenario. "Nothing has happened yet. Do you know what you need? A pick-me-up. I'll come around yours tomorrow."

. . .

The next day, she takes me to our go-to nail salon in Lewisham.

"Everything will work out," she says, throwing me a concerned glance. "Try not to be in your head."

We're sitting side by side across from our nail technicians in the manicure section. While Shona has opted for three-dimensional acrylics with a sunflower pattern, I've gone for something that matches my mood: jet black. On a good day, I would have gone for number 137: a glittery teal polish.

The nail technician adds another coat on my right-hand nails. I dry my left under the LED UV lamp. "I just keep thinking about how Wale would react if he found out."

"Jeez, how bad is this book?" Shona says. The nail technician prods her to keep still.

I pull a face. "I was angry, Shona. I didn't hold back. I took a dig at his finances. Said he was rubbish in bed."

Shona's eyes go wide.

"Of course, I was exaggerating," I add quickly.

"So what? You faked a few orgasms," she says nonchalantly. "We've all been there before."

Across the table, her nail technician loudly clears her throat.

"You see, this is exactly what I'm nervous about," I say, lowering my voice. "People not being able to distinguish fact from fiction. What if word gets out that we dated? Everyone will assume that everything I wrote about him is true!"

"Okay, you're getting ahead of yourself," Shona says. "Realistically, the only other person who would know that *The Ultimate Payback* is based on him is Wale."

"Still!" I cry, not entirely convinced. "It doesn't sit right with me. How would *you* feel if your ex published a book about you and filled it with exaggeration and lies?"

Shona's expression turns serious. Her lips purse into a straight line. "I'd kill him," she says sharply. "Sue him for every penny he has. Cuss him out on Twitter."

I dip my chin as if to say, *Exactly*.

"And it's about having principles," I say with a sigh. "How can I write a memoir debunking the very things I portrayed him to be?"

A jerk.

A bad boy.

A cheater.

Each accusation is a scream in my head.

My pulse begins to race faster. I feel nauseous.

"I still think you're overworrying," Shona says, eyeing her nails. "Who knows? This book might not even go anywhere. If Mayee couldn't sell *Wildest Dreams*, which you had been working on for years, may I add, what makes you think the book that you blasted out in a matter of weeks will fare any better? And you wrote it as part of your healing process," she adds. "Breakups are painful; Wale will understand. *And* you're a writer for goodness' sake! Why wouldn't he end up in your book? Inspiration has to come from somewhere."

"I know, I know, but things are different now." My lips fall into a sulk. "I feel like he's beginning to trust me again. I . . ."

Shona swivels her head, as if she misheard. Then, in a quiet voice, she says, "You've fallen for him, haven't you?"

I stare at her, my throat thick with emotion, and then, slowly, I nod.

I don't know exactly when it happened—I've been in denial for quite some time—but now there's the possibility that I could lose Wale for good, I know I have. I believe he has too. Although he hasn't said it, I can tell through his actions; the way he looks at me. Whatever happens, this book cannot stand in the way of our second chance.

"Have you spoken to him?" says Shona after quietly studying my face.

I adjust my bag on my lap and shake my head. "Not since the photo shoot," I reply. "Though he keeps sending me voice notes. He thinks I'm still working on *Love Drive*. He keeps checking in on me."

Shona maintains a neutral expression to stop me from spiraling.

"Did he say how it went with Kojo?" she asks as she studiously watches the nail technician apply her acrylics.

"Nah. He probably thinks I've got bigger shit to deal with."

I inhale a waft of acetone. The sound of my nails being filed down fills the silence. I'm conscious that I'm turning into that grumpy friend who brings the mood down.

"Congrats again on the Spotify gala sponsorship!" I say, forcing cheer into my voice.

Shona brightens. "Thanks, babe. I had a contact there who owed me a favor."

"How's everything going with the gala, anyway? I can't believe it's in three weeks. And what's it like working with Wale?"

"I'm not gonna lie, hun, we actually work really well together."

I cough. "Is the world ending? Are pigs flying?"

She laughs.

With her persuasion, Wale has managed to convince Kathy to make the news of ACE's impending closure public. Now they have set up a crowdfunder, which they can use in their publicity and marketing to drive donations. They have also decided to host a small awards ceremony toward the end of the evening.

"We thought it would be nice to honor Kathy," Shona says. "Ooh, speaking of the gala, we need to go dress shopping." She starts talking about the type of dresses she wants to try.

I'm waiting for the countdown on the nail-drying lamp to reach zero when my phone vibrates. I wait for the remaining seconds before I remove my hand.

It's Fonzo. We have arranged to do his interview today and he's ten minutes away.

"Fonzo," I say to Shona. "You seen him recently?"

"No. Why?"

"Oh, no reason." I text Fonzo back:

> **Temi:**
> See you soon.

A short moment later, Shona gets out her purse to pay for our nails. I hug her from behind. "Thank you. You're the best. Next appointment is on me."

She pecks the side of my head. "Anytime, babe. Besides, your nails were looking scraggly."

I shove her.

We're making our way out of the door when Shona bumps straight into Fonzo's chest.

Perfect timing.

He's wearing an open-buttoned pink shirt with a vest underneath, denim shorts, and Converse.

"What you doing here?" she asks at the same time Fonzo says, "Hey!"

"The same reason you're here." He wiggles his fingers. "Got a nail appointment." Shona doesn't laugh. Fonzo coughs into his hand. "I'm meeting up with Temi."

"Oh." She turns to me with a dubious expression.

"It's for Wale's memoir," I say quickly. "I'm interviewing him."

"Well, let me not hold you guys up." Shona turns to hug me goodbye.

"I hear you're helping out with the gala," Fonzo says—it comes out as an outburst. "If you don't mind, I would love to get your thoughts on some photos I've taken. I've done a series with some of the carers who are supported by ACE. I need some help narrowing down which ones I should exhibit on the night. Temi says you have a good eye."

"Oh, did she now?"

I avoid her gaze.

"You reckon you can help?" Fonzo rubs a hand over his collarbone. Shona looks at him for a few seconds.

What are you waiting for then? I want to say. *Say yes!*

"Yeah, sure," she says finally with a half shrug.

Fonzo whips out his phone at lightning speed. And then drops it and has to bend down to retrieve it.

"Nice nails," he says as Shona puts in her number. She hands him back his phone and he quickly gives her a missed call.

"Right, I'm off," she says as I fight the urge to celebrate. *Finally.*

We hug and, just as I'm about to release her, she says in my ear, "I know what you're doing."

28

```
Wale_Memoir_Draft1.doc
Target word count: 10,000
Current word count: 12,062
Four weeks to go . . .
```

We go to Greenwich Park, where we perch under a tree with a view of a small lake and a few ducks swimming. Once we're seated comfortably, I pull out my laptop and phone, mulling over how to make the best of this interview. With only four weeks to go until I have to submit my first draft, I need to make headway. Fast.

So far I've written more than forty pages, including how sensitive Wale was growing up and how he flourished in his charity job—two things the public would be surprised to learn about him. I'm planning to use my time with Fonzo to find out more about Wale's teenage years and to pick his brains on some other misconceptions people may have of him.

Fonzo tries to get into a comfortable position. He resorts to hugging his knees. "Before we get started," he says, pulling the tongue of his Converse, "I just want to say I'm sorry to hear what happened with Kojo. That guy is the worst. Are you okay?"

I feel touched by Fonzo's concern and I'm glad that Wale opened up to his best friend about it. "I'm better. Thank you for asking. You good to get started?"

"Ready when you are."

Fonzo paints a picture of his oldest childhood friend. He uses some of the words his parents did—sensitive, quiet. But he also talks about the silliness and the laughter that flowed when Wale was comfortable—playing FIFA or doing homework in Fonzo's kitchen. He doesn't mention anything about Wale's caring experience. I guess he wants to respect his privacy.

"So, at what point did he come out of his shell?" I ask.

Fonzo refolds his white cotton socks, his long legs peppered with stray hairs. "Definitely secondary school," he says without missing a beat.

He tells me about a more cheeky, outgoing Wale who grew more confident after he got his teeth straightened. He was never one of the popular kids at the all-boys state school but, unlike Fonzo, he sought their validation.

"Why is that?" I ask with genuine curiosity.

Fonzo ponders. "I guess gaining the right type of respect boosted his confidence. Made him feel like a top dog."

He then goes on to share a few anecdotes about the things they got up to both in and out of the classroom, including having a water-bomb fight, which saw their poor French teacher get caught up in the cross fire.

"Sorry, I'm going off topic," he says after laughing at the memory. He nods to my laptop. "Wale tells me you both drew up a list of things people assume about him. If you like I can share my two cents on a few?"

"Good idea." I retrieve the document and turn my laptop around.

"People assume that I'm scared to love," he says, reading aloud. I feel my cheeks blush. At the time, I wasn't too sure if Wale had only said that to reassure me that he had always felt the same way I'd felt about him, even if he hadn't vocalized it as openly. But then, Fonzo says, "You know about his ex-girlfriend Cammie, right? Well, BC Wale wasn't scared to love but AC Wale . . ." His voice trails.

So, I got the AC Wale, I can't help but think. "Tell me, what was BC Wale like?"

Fonzo takes off his glasses and cleans each lens on the hem of his shirt. "BC Wale was a sucker for love," he says. "You know those Black American romance movies? Yeah, he was obsessed with those. I think seeing Black love made him aspire to be in a long-term relationship."

I smile. "Yeah, he told me he watched *The Best Man* parts one and two, like, twenty times."

"Do you know how he met Cammie?"

"Yeah, in the library."

Wale had told me how Cammie would usually study in the quiet section, which made it difficult to go speak to her in person—unless he was prepared for a potential public rejection. Apparently, he wasn't as confident as he is now. So, on the way to the toilets he dropped her a handwritten note. She later dropped one back and the rest was history.

"He really liked her, Temi. And I mean *really* liked her to the point he was calling me, like, every day to tell me about her. Okay, maybe not every day, but you know what I mean."

"It's so hard to believe that Wale didn't have the courage to speak to her," I say. "The other day, he told me he felt he wasn't in her league."

Fonzo stares at me. "Temi, the Wale you see today isn't the Wale back then." He sighs. "He's going to hate me for this." But still, he pulls out his phone and swipes a few times before handing it to me.

The second my eyes land on the screen, my brows quirk. It's as though I'm looking at one of those "before they were famous" pictures. Gone are the tattoos, the beard, the muscles. Wale was slim—but not as slim as Kojo had said. He was still handsome; he just didn't have that swag.

"Okay, I've got a visual image." I hand Fonzo his phone back.

"Wale was besotted. He couldn't believe his luck. I think he felt it was a privilege to be with her, so he did everything he could to make her happy. But Cammie liked the finer things in life. And Wale didn't have money like that. Still, he did what he could to make her happy, to make them work. He surprised her with gifts, took her to fancy restaurants. He was so in love with her, Temi, he even introduced her to his parents."

My shock must have shown on my face because Fonzo says, "Yeah. That was a massive deal for him."

"This is going to sound strange, Fonzo, but I never really got the full story of what led to their breakup. Wale said it made him angry just thinking about it. He said she made him feel like nothing."

At the time, I didn't pry. After all, we had agreed to take things slow, and so I had to respect our decision. In truth, though, I had agreed to go at *his* pace, which was a lot slower than I'd have liked. *He will tell me when he's ready*, I thought. "We don't have to talk about it if you don't want to," I would say. I didn't want to do anything that would push him away or make him have doubts about going exclusive, especially as when we first started talking he'd told me he wasn't actively looking for a relationship. And so, if it meant shying away from asking the deep, important questions, that was what I was going to do.

But if Fonzo is saying that "AC Wale" is scared to love, then *something* must have happened in their relationship. Something major.

Now Fonzo looks visibly torn over how much he should share while also respecting Wale's boundaries. He reads aloud again: "People assume that I'm a cheater." And when his eyes ping back to me, he adds, "How ironic."

29

```
Wale_Memoir_Draft1.doc
Target word count: 18,000
Current word count: 15,108
Just over three weeks to go . . .
```

Over the next few days, Fonzo's interview continues to whir in my head, so I set up camp in a café near my flat to continue working on Wale's memoir. Wale has a few press commitments, so I won't be able to see him until later on during the week.

The more I find out about Wale, the more I realize that I hardly knew him at all. I was so blinded by his charisma and good looks and maybe even the excitement of getting into a relationship that I didn't want to accept that he was emotionally unavailable.

It's like having a chocolate cake. You know it isn't healthy and has a ton of calories. And yet, you have it anyway because it looks good and it also makes you *feel* good—until it doesn't.

Wale made me feel good. Better than good, even. He made me feel alive. He made me feel happy. Special. Chosen. And yet, I felt these things without him being completely vulnerable with me. Maybe I was in love with the idea of being in love. And who can blame me? How often do you meet the man of your dreams in person and have an instant connection with them so electrifying you can't imagine life before they were in it?

My feelings for him then were loud. Like a swarm of bees that never stopped buzzing.

But my feelings now are different. They're quiet. Deep. Growing in depth and intensity the more layers he peels back and the more I discover about him. He feels something, too—I sense it—but he's following my lead, gauging each interaction, being patient, playing chess. At some point, though, we're going to have to have a conversation. What do we both want from each other once the memoir project is done? Let's be real. We've crossed the line of keeping things "professional" a long time ago.

After I end up rewriting a paragraph for the third time, I stop. I can only do so much. I need to get the full story about Cammie. From Wale.

I grab my phone and message him, asking if he's got time to fit in a quick meeting. Forty minutes later, I receive a text from Wale saying that he's waiting outside in his car. I gather my belongings and go out to meet him.

"I could have met you in the café," he says as I shut the door behind me.

I lean over to give him a hug and get a lungful of his scent: half cologne, half something distinctly his. "It's okay," I tell him, sitting back. "I actually wanted to speak to you in private."

Wale looks at me as if we're about to talk about something serious. He angles himself toward me. "Okay, but first: How did it go with Mayee?" he says.

His question takes me by surprise—not because I hadn't anticipated it, I just wasn't expecting it yet. Thankfully, I had already thought about what I was going to say.

"I told her the truth." My voice comes out crisp and clear.

"You did? Wow. How did she take it?"

After talking it out with Shona, I had decided there was no point telling Wale about *The Ultimate Payback*, especially as it might end up leading to nothing. I would just be causing a fire for no reason. Why ignite the flame? And yet, something is nudging me to tell Wale the entire truth.

"She was really disappointed in me, Wale, so I . . ."

Wale puts a hand on my shoulder, empathy flooding his eyes.

I swallow my words. "So, I told her I was extremely sorry. And asked her to give me a second chance."

Wale nods. "I'm proud of you, Tems," he says, giving my shoulder a squeeze. "And you should be proud of yourself. What you did takes guts."

His words tighten my throat and I can barely hear myself when I say, "Thanks." Except I don't feel proud—I wish I could be completely honest with him, but something is preventing me from telling him about *The Ultimate Payback*.

"I take it she didn't let you go, then?"

"No." My voice comes out a strangled whisper from the discomfort of it all. I decide to change tack. "Wale, can I talk to you about something?"

"Yeah, sure." He adjusts his sitting position again.

"Did Cammie cheat on you?" I ask in one breath.

Wale's lips part. He stares at me, unblinking, like a frozen still. He clears his throat. "Fonzo messaged me that you interviewed him."

"In his defense, he didn't say it outright. Wale, that must have been heartbreaking. Why didn't you tell me?"

Wale purses his lips as if he's giving my question serious thought. "Record me," he says.

I'm so taken aback by his words that it takes me a second to understand what he means. I snap into action, get out my phone, and hit record.

"It was savage—the way I found out," he says with mock humor. But I can tell from the way he takes a deep breath that he's still trying to work through the hurt, make sense of it all. Cammie and Wale broke up two years back, which isn't that long ago. I'm still working through my baggage with Seth seven years later so I'm familiar with how long it can take.

"In hindsight," he carries on, "the signs were there." He looks reflective. "She kept blowing me off, saying she was too busy studying. She was doing her master's up in Hull. So, one day, I thought I'd do the sweet boy thing and drive up to surprise her." When he sees my expression, he says, "Yeah, I know. Five hours. In the rain too."

"Then what happened?" I ask gently. Wale has gone silent. He's staring out of the front window at the silver parked car in front. I hate seeing him like this. I know how it feels to be betrayed. To be blindsided.

"There was a Sainsbury's not too far from where she was staying," he says finally, dragging a hand over his mouth. "I stopped off to grab a bottle of wine. And who did I see holding hands with another man in the alcohol aisle?"

Despite myself, my mouth falls open. I can't imagine the depth of betrayal he'd felt.

"And what did you do?" I ask softly. Wale has fallen silent again. He looks so bereft, I wonder if he's trying his best not to cry. And then, eventually, he says, "Nothing. I did absolutely nothing. Well, not there and then. I did confront her on the phone later on. But in the moment..." He shakes his head. "I froze."

I reach past the gear stick and put a hand on his knee. My chest physically aches as if it's been cracked. I know what that feels like—to not do anything in the moment. To live with regret.

Wale swipes the back of his hand under his nose. He sniffs. "I went back to my car," he says. "And I waited. I waited until they came out. And when they did, I watched them. They were smiling, laughing, holding hands still. She got into his car. He drove a Porsche. You know, as I was sitting there, I was observing *every* little detail so that I could use it to confront her later. At least, that's what I told myself to make me feel better for not doing anything. When, really, I was sizing up the guy. Comparing myself to him. He was hench. Well put together. Going by his car, he was obviously making good money. He seemed"—Wale's throat juts out as he swallows—"much more of a man than me."

I squeeze his knee then, my heart breaking into a million pieces. Wale places his hand over mine. I feel glad that I'm here to provide comfort in this moment. As he has been doing for me.

"How did she react when you did speak to her?" I gently stroke my thumb over his skin.

"Hysterical," he replies. "Though I think she was more upset that she got caught. She couldn't stop saying how sorry she was, that she didn't mean to hurt me. But not once did she fight for me. Not that I would have taken her back," he adds quickly. "But at least that would have made me feel that she actually did love me. It was like I meant nothing to her. That she was only with me because she felt sorry for me."

I shake my head, enraged and disturbed in equal parts. His every word crushing my soul. "Gosh, I can't imagine how you must have felt. How does one even get over that?"

"Yeah, I was in a dark place," Wale says, staring off. "I shut out the world around me, became a recluse, bottled all my feelings. Not even Fonzo could get through to me. Though it was him who suggested I sign up for the gym after I said I didn't need therapy. He thought it would help get my mind off things. And that's how I met Kojo," he says, turning his head toward me a little.

"It's okay." I squeeze his hand. "Go on."

"I was in the changing room," Wale continues, "and I just broke down. It was Kojo who found me. I was a mess. He said, 'Yo, bro,' put a hand on my shoulder, and gave me a hug. It meant a lot." He sits in the silence before carrying on. "Here was I, a complete stranger, getting snot on another grown-ass man's clothes." He chokes out a small laugh. "Kojo took me for a drink. I told him everything. He listened."

Now it all makes sense.

"Kojo helped you get back on your feet," I say as Wale retreats into another one of his quiet moments.

He closes his eyes briefly and draws a long stream of air into his nose. "Yeah," he says, breathing out. "We started hanging out together, going to the gym. He even came with me to get my first tattoo. He encouraged me to work on myself, not necessarily to prove something to my ex, but to do it for me. And that's what I did." He sighs. "I put dating on the back burner, started lifting weights. The crazy thing is, the more I focused on myself, the more female attention I got. I guess the new look helped." With a small smile, he nods to his tatted arms.

"I wish you'd told me," I whisper. We interlock fingers. "I wouldn't have judged you. Remember when I overheard Seth. I froze too."

He gives me a squeeze. "I felt embarrassed," he says after a silent beat, his voice small. "I'm supposed to be a man."

The meekness in his voice rips me in half. Does he not see it? That this—opening up—is what *makes* him a man? I'm no therapist, but I think Wale has a masculinity complex.

"It sounds petty," he's saying now, "but part of the reason why I said yes to going on *The Villa* was so that Cammie could see the new me."

"I get it." My mind recalls me bumping into Seth. I wanted him to know that I was doing well too. "You wanted Cammie to see you thriving and unbothered. But what I don't get," I say slowly, "is why you decided to get with me. Granted it was years later, but you even said you weren't looking for a relationship."

"Because I really liked you, Temi," he says, looking at me dead on. And for what feels like an eternity, we both stare at each other. I understand that people can change their mind. But he wasn't ready for a relationship when we got together. I got the AC Wale. With all the baggage.

Wale appears to read something in my face because he apologizes. "I'm sorry that I wasn't completely honest. But please understand, it was never to do with you. I just had my guard up; I needed to protect myself. I thought taking things slow would help. But, in the end, I had one foot in and one foot out. It was like I was waiting for you to go behind my back. Waiting for history to repeat itself."

"That's why you didn't drop out of the show," I say, more to myself than him. *The Villa*—it was his backup plan.

"It's also why I became withdrawn," he says, following it up with a deliberate pause. "I'm talking about after I found out you were meeting up with Seth. Temi, why didn't you tell me? Especially if it was just to discuss a job opportunity. Though I would have thought you'd want nothing to do with him."

"I didn't!" My voice comes out with a tinge of exasperation.

"I don't understand, Temi. Please help me understand."

The earnestness in his voice breaks me. It's time Wale knows the truth.

"There was no job." I look straight ahead, directing my words to the windscreen now. "Seth works in publishing as an assistant editor."

I can't bring myself to look at Wale, to see the shock in his eyes as he makes the connections. Wale remains perfectly still, his strong gaze on me.

"I bumped into him—at Waitrose of all places," I carry on. "We got chatting. I tried to keep things cordial. I didn't want him to think that what he did still had a hold on me. And then"—I sigh—"he tells me what he does for a living. I couldn't believe it, Wale. I thought, *Maybe it's a sign.* And so, I told him about *Wildest Dreams*. He seemed really, really excited by it, but he had to shoot off—he was on his lunch break. He said we should discuss it over coffee. And that's when we exchanged numbers."

I wait for Wale to say something. He reaches for my hand. I turn to him.

My heart melts. He's still looking at me with such gentleness in his eyes. Of course, Wale wasn't going to judge me. All this time, I projected my shame on to him.

"Over the next few days"—I heave out a breath—"I was going out of my mind. I had been rejected by nine publishers. It felt like Seth was my only hope. I thought, what if bumping into him wasn't just some weird coincidence? That's why I didn't mention anything sooner. To be honest, I was afraid you'd persuade me out of it. But the more I tried to convince myself to meet him, the more wrong it felt. My spirit just felt unsettled. My main character is unapologetically plus size and unapologetically Black. Why in the world would I entrust my book to him? He wasn't prepared to stand up for me. I didn't want you to know that I even contemplated selling out and *that's* why I didn't tell you the truth." My voice cracks on the final word.

Wale doesn't say anything but the silence is comfortable—he brushes light strokes over my thumb as if to say, *I'm here*. The anxiety, the fear, all those big feelings and worries I had about telling him, disappear. Just like that.

"I'm sorry I wasn't honest with you." My voice is just above a whisper. "I didn't want you to think that I have no integrity, no values. But now that I know about you and Cammie, I can understand how seeing a text from my ex was triggering, and why you struggle to trust."

"I'm sorry I didn't tell you about Cammie," Wale says faintly.

"It's okay," I say.

His lip hitches up just a fraction. "I'm glad we can be real like this."

"Me too." I smile back. "Shame it took us forever to get here, though."

We laugh a little and continue to stare at each other, neither of us willing to break the spell. Wale's gaze is unwavering and so tenderly familiar that I feel a tingle of déjà vu—whenever he dropped me off in the past, he would seal the evening with a goodbye kiss. The very thought sends prickly goose bumps down my arms. Now, suddenly, the car is too hot, too small. My eyes make an involuntary fall down to his lips. My breath is shallow and we're leaning over the cup holder and gear stick toward each other. Tentatively, his lips brush mine first, and when I shift toward him, my phone slides from my lap onto the floor with a thud. It doesn't snap us out of the spell; instead, he presses into me, hard. A crackle of fireworks explodes inside of my belly as I give in to the sensation: nostalgia, relief, wanting, all rolled into one. Effortlessly, our tongues find their rhythm. It's as if we've never been apart, and yet the kiss feels urgent—as though this is our last chance.

Wale cups the back of my head. I trail my fingers along the sides of his face. It's impossible to stop.

"I miss you," he says gruffly.

He kisses me fervently, passionately.

I'm buzzing so much that the vibration of my phone doesn't feel like it's coming from outside my body.

"Don't you wanna get it?" Wale says, his voice husky, his breath warm.

I reply by kissing the soft skin on his neck. "Not really."

I feel Wale's lips curve into a smile. His hand brushes my boobs. I slide a hand around the nape of his neck. He lifts my chin and trails kisses along my jawline. I feel the flicker of his tongue against my earlobe and I bite my lip to stifle a loud moan.

The moment is punctured by my phone buzzing again. I hadn't even realized it had stopped.

"You should probably get that," he says, reclining into the driver's seat.

"I'll put it on silent."

Breathless, I bend over and pick up my phone from where it had slid on the floor.

I freeze.

"Shit, it's Mayee."

"Again?" Wale sits forward. "I'm starting to think I'm some sort of omen or something. Aren't you going to pick it up?" He puts a hand on my knee.

Clearing my throat, I pick up the call. *The Ultimate Payback* is like a siren in my head. No, it's only been a few days. There's no way Dionne could have read it just yet.

"Mayee, hi!"

"Temi! Thank God, you picked up. I've got some major, major news for you. Are you sitting down?"

Wale lets out a small gasp. Oh crap, he can probably hear her.

"Just a sec," I squeak, turning to clamber out of the car.

"Guess who just got offered a book deal?!"

My body turns ice cold as I get a blast of breeze while I slam the door behind me. I pace a few steps away from the car. *It can't be.*

"For which book?" I ask.

Mayee laughs as if she's surprised that this is the first thing I say. "*The Ultimate Payback*, of course. And guess what? Dionne's offering high five figures."

Just like that, my greatest dreams and my biggest nightmare become reality.

My emotions are so overwhelming that I have to choke back some tears, drawing looks from a few pedestrians walking by. I drag a shaky hand over my hair, my lips juddering.

"Aww, Temi. You deserve it," Mayee says.

I can barely speak. All I keep thinking is *Wale, Wale, Wale*.

I glance at him as he watches me from behind his car's front window. He grins and gives me two thumbs up.

"Is it okay if I call you back when I get home?" I say tearily.

"Of course. Take a moment. I know this news is so sudden."

She congratulates me again and we end the call.

My head is so hot; I bend over and put my hands on my knees. I don't know what I'm going to do. I'm fucked.

And then I feel a hand pull me to an upright position; my body is smothered into Wale's chest.

"You did it!" he cries. "They loved *Wildest Dreams*!"

30

```
Wale_Memoir_Draft1.doc
Target word count: 18,000
Current word count: 16,062
Just over three weeks to go . . .
```

I always thought I would be too excited to sleep on the day I got a book deal. And I'm wide awake all right. But it's adrenaline and anxiety rather than excitement keeping me up. After Wale helped me back into his car, he drove me home while I sat in silence, only managing to utter a few words—"I can't believe it." He thought I was still in shock, so he talked instead, filling the suffocating air with his pure joy.

If the stakes were high before, they're monumental now. A high five-figure book deal with the world's biggest publisher is any writer's dream. I have manifested, wished, visualized this very moment. Although I've never been in it for the money, I would be able to write full time for a good number of years.

But what about Wale?

Wale would be so hurt if I published a book that played into his biggest insecurities. Especially now that I've earned his trust.

Only a few hours ago, I told him about Seth and how, ultimately, I couldn't compromise my morals and my values. And now I'm compromising them.

I begin to question myself. My integrity.

After all, it was integrity that led me to tell Wale what happened with Kojo. It was also integrity that prompted me to tell Mayee the truth about *Love Drive*. So, what was it when I emailed Mayee a copy of *The Ultimate Payback*?

Desperation?

Fear?

Relentless ambition?

Am I actually willing to do *anything* to get published?

I don't know what to do. There's so much on the line. And if I tell Wale, would he still want me to write his memoir? I'm really, really invested now.

But, more importantly, I care about him. I love him. I was hoping we would get our second chance.

I think about our kiss.

My tears soak my pillow.

The next morning, I do not feel any better. I am tired to my bones. But I only have a little more than three weeks until I have to submit Wale's memoir, so I need to put aside my emotions. When I called Mayee back yesterday, she said Dionne wanted to meet me next Monday. Naturally, *The Ultimate Payback* is going to need a good edit. And while Dionne probably won't be keen on me changing the plot, she may be more open to me tweaking a few things so that the indirect references to Wale aren't so damning. But until we've had that conversation, I'll need to somehow avoid seeing him this weekend. Thankfully, I'm going up to Oxford for Rosemary's celebration lunch on Sunday. Which leaves just today—Saturday. I'm hoping he's super busy.

I read and annotate Wale's interview transcript—although it reads more like an outpouring from the heart. I type a few titles before finally settling on one.

People assume that I'm a heartbreaker
The truth is I've been heartbroken

I write. For hours. Getting lost in the desire to do right by Wale. I don't even stop to cook, ordering a LEON takeaway instead. Ten minutes later, I hear a knock. That was quick.

"Wale!" I cry after I open the door.

Wale is standing at the entrance with an actual djembe under his arm. With a grin, he slaps the drumhead with his bare hands and sings along to the beat, bending his back a little while bopping his knees. I recognize the song instantly. It's one of those West African tunes that I used to hear often at my parents' church.

"What are you doing?" I tug him inside before the neighbors complain.

"Pala lalalala!"

"Wale!"

"Blow your trumpet! Pala la la la."

"Wale!"

Finally, he stops, but not without giving a few last whacks on his drum. He flashes me a grin. I haven't seen him this happy.

"I'm celebrating!" he says. "Tell me. How does it feel?"

Fuck.

"Um, insane," I shrill, rubbing my arms.

"Yeah, man. It's *crazy*, still. Hope you don't mind me stopping by?"

I bite my lip. "Actually, I'm kinda busy working on your memoir."

"Temi, fuck that. We need to go out and celebrate. Me, you, Shona, and Fonzo."

"Wale, I've got a deadline—"

"And you've just been offered a book deal. I'm sure you can spare at least an hour."

If I persist and keep saying no, he'll think something's up and start to ask questions. I need to act normal. Well, I need to act as if I'm really excited about this book deal.

"You're right," I say, twisting my lips into a smile. "But give me a couple hours, though, to finish a few things. And whatever you do"—I raise a finger—"do not bring that drum."

Wale feigns disappointment. "No? I had a special performance planned and everything."

"And I don't want to go anywhere fancy," I add. The last thing I need is Wale splashing on me. "Whatever Shona recommends goes." I called her last night, so she's clued up on everything.

"Okay, no drums. No bougie restaurants. Anything else?"

I shake my head.

"Right, I'll leave you to crack on," he says, hoisting his drum under his arm. He lingers at the door for a moment and then he reaches forward to kiss me. I see it coming so I quickly offer him my cheek instead. I refuse to make the next few hours even more agonizing. But from the embarrassed look he gives me after, I think I have.

"See you in a bit," he mutters.

He turns and leaves.

. . .

Thankfully, Shona sticks to the brief. We meet at Camden Market—much less stressful than a sit-down meal. It would be even less stressful if Fonzo and Shona stopped walking ahead, but at the same time it's really sweet watching them bond.

Breathing in a concoction of grilled meat, pizza, and fries, Wale and I browse various street food vendors lined with messy huddles of people. With every turn we take, there is another type of music playing. The buzz is a welcome distraction.

"Seen anything you like?" he says as I peer at a stand: JOLLOF MAMA: NIGERIA'S FINEST FOOD WITH A TWIST. A sweaty-faced chef is sautéing a steaming pan of prawns, spring onions, and chili seasoning, while a woman in a head tie serves foam takeaway boxes to the customers. On a normal day, I would have gone for something on their menu. Or from the vibrant Venezuelan stall a few yards back. But I'm feeling nauseous. Best to avoid spice.

"Not yet," I say again, wishing the stall a silent goodbye. At this rate, I'm going to end up getting an egg-and-cress sandwich from Boots.

We resume what I hope is a comfortable silence. I've managed to field most of Wale's overexcited questions by reminding him that I won't know anything until I meet Dionne on Monday. I go back to pretending to study the menus. I'm so conscious about acting normal that I'm finding it hard to relax.

"Do you know what I'm in the mood for?" Wale cuts through my hyperactive thoughts. I turn to him. He's wearing his face mask. "Something with lots of tzatziki in it," he finishes.

"Well, you're in luck. The gods have heard you." I nod to the Greek food stall across from us.

"Hey, Shona! Fonzo!" I yell.

But Fonzo and Shona are too busy laughing and chatting.

"We'll catch up with them later," Wale suggests, already making a beeline toward the kiosk.

Just my luck.

I join Wale in the queue. The smell of truffle aioli tickles the inside of my nostrils.

"The classic souvlaki wrap looks good," he says after surveying the list of sandwiches written on the chalkboard. "I think I'll get the one with the Halloumi."

"Excellent choice." I pretend to contemplate the menu.

The vibe is giving awkward first date. This conversation is taking effort.

"So," Wale says after a moment, his hands in his pockets, "how did your parents react?"

"My parents?" *Shit, I should have prepared for this.* "Um . . . I haven't told them yet. I'm seeing them tomorrow."

Wale's smile reaches his eyes. "They're going to lose their minds. How do *you* think they'll react?"

Truthfully, I hadn't considered telling my parents until now. "Actually, I'm not sure if I want to tell them just yet. They're throwing a celebration lunch for my childhood friend. She recently finished med school. I don't want to steal the limelight."

Wale looks at me as though I'm barking mad. He shakes his head. "Temi, man! You're too modest. First, you didn't wanna go out and celebrate. Now you wanna delay telling your parents. *Pshh.* If I were you, I'd be shouting from the rooftops."

I giggle nervously. "I know. I saw the drums."

He laughs. "Hey, remember back in March when it was your dad's birthday?"

"I remember my dad's birthday, yes."

He squints at me. "Well then, you'll remember that he planned a special family trip to Morocco. You remember that? The one you missed out on?"

"I couldn't afford to go. I told you that."

The line moves forward. We take a few steps.

"But you said your parents offered to cover your flights *and* hotel, and yet you *still* turned them down—"

"Okay, where are you going with this?" I fold my arms.

"Hold up. Let me land." We take another step. "Now, you told me that you didn't wanna go for two reasons. One: you wanted to avoid being interrogated about your choice of career—to become an author. And two: you felt guilty that they were still covering for you and paying for things. Well, now you have an opportunity to tell them that your plan worked. You took a risk by not going down the traditional route and you achieved your wildest dreams. Excuse the pun." He laughs.

With a faint smile, I think back to that conversation. We were lying in my bed, my head on his chest while his fingers twirled in my natural curls. He tried his hardest to persuade me to go to Morocco, but I was convinced I wouldn't enjoy it.

"You're right," I say softly. "Deep down I know they're proud of me but I always struggled to shake the thought that they're desperate to say 'I told you so.'"

Wale places a hand on my shoulder and my body tingles from the touch. I'm transported back into his car again. "Trust me." His dark eyes bore into mine. "They're proud of you."

My heart squeezes. That word again. *Trust.*

"Next customer, please!"

Somehow, we've reached the front.

We place our orders—I go for a simple rice bowl. The woman tells us there'll be a ten-minute wait, so we're each given a pager. We stand off toward the side. Neither of us is saying anything. And I seem to be transfixed by a watermelon-patterned tote bag on the shoulder of a lady who is walking by.

"Let me call Shona," I say finally.

"I get it. It's awkward."

My heart jumps to my throat.

Wale pulls off his face mask. "Should we . . . talk about yesterday?"

I stare at him.

"Ohmigod, Wale from *The Villa*!" a female voice cries.

We turn our heads. Two South Asian women are gawking at him.

"Mind if we get a selfie?" the one with glasses says. She's already got out her phone.

"Yeah. Sure," Wale replies with a small smile.

The women get into position. I make myself useful by taking a few shots. I hand the glasses-wearing woman back her phone. She studies the photos.

"You know, I wasn't a big fan of you on the show," says the other woman while her friend continues her inspection.

Wale lets out a startled laugh. "Thanks. Don't worry. I wouldn't be either."

"I love what you're doing now, though," the woman says. "I look after my nan. She has dementia. God, it's hard. Thanks for raising awareness. I donated the other day."

Satisfied with their photos, the women thank both me and Wale and go on their merry way. Wale and I turn to each other, stunned.

"Hmm. Maybe I don't need this anymore." He holds his face mask as though it's a dirty diaper and throws it in the bin. He turns to me. "As you were saying . . ." he prompts after a short moment.

"I wasn't saying anything."

"Yeah, I know. You were being awkward. Do you regret it? 'Cause I don't." His brows knead together as his eyes search my face, questioning.

Without meaning to, my gaze makes a swift descent to his lips and then, quickly, I bring it back up. He can't read my mind. Otherwise, he *will* kiss me and I'll feel even worse knowing I'm keeping this big secret from him. I just need Monday to hurry up and be here already. I need to know from Dionne how much of *The Ultimate Payback* I can change before I can tell Wale about it.

Wale, reading into my silence, says, "Aight. Cool," with a slow nod.

"No, I don't regret it. It's just . . ." I don't know where my words are heading.

"You wanna keep things professional?"

The low thrum of disappointment in Wale's voice makes my eyes sting. Every part of me wants to be in his arms. I want to kiss him senseless, tell him that this isn't what I want for either of us, and beg him to please ask me the question again on Monday, my answer might be different.

I hope.

Bitter guilt rises in my chest like poison in a syringe. I swallow. "I just need time . . . to think things through. Properly."

Wale looks at me in silence. He's absorbing what I've said. Then he smiles, gentle, as if it took effort. "Noted."

31

```
Wale_Memoir_Draft1.doc
Target word count: 20,000
Current word count: 18,042
Three weeks to go . . .
```

It's just a small celebration lunch.

It's Sunday and I'm with Shona outside my parents' house. If I can survive an awkward evening with Wale, I'm sure I can manage the next few hours.

I open the door to a chorus of laughter bursting from the living room. Shona and I didn't intend to be late, but our train to Oxford was canceled and the next one wasn't due for an hour. At least it gave me time to continue working on Wale's memoir.

Following the glorious smell of freshly made jollof rice, we pass the kitchen, where I catch sight of a massive cake box on the marble countertop.

"At last! They're here!" I hear Mum say as Dad comes over to greet me.

We do the round of hugs, apologizing for our lateness before remarking how good it is to see everyone. Aunty Anu looks just as I remembered only older. Her sons, Junior and Ade, have surpassed me in height and Rosemary, she's . . . smiling.

"Temi! Long time!" With a squeal, she swoops me into her arms.

Her microbraids smell of coconut oil. She's dressed plainly—a blue sweater and dark jeans—and she isn't wearing a scrap of makeup.

As she squeezes my shoulders, I remember how bubbly and sunshiney she always was. Maybe I was overthinking the tension between us.

We sit around the dining table, which is overflowing with food. Red Le Creuset pots are full to the brim with mouthwatering dishes, from beef stew to boiled yams. After blessing the food—and giving an honorable mention to Rosemary—Dad floods Rosemary with questions about her time in med school. I'm grateful the spotlight is on her. I still don't feel ready to share my news.

"So, Shona, is it?" Aunty Anu fluffs her rice. Her Senegalese twists look freshly done. "What is it that you do, my dear?"

My body stiffens. Maybe I was hopeful too soon.

Shona covers her mouth until she swallows. "I work for an events company that puts on music events. But I also have my side hustle as an events planner."

"Beats life as an estate agent," says Junior with a chuckle, his shoulders bobbing under his tweed shirt.

"How about you?" Shona directs her question at Ade before Aunty Anu can ask me.

"Aerospace engineer." Ade says this as if it's common to build spacecraft for a living.

To my relief, his profession is now the hot topic. Dad has ninety-nine questions; I chip in, too, so that my quietness doesn't raise any concern. Even though I do have a proper job now, any mention of it is bound to get Mum and Dad talking about my book.

"And how about you, darling?" Aunty Anu offers me a warm smile. She's giving me one of those "I haven't forgotten about you" expressions, but honestly, I wish she had.

I mumble my answer. "Oh, I'm just doing some freelance ghostwriting work."

"She's writing a memoir," Mum puts in proudly. Then in a loud whisper: "For a celebrity."

Rosemary says, "Oooh," while Shona coughs and pats her chest.

"No offense to Wale," she says, spluttering a laugh, "but I'd hardly call him a celebrity."

Under the table, I whack my knee against hers. But it's already too late.

"Wale? Who's Wale?" Dad asks.

Junior cries, "Wait, are you talking about Wale the rapper?"

"Wale the rapper is an A-list celebrity," Ade says seriously.

Rosemary scrunches her face. "Is he?"

To my horror, the siblings begin to debate on the celebrity status of the American Nigerian rapper.

"It's Wale from *The Villa*!" I finally announce, bringing the dispute to an abrupt end. "I'm ghostwriting a memoir for Wale Bandele."

Dad grimaces. "Wait, you're not talking about that trashy dating show, are you?"

Rosemary cries, "Oh, I love that show!"

"Ohhh, *that* Wale," Junior says.

Aunty Anu, who has been smiling at me the entire time, says, "I don't know who that is but that's nice."

I tuck back into my food, my body suddenly clammy and warm. "I can't really share details about it," I say gruffly. "It's confidential."

"He's clearly in it for the money," Dad says, and my head jerks up.

"No, he's not! And his memoir is actually inspiring. It touches on Black masculinity and stereotypical assumptions people make about him." I must sound incredibly defensive because Shona places a hand on my knee.

"So, you're a ghostwriter." Ade says the word as if he's trying it out for the first time. "That's different. I don't think I've ever met one before."

Rosemary fiddles with one of her tiny braids. "Temi used to write

The Re-Write **183**

stories back at school. Don't you remember?" She glances at me. "Have you thought about writing a book?" She asks this airily, as if writing a novel is one of the easiest things in the world.

Still riled up from earlier, I stare at her as she shovels down another mouthful of food.

"I have," I reply.

"She means she has written a novel," Shona clarifies. "She actually has an agent."

"Oh, wow! That's awesome!" Rosemary exclaims with the enthusiasm of a kids' TV presenter.

"Nice one, Temi," Junior says. "What is it called? What is it about?"

I give a quick, half-hearted summary of *Wildest Dreams*.

Rosemary beams. "So, when is it coming out?"

I purse my lips.

"She's still waiting to hear back from publishers," Mum says, filling in the lull.

"Well, either way, writing a book is a massive achievement." Rosemary grins.

I give her a sheepish "Thanks."

"What is it? Only two percent of people who write a book actually get it published?" she carries on. "Two percent! How tiny is that!"

My parents are looking at me. I can't quite read their faces.

"Yeah, it's hard to get published but by no means is it impossible," I find myself saying.

"Of course. Absolutely," Rosemary says, a hand on her chest. "I just read an article about it in the *Guardian* the other day."

"So, what else did this article say?" Dad reaches for the salad bowl, his interest suddenly piqued.

"Oh gosh. A lot." Rosemary blows air through her pursed lips. "The author was saying how you'd be lucky to even sell ten copies and that the majority of authors make peanuts. He said he wouldn't even encourage his own kids to try and get traditionally published. Only if you can accept a life of rejection and disappointment. Oh, but that doesn't mean things can't be different for you," she adds quickly, suddenly remembering I'm sat opposite her at the table.

There's a stifling silence. Cutlery scrapes against plates.

My parents are deeply disquieted. Dad is fluffing his rice back and forth on his plate, Mum is sipping her drink, avoiding eye contact. It's as though they are embarrassed for me.

Finally, Dad says, "Do you have any thoughts on this, Temi?" His voice is evenly measured. He seems to genuinely want to hear my opinion.

I twist the spine of my glass, the truth teetering at the tip of my tongue. It's so frustrating. I could stop them worrying with one little sentence.

As though suddenly realizing the awkward position she has put me in, Rosemary says, "But who needs money to be happy! And there's always the option to self-publish—"

"I've already got a publishing deal."

The impact of my words ripples through the room.

"I didn't want to say anything because today is your day. But Ocean Books offered me a book deal."

There's a short gasp as Mum's hand flies to her mouth. "When did this happen?"

"Just the other day."

Dad jumps to his feet. "Come here, you." He swoops down and hugs me from the side, showering my head with a flurry of kisses.

Mum scurries over. "I can't believe it! Why didn't you say?"

A strange feeling unfurls behind my abdomen, almost as if I've just accepted an award that I didn't work for. I push the feeling down. The news is out now.

32

At last. It's Monday.

I'm at Ocean Books' office waiting in the lobby for Dionne. I can't stop staring at the wide selection of books on display, protected behind shiny glass.

Now that my parents know about my deal, I *have* to find a way to make *The Ultimate Payback* work. I told them it was one of those cringe stories that I had written during my Wattpad days, which I was convinced would amount to nothing. To my surprise, they lapped it up.

Tapping my jet-black nails against the arm of the leather chair, I watch as a conveyor belt of people (notably white) swipe into the building.

Ocean Books was on my vision board. This is supposed to be a good moment for me.

"Temi?"

A woman with a pink pixie haircut and DON'T LOOK! printed across her T-shirt rolls her wheelchair in my direction.

I rise to my feet. My handbag, which I had forgotten was on my lap, falls on the floor. Great first impression.

"Hi, I'm Dionne," she says, helping me pick it up. "Hope you don't mind, but I'm a hugger." She hugs me like we're friends meeting up for drinks. I relax a bit. I like her already.

Dionne leads me to a bustling canteen where the walls and furniture are all in Ocean's distinctive purple-blue colors. After buying me a flapjack and a bottle of orange juice, we sit at a table by the window. We get on like a house on fire. I tell her my age, my heritage, my love for reading and writing, and about my ridiculous eyewear collection (today I'm wearing Shakira). She tells me about herself, too: she's Australian and when she is not reading or editing, she likes to knit.

"Okay, now that we know a bit more about each other," she says, her eyes twinkling as she grins, "can I just take a moment to fangirl over *The Ultimate Payback*? My God! What a cracking novel! How did you come up with it? How long did it take to write?"

I cross my ankles nervously under the table. "Oh, about a month or so."

"A month! God, you're speedy. That's good to know, as I was thinking you could write a sequel."

"A sequel?!"

Dionne grins, oblivious to my state of panic. "And did Mayee tell you that I read it in one sitting?"

"Seriously? I mean, wow, thank you." Though I'm flattered, I'm shocked that she is responding so positively to something so filled with negativity. "Sorry"—I clear my throat—"may I ask what you responded to in the manuscript?"

"Honestly?" She raises a brow as if she's about to make a confession. "Pretty much everything."

Oh dear.

"From Sophie's sass levels to Wayne's beautiful, tatted-up body. Some of the things she writes in her exposé are just comedy gold. And so relatable!"

I try to disguise my wince. Then she reaches into her Ocean-branded tote bag, pulls out a stack of paper, and places it on the table.

It's my manuscript.

My actual manuscript.

Over 350 pages printed out in its full glory.

On the front, Dionne has scribbled "Love this!" next to where I'd typed *The Ultimate Payback*.

I guess there's no point asking whether I can change the title.

"I highlighted so many sentences," Dionne says. She's thumbing her way through the printout to reveal the pink and yellow sections. "Ooh, like this scene." She stops. "It's the one where Sophie and Wayne have sex, and it's so bad, she spends the whole time thinking about what she'll make herself for lunch."

I try not to pull a face. That had never happened. But if Wale reads this, he will question whether I faked every one of my orgasms. It'll crush him. Massively.

"Oh, and this one." Dionne stops again and I try my best not to groan. "When Wayne puts on a front that he's loaded, only to have his card declined at a swanky restaurant. Talk about awkward."

I remember the night I wrote that scene. It was right after I'd finished watching another frustrating episode of *The Villa*.

"So, tell me more about your writing process," she says, turning the printout over. On the last page, she has drawn a star at the bottom with the words "Smash hit." "Mayee told me how you're a ghostwriter for a reality TV star. How cool is that? Is that what sparked the idea, then?"

I nearly choke on my flapjack. "Actually, it's inspired by my ex."

Dionne's mouth shrinks into a small O. "You see, this is why you should never piss off writers. You might end up in their next book." She laughs. "So, what did he do? Don't tell me he cheated?"

"No," I say quickly. I know Wale hates that word. "He lied. By omission."

Dionne shakes her head and sighs. "I'm sorry you had to go through that. At least you had the last laugh."

"Well, that's the thing . . ." I break a piece of my flapjack and lower it. "I actually don't want my ex to know that my book is based on him. Is there any way I could change it somehow?" I really hope Dionne is open to me making some serious revisions, otherwise I don't know what I'm going to do.

"Do you mean changing the bits you're uncomfortable with? Absolutely," she says.

Her words are like music to my ears. I feel so much lighter.

"Don't worry. We can change anything that is too obvious. It's not like you're asking that we change the entire plot now, are you? Unless your ex is a reality TV star?" She laughs again.

I can't bring myself to laugh along.

No—I knew that change wouldn't be possible. It would produce an entirely different book. But perhaps if Wale realizes that only the concept is based on him, on us, he won't be so hurt.

My mind whirring, I nibble on my flapjack even though I no longer have an appetite.

"Now that explains the ending," Dionne says, studying my face. "Why Sophie ends up with someone else as opposed to reconciling with Wayne. But I actually think they *should* get back together. Readers love a good second chance romance."

I force a smile and nod. She's right. I'm one of those readers. And as a die-hard romance lover, I knew Sophie and Wayne were meant to find their way back to each other's arms, that I was supposed to give them their "happily ever after." I was just too angry with Wale.

But I'm not anymore.

No matter how much I can say it's only fiction, there will always be a part of him that will question what I really think about him. And if the public does find out that he's my ex, they will not be able to draw a line between what is true and what is not. He will be the center of an online furor. It will feed into his paranoia, make him trust less. I will be that ex-girlfriend who's responsible for his emotional trauma for years to come—Cammie 2.0. Worst of all, unlike Sophie and Wayne, we will never get our second chance as Wale may never speak to me again.

I *have* to find a way to get this book right. I have to.

33

Later that day . . .

Monday Sept 9, 12:44 p.m.
From: Watts, Dionne
To: Li, Mayee; Ojo, Temi

Subject: Press release

Hi both!

Hope you're enjoying the little bit of sunshine!

Temi—so lovely meeting you this morning. I hope I didn't scare you off with my fangirl ramblings! I'm really looking forward to us working together. 😊

I've written and attached a press release to announce your deal. This will go out to our main industry publications (*Books Today*, *In Book News* etc.) later today. Mayee, are you able to let me know if you're happy with it? I'll post on Twitter, and then you can both retweet from there, if you like.

Last thing, Mayee, regarding your email about when to expect the contract, I'm chasing Legal as we speak!

Any questions, let me know.

Dionne xx

Monday Sept 9, 12:54 p.m.
From: Ojo, Temi
To: Li, Mayee; Watts, Dionne

Hi Dionne,

So lovely meeting you too! Don't worry, you didn't scare me off. However, I'm still overwhelmed by the idea of writing a sequel. But like you said—we can cross that bridge when we come to it.

Enjoy the little bit of sunshine too.

Temi xx

Monday Sept 9, 13:26 p.m.
From: Watts, Dionne
To: Li, Mayee
Cc: Ojo, Temi

Mayee—sorry to nudge, but are you able to read and approve the press release soon? The guys from *Books Today* and co need it in the next hour and I'm about to go into a two-hour meeting.

D x

Monday Sept 9, 13:28 p.m.
From: Li, Mayee
To: Ojo, Temi; Watts, Dionne

Apologies. In a meeting. If easier I can send it to them directly?

Mayee

Monday Sept 9, 13:29 p.m.
From: Watts, Dionne
To: Li, Mayee; Ojo, Temi

Perfect!

D x

Monday Sept 9, 13:29 p.m.
From: Watts, Dionne
To: Li, Mayee; Ojo, Temi

PS—I forgot to include a headline for the press release. Feel free to add one!

D x

34

```
Wale_Memoir_Draft1.doc
Target word count: 22,000
Current word count: 23,062
Just under three weeks to go . . .
```

The next day, I'm slightly more peaceful than before the meeting with Dionne and have even made good progress on Wale's memoir. With the help of Wale's interviews on podcasts and the radio, I've managed to draft another chapter. I've titled it:

> **People assume that I'm a bad boy**
> **The truth is I just look like one**

The words came very quickly. It helps that I *know* him. It also helps that I have a new working laptop.

Now that I have heard from Dionne's own mouth that I can edit anything in my manuscript that I'm uncomfortable with, I feel a lot more prepared to have the talk with Wale. He'll demand to read my manuscript, I know. I'm just going to have to keep telling him that it's not the final version.

I put my playlist on pause. Scrolling down the document, I give it a quick skim. Given everything I've dealt with in the last few weeks, I'm pretty impressed with how much I've done. I've written about how Wale's overuse of the word "fine" stems from childhood—he was sensitive and not so great at standing up for himself, unlike his bonus family.

I've been able to interweave the stuff he told me about his physical transformation to write the new chapter about the assumptions people make about him based off his physical appearance. I've written about his first love and his first heartbreak, and how quick some are to write him off as a cheater when, in fact, he's experienced the painful devastation of being cheated on. I've also written about how his job at ACE charity was not merely a stopgap until he found something fancier and more high-paying.

But still, there's something missing: context. The backdrop to how and why he's become the person he is today. And I know what the missing thing is. I need to somehow get Wale comfortable enough to share his experience as a carer.

Grabbing my phone, I ring Wale. I haven't spoken to him directly since our conversation at Camden Market. Instead, we've been exchanging voice notes, mainly for him to clarify things thrown up by the writing process. He picks up straight away.

"That's crazy. I was just thinking about you," he says. "I mean, I was just about to call you to talk about work."

"Oh. What a coincidence. I'm calling to talk about work too."

Silence.

"Do you wanna go first?" he says.

"Yes, right." I clear my throat. "First off, you'll be pleased to know I'm making really good progress with your memoir."

"Nice."

"But I feel like there's something missing. Your home life. Wale, I know I can't interview your parents—"

"That's why I was calling. What are you doing later today around seven?"

"I'm free," I say softly. "Anansi Books will be closed, though."

"Actually, I was thinking we could talk at Fonzo's. I stayed at his place last night."

"Perfect."

"I'll text you the address now . . . anything else?"

The Ultimate Payback floats to mind. But if I tell him now, he won't open up later on. And I need him to.

"Not that I can think of. See you at seven."

I end the call and lower my phone. On the one hand, I'm touched that Wale is now in a space where he is mentally ready to talk about his family but, on the other, must our interaction be so stiff? Now that I've spoken to Dionne, I hope we can pick up from when we last kissed.

I'm replaying the soft brush of his lips on mine when my phone vibrates. It's an email from Dionne.

> Tuesday Sept 10, 15:08 p.m.
> From: Watts, Dionne
> To: Li, Mayee; Ojo, Temi
>
> **Subject:** Press release
>
> Temi, not sure if you've seen but the press release is out! Feel free to retweet!
>
> Mayee—thanks for finalizing and sending it directly to *Books Today* and co yesterday.
>
> D x

I check Twitter.

> **DionneWattsOceanBooks**
> Excited to be the lucky editor to snap up *The Ultimate Payback*! Can't wait to publish this HOT debut by @TemiOjoWriter next year! 🗣️📚
>
>> **BooksToday** British Nigerian author lands high five-figures deal with Ocean Books after writing book inspired by ex. Read more here

The Re-Write

I balk.

Fuck! Why the heck did Mayee pick that headline? Did she really have to mention my ex?!

And then I remember. Although I was partially honest with Dionne, I've been nowhere close to that with Mayee.

I stare at the tweet. Wale is not on Twitter, so I can technically get away with reposting.

TemiOjoWriter
Can't believe my dreams have come true! 🙇 🙇 🙇 😸 😸 😸

> **BooksToday** British Nigerian author lands five-figures deal with Ocean Books after writing book inspired by ex. Read more here

Twenty minutes later, I have a change of heart.
I delete the tweet.

35

I get to Fonzo's flat at seven on the dot. After Wale buzzes me up, I take the elevator to the fifth floor, checking my outfit in the mirror: a mango-orange Bershka top tucked into a denim white skirt. Cute. Though it's only been three days, I'm looking forward to seeing him.

"Hey," he says after he opens the door. He's wearing white socks and slippers with a plain T-shirt over jogging bottoms. I smile. Even in loungewear, he still manages to look ridiculously fit.

We hug at the entrance, our bodies melting into each other, balmy and warm. I shiver at the memory of our kiss. And then I smell something. A waft of aromatic spices fills the short hallway.

"Is Fonzo cooking?" I ask, letting go of him.

"Why Fonzo? I could be the chef."

"Wale, you nearly set off the fire alarm when you attempted to make party jollof that time at my flat."

He smirks. "But you ate my sausage, though."

I give him a "Behave" look.

With a snicker, he says, "Fonzo's out at the moment."

My heart should not be beating like this.

So, it's just me and Wale.

Alone.

Again.

In my head, I throw myself at him, he passionately kisses me back and presses his body on mine against the wall.

"He's gone to the cinema with Shona," he says, halting my spiraling imagination.

"Oh" is all I can manage to say. Shona did not mention this. And then I notice his lips. They're twitching. "Okay, why are you smiling like that?"

Wale goes behind me and puts his hands on my shoulders. Something is up. He guides me down the cold-tiled hallway and through an open door.

"Surprise!" he cries.

I gaze around the room, my feet rooted to the spot.

Wale has turned Fonzo's living room into a real-life Pinterest board. Tasseled pashminas are draped over a shaggy black rug. They're laid out like a picnic blanket with satin and velvet cushions scattered on top. It's giving Arabian Nights. It's giving—

I gasp. "Morocco!"

Wale's smile is the giveaway. Rotating slowly, I take in my surroundings.

He has carefully arranged a silver-plated tray to hold a traditional Moroccan tea set. There are antique metal lanterns with tea light candles around the edges of the room. He's even got a ceramic tagine pot and wait—is that an actual shisha?

"Wale . . ." I'm breathless. I push through the tears gathering in my throat. "I can't believe . . . I don't know what to say."

"Oh shit. I forgot something." He grabs the remote control and presses a button.

A flute melody plays over a riff of darbukas. He rolls his hips. I laugh. If he hadn't put in so much effort with the presentation, I'd grab a cushion and throw it at his head.

"So"—he spreads his arms—"what do you think?"

I feel as though I'm having one of those surreal, good dreams that you never want to wake up from. Guilt rises inside of me like a wave. He needs to know.

"Why?" My voice comes out crackled. "Why would you go to all this effort?"

Wale peers around himself as though trying to see the gesture through my eyes. "Well, you weren't able to go to Morocco that time with your parents, so I thought, hey, why not bring Morocco to you? Consider this a continuation of your book deal celebration. Part two." Then, quickly, he adds, "I hope I'm not overstepping your boundaries."

The wave is threatening to overwhelm me. But I don't know what to say; he's gone to so much trouble. And my admission won't just ruin the evening, it will ruin everything. Our business relationship, our friendship . . . I feel an ache deep down to my core when I think back to our kiss. Us.

I begin to shake my head. "Wale, I appreciate this. I really do. But I don't deserve it."

Wale walks over and places a hand on my shoulder. "You deserve every good thing in life." His voice has taken on a new edge. Measured and sincere. He's heart-achingly sweet. "You're a good person and not enough good things happen to good people."

I cast a sidelong glance at the pashminas. It hurts to look at him.

To my relief, his phone vibrates.

His brows turn inward as he glances at the screen. He answers it. "Hello?" he says tentatively. "I told you! Delete my number!"

He ends the call.

"Who was that? Cold call?"

He stuffs his phone back into his pocket and runs a hand over his hair before letting out a sharp breath. "Kojo," he says, and I blink.

I haven't thought about Kojo since getting my book deal.

"I thought you blocked his number?" I ask.

"I did," Wale says. "Still, he's been trying to reach me. First through a different Insta account. Now this."

I scoff. "Well, you're not the only one he should be saying sorry to. Not that I need or want his apology."

"Well, actually, he . . . don't worry about it."

"No. Go on. You might as well say."

Wale lets out a resigned sigh. "He's got it in his head that you're only using me."

My shock shows on my face.

"That's why I didn't wanna say anything," Wale says. "It's stupid."

My heart is beating so fast, it feels as though it's going to crash right through my chest. I force a weak laugh. "So, what? He thinks I'm using you to gain clout?"

"For content," Wale says, and I release a breath of disbelief. "Not social media content but content for your writing. He thinks you're out for revenge. Why else would you write my memoir?"

I feel winded—as though the rug has been pulled from underneath my feet and I'm suspended in the air, about to hit the floor. The last time I felt like this was when Wale confronted me about Seth's message on my phone. I can't believe that Kojo is getting back at me like this.

Wale must have noticed the shock in my face because he touches my arm. "Temi, he's just trying to get one on you. Don't worry. I've blocked him."

My throat feels too dry to speak. I manage a weak nod. Even if I wanted to come clean, there's no way I can tell him now.

36

I fluff my rice into my lamb-and-artichoke tagine, which Wale had in fact ordered from Uber Eats. We're sitting on the floor beside each other with our backs against the sofa, our legs sprawled out toward the nest of cushions and pashminas. It should be lovely—it is lovely—but Kojo's call has punctured my mood. I keep asking myself whether I should just bite the bullet and tell him now, but I can't bring myself to do it.

"I've got another surprise for you," Wale says.

I let out an involuntary groan. As sweet as it is, I don't think I can take another surprise.

Wale laughs. "I promise it's the last one." He motions his head. "Look under that cushion."

I crawl over and reach under the teal velvet cushion. My fingers make contact with a slim, cool surface. I pull out an old notebook with his name on the front.

"You know how I used to journal as a kid?"

My eyes widen.

"No, it's not that. The one in your hand is my English notebook from year seven, I believe. I found it when I was looking for the journal."

I flick through the short pages and get a glimpse of black and blue slanted handwriting. I've been so in my head, I've forgotten I'm here to interview him.

I clear my throat. "Are there stories in here that you think will be relevant to your memoir?"

Wale shakes his head. "Not stories, no. Doodles and thoughts, maybe. I used to do this thing as a kid where I would write in the blank pages toward the back—you know, so that the teacher wouldn't see. Normally I would rip the pages out, but there's still one in there." He motions at me to have a look.

This time I flick through the notebook by starting from the back. There aren't that many pages, so I turn each one individually.

And then I see it.

My heart stills.

I wish my mum was normal.

I look up at Wale. He is resolute.

"I'm ready," he says.

Shakily, I snap into action and hit the record button. I don't even know if *I'm* ready. Wale props a cushion under his head to lie flat on the floor. I wonder if this is how he sits when he's in therapy.

He licks his lips and then he says it.

"My mum's a recovering alcoholic."

After Kathy told me that he was a carer, I had a gut feeling that Wale looked after his mum. And I knew it must be something taboo or something that had stigma attached to it, because Wale was completely mute about it. So, I had quietly convinced myself she had a mental illness. Alcoholism isn't the first thing that comes to mind when someone tells you they're a carer.

The next few seconds are silent. Wale doesn't say anything or tilt his head to glance at my reaction. Although he's physically in the room, he's no longer here. I want to lie on the floor next to him, but I don't know if it's the right thing to do. Instead, I remain where I am—sitting sideways beside his feet, one hand clutching my ankle.

"I'm her carer," he eventually says, his voice gravelly.

My throat pricks. I know it took a lot for him to admit that.

"We all were, are. Me. Dad. Ayo. I've been looking after her since I was a kid." He licks his lips again. "It all started when she lost her job. Actually, it began way before then. My mum said she had a traumatic childhood. But the drinking started after she got fired. She worked as a chef at this fancy restaurant. Apparently, she got caught drinking on the job. And it wasn't the first time either. We all thought she'd get another job. My mum's a *really* good cook. But then"—he lets out a long sigh—"I would come home from school and see her passed out on the sofa. At first, I thought she was just mad tired. Until Dad found the bottles."

My heart squeezes.

"I can't remember how it got from there to it being normal—seeing my mum drunk." He says the word as though he's swallowed a mouthful of bleach, his face grimacing. "Temi, I was so embarrassed. Drinking was what the homeless people on the streets did, not Mum."

His pain is unbearable. I put a hand on his leg and give it a light squeeze. The skin-to-skin contact must reassure him because the memories pour out, like an emotional montage: the slow loss of a funny, loving mother; the uptick in concerning behavior—from the incoherent ramblings and the jarring singing to the sporadic bursts of loud music. Sometimes these behaviors took place behind the four walls of their home. But sometimes they spilled out on to the streets.

"Everybody knew," Wale says with a low sigh. "Neighbors, teachers. A few kids at school used to call my mum an 'alki.'" His voice breaks at that. I keep my hand on his leg like an anchor. "That's how I got closer to Fonzo's family. After school, me and my brother would hang out at the barbershop or Anansi Books. I hated going home. Hated it. And Dad was always working. I guess he hated being at home too."

"Did he try and help her?"

"Professional help?" Wale sniffs. "Yeah, eventually. But mostly, he kept things hush-hush. It was this thing that we just didn't talk about. But when Mum continued to act . . . wild, he went to church. Obviously, her alcoholism couldn't be prayed away. But the people there did float the idea of rehab. The only thing with rehab is"—his chest falls as he exhales heavily—"you have to be willing to go. You can't *force* someone. It's never effective when you do. And so, when Dad was at his wits' end, he gave Mum an ultimatum: you either get sober or I'm leaving you and taking the kids."

I stop overthinking. I crawl nearer and curl up next to him, resting my head against his chest—a little, helpless gesture to acknowledge his pain. Wale wraps his arm around my shoulder, and as I sink into his warm body, I feel him physically relax.

"The ultimatum worked for a bit. Until it didn't," he carries on. "Dad tried to get her back into cooking by enrolling her in these classes. Not like she needed it. It was his way of keeping her busy. But whenever she was out, she couldn't resist." His words come out faster now, like water flowing through a burst pipe. "When she got caught, she would promise that she'd do better next time, that we should give her grace, that she loved us. And I would think, 'Yeah? Then why do you keep drinking, then?' I dunno. Maybe that's why I struggle with that word." I feel his head shift to look down at me. My breath hitches in my throat.

I think back to that day when I told him I was falling for him. He told me he did have deep feelings for me but would rather express them through actions than words. At the time, I couldn't understand why he wouldn't just say it—after all, I wasn't expecting him to use the L-word. Now I know it's a much bigger story. Much bigger than me.

"Cammie said she loved me and she cheated on me. And then you have my dad who never said the word at all. I think he thought saying it would make me and my brother weak. Less of a man."

Lacing my fingers with his, I twist onto my side and look at him. He doesn't make eye contact.

His throat bobs as he swallows down the pain. "My dad—he's one of those strong African men who shows no emotion. I frustrated him 'cause I was sensitive and cried all the time. He didn't think I was setting a good example for my younger brother. I will never forget the first time my mum went to rehab; I cried when my dad came home without her. Ayo too. When my dad saw, he didn't hug me. He told me off. He told me to stop crying. That he didn't raise his son to be weak . . ." His voice trails. I rub small circles between his thumb and finger to let him know that I'm here.

Wale doesn't say anything for a very long time but his jaw hardens as he delves deeper into his thoughts, his features writhing with anguish.

"My therapist," he says, changing tack, "thinks I have a skewed perception of what it means to be a man. She says the boy in me and my adult self are at war with each other. A part of me wants to lean in to my sensitive side but another part wants to hold back because as soon as you show your soft side, people take advantage of you. It's exhausting constantly having to rein yourself in. I just wanna be able to feel, y'know?" He licks his lips. "I dunno. Maybe my memoir will help another Black man who feels as though he has to be strong all the time." And with a small laugh, he turns to me and says, "No pressure."

And that's when I see it.

His eyes are shimmering with tears, a dam waiting to break.

My lips quiver. "You don't have to be strong now." I'm crying too.

Finally, Wale blinks. A single tear falls.

And as I lean in and hug him tighter, more tears come—tears he has been holding back for years. At last, he allows himself to feel. At last, he takes his armor off.

37

I don't know how long we've been lying like this. At some point our legs became intertwined, my thighs peeping out a little from under my skirt. After a few tears, Wale dabbed his wet eyes and kept telling his story.

He tells me about his experience as a carer. How Aunty Shirley would send him and his brother home with a ziplock bag of Jamaican fried dumplings, which they would have with baked beans when there was no food in the fridge. How he would work a brush through his mother's brittle hair when it got too matted, cutting the split ends and moisturizing her scalp. He recalled how his scrawny arms gained a little muscle from going to the launderette when the washing machine broke down.

"Kathy was a godsend." He discovered the charity when his dad came home with a bunch of leaflets after dropping Mum at rehab. It was the first time he came across the term "carer." One day after school, he decided to pay ACE a visit. He's never looked back.

"We met other young carers, got vouchers for school supplies," Wale says. "Dad didn't like the idea of us being a charity case, but at least me and my brother didn't starve."

"Will he be attending the charity gala?"

"Ayo lives abroad, remember?"

"I meant your dad."

There is a silence before Wale says, "No. We're still not on the best of terms since I went on the show."

I brush a light hand against his chest. "And how's your mum doing now?" I ask because it would be strange not to. The question has been at the back of my mind for this whole conversation.

"She's doing okay, y'know. Coming up to almost five years now, completely sober. But"—a heavy breath racks out of him—"the drinking has taken a toll on her health, so she's very . . . fragile. Sometimes depressed."

"I'm so sorry," I whisper. "Wale, I don't know what to say. You've been so brave. You . . ." It frustrates me that I can't put into words how highly I think of him.

"You've actually seen her."

I lift my head from his chest.

"That day when you showed up at my football match. My mum and Ayo were there," he goes on. "That's partly why I was acting so strangely; I wasn't ready to introduce her to you yet."

I lower my head back down again. I can hear his heartbeat. I wish I could recall her face. "Sorry for making such a massive deal about meeting each other's parents," I say guiltily.

"You didn't know." He takes my hand and skims his thumb over my skin with such tender affection, warmth fills the fissures in my heart. "I was nervous you'd look at her and have questions about her health. I just need to get over the . . . shame."

I tighten my grip.

"She'd like you, though," he says more brightly.

"Oh, yeah?" I lift my chin.

Wale props himself up on his elbow so he can see me. "Course, man. How can she not. You're kind, ambitious, beautiful." He lingers on the word as if I'm breathtaking. And just like that, a spell is cast—neither one of us breaks eye contact. "I've really, *really* missed your face," he says, his voice a low rasp, his eyes drunk with longing.

"Just my face?" I was aiming for playful but it comes out suggestive.

Suddenly, there's a shift. Wale's eyes flick down to my cleavage, then up to my lips. Desire roars through my veins.

Like me, he wants to reignite what we sparked in the car. We're teetering on a tightrope, the temptation growing too much to resist.

And then he kisses me. It's dizzying. Wale cups the back of my head, switching from gentle to urgent. I am losing my reason. Lust and relief—that's what it feels like, as our tongues intertwine, our breath becoming one. This time we kiss with no hesitation. We're both fully committed, we're both in it. Wildfire.

The pressure of his tongue is setting me alight. We subside to the floor again. Wale rolls on top of me. My hands skim over his shoulder blades—his back is so strong—before slipping into the neck of his top. Every cell inside of me sings with euphoria at the touch of his smooth, warm skin. Everything about him is so familiar, and yet new.

We're grinding now, slow, rhythmic movements, the fabric around his crotch rubbing against my pretty lace knickers (I wore them just in case). He pushes my skirt up my leg, gripping my thigh. I nearly explode.

"God, I've missed you," I breathe out, giving in.

"Oh, yeah? Show me."

I shove him the other way so that I can climb on top of him.

But then, Wale says, "Shit!" with alarm and zero lust.

I stop. "Are you okay?"

He sits up and twists his neck to look over the back of his top. And that's when I notice the crumpled takeaway box lying on the floor right behind him. I try to hold it in, but the giggles rise up.

I've pushed the man into his food.

"How bad is it?" I ask, trying to hold it together.

Wale pulls the back of his top around to show me the mess—a pickle-green splodge with grains of couscous attached. Truthfully, it looks like baby puke.

I snort.

"Oh, you think it's funny, huh?" Wale yanks off his top, and I yelp as he rubs it on my head. He's laughing now.

I scream and push him away. "Do you not know how long deep conditioning—"

He's not bare chested but he might as well be. I stare at his inked biceps poking out of the arms of his vest.

Wale is too busy inspecting the stain on his top to see me gawking. I crawl closer but when I try to kiss him, he retreats a little.

A flash of hurt washes through me. I didn't see that coming.

"I wanna respect your wishes," he says, tucking one of my loose curls behind my ear. "Let's figure out whatever this is once the memoir is done."

"But we don't have to have sex," I say a little too quickly. "We can just make out. If you want?"

Wale looks me up and down, a smile coiling the corner of his lips. "Trust me. I won't be the only one with my top off," he says. He glances around the room and stops. "Fancy doing shisha?"

38

The following evening, I jump on the train to meet Shona at Peckham Rye Station. We're going dress shopping for the gala—she recently discovered this amazing African-centric boutique on Instagram and said we *have* to check it out.

I slide through the ticket barriers and there she is, smiling ear to ear, her long braids tied back into a ponytail. She must have had a lot of fun with Fonzo last night. I wonder if she will mention anything.

"Someone's glowing," I point out as we fall into a hug.

Shona frowns, amused. "It's just sweat, babe. The train was rammed." She loops her arm into mine and, over the loud backdrop of an evangelical street preacher, she tells me about her disastrous journey while we walk down the busy high street. We turn into an indoor market flanked with small shops.

"This boutique," I say, breathing in the stuffy air, "they cater for plus-size people, right?"

Shona drags her attention from a kiosk selling traditional Afro-Caribbean herbal medicine. "Of course, hun," she says. "I wouldn't suggest we go otherwise. Ooh—I think this is it."

We stop outside a shop with the name NANA BADU in giant kente colors at the top. In the window display is a dramatic but elegant maxi dress and a geometric-patterned jumpsuit. A Jill Scott song is playing. I love it already.

We head inside and I'm overwhelmed with color. Loud, vibrant, in-your-face color. So us.

Excitedly, Shona and I trawl through each rack, pulling out exquisite dresses made from lace and Ankara fabric. When our hands become too full, we head into one of the changing rooms to try them on.

"What do you think?" she says after she puts on her first dress—it has a patterned frilly skirt with a plunging neckline.

I click my fingers. "Yasss, girl! I love it!"

She vogues—posing like a model at the end of a runway.

I step into the opening of my first gown—a gorgeous off-shoulder ruched dress with a thigh slit.

"Let me zip you up," Shona offers.

I hold the bodice against my chest and turn my back toward her.

"And do you know who else will love it?" I ask with a twitching smirk. I catch Shona's confused expression in the mirror.

"No. Who?" she says.

"Fonzo."

She lets go of the zip and slaps my bum.

I crack up. "Hey! What was that for? I know you guys went on a date last night."

In the mirror I watch her arch her hand toward the center of her back, clasp the zipper, and pull it right down. *Wow.*

"Well?" I prod.

"Okay, fine." She whips around. She pushes her bottom lip out and in a quiet voice says, "Temi, I really like him."

I screech as if she's just announced that she's engaged and then I thrust my arms around her, squeezing her tight. For Shona to say those four words must mean she likes him a lot.

"Details. Spill," I demand as I turn around again. This time she zips me up straight away.

"Ooh, I'm loving this high slit on you," she coos. "Let's see it without your socks."

"Don't worry about my damn socks, woman! Spill!"

While we try on different dresses, Shona fills me in. It all started when Fonzo invited her to his studio to help pick out some photographs

The Re-Write

for the gala. The light was good and he began to snap a few pictures of her. At first, she told him to stop, but then he showed her the photos. She was so impressed by his skills that she literally let her hair down and told him to take another. It then progressed into a laughter-filled photo shoot. She felt so comfortable around him.

"I told him I was happy to pay for the photos. And do you know what he said? I could pay by going on a date with him."

A squeal lurches out of me. "Go, Fonzo! I never knew he had it in him. So, you went on a date. Did you kiss?"

Shona covers her blushing face with the silk underlay of her second dress.

I gasp. "I knew it!"

It's so nice to see Shona genuinely excited about dating again. I always wondered when she would meet someone and what that person would be like. They would need to make her feel safe enough to let her guard down. I'm glad she's realized that you can't paint all men with the same brush, that it's okay to open your heart again.

"You guys are officially my favorite couple," I say, bending to take off my socks. "You need a name. How about Shonza?"

She laughs and neatens the bow that she had tied around her waist. "Now we can go on double dates," she says so casually she might as well be telling me the weather.

"Huh?"

"Don't 'huh' me, missus. What were *you* up to last night? Fonzo told me there were pashminas and shisha."

I try to paint Shona a picture, melting as I think about the effort Wale put in. I told her how soft Wale was with me, how emotionally mature he now is.

"Did *you* kiss?" she asks, hurling the question back in my face.

Sucking in my lips, I look side to side.

"You more than kissed, didn't you? Okay, what base?"

"We only kissed, Shona! Well, there was some touching."

She looks at me as if to say, *Yeah, I know.*

"So, where does that leave things with *The Ultimate Payback*?" she says, reaching for another lovely dress.

I twiddle my fingers in front of my stomach and take a deep breath. "I've decided that I'm not going to publish it."

Shona drops the dress she's holding; the hanger clatters on the floor.

"What! Are you serious? You told me that Dionne was happy for you to make some changes."

Shakily, I nod. Tears are stinging my eyes.

Shona bounds forward and pulls me into her. My chest burns with the ache you get when you do the right but hard thing.

Now that I've said it aloud, there's no going back.

When I returned home last night, two things were undeniably clear: I had fallen deeply for Wale and I had earned back his trust. And because of this I knew I wouldn't be able to look myself in the mirror if I signed the deal. Since agreeing to it, I've been split into two: my ambition versus my morals. The very fact I was so unsettled tells me everything. And then yesterday happened. And I had to face the possibility of losing the man I love. And I cannot go through that again. Not even for the money and chance at success.

"And there's also the fact that Dionne wants me to write a sequel," I go on as I try to rationalize my very big decision. "Not to mention the burden of promoting a book I had no business putting out."

Shona looks at me tenderly. "Are you going to call Mayee?"

"Tomorrow." I breathe air out of my nose, the anxiety already creeping in. "I know she will be pissed . . ." I stop myself from thinking about the consequences for fear of spiraling.

Shona's eyes are welling. "Well, whatever happens, I'll be right here to support you."

We go back to trying all the dresses. Shona and I whittle it down to one each. While I've gone for a show-stopping maxi-print ball gown, Shona has opted for a floor-length mermaid with an elastic waist and an oversize rosette over the shoulder.

Finally, we head toward the till, where a dark-skinned lady in a crop top is waiting. She takes our garments, flashing a gem on her side tooth as she smiles.

While she folds the dresses, Shona scrolls on her phone. I pinch one of the many business cards on the counter. I'm about to put it in my purse when I do a double take.

"Oh my gosh! That's my dream dress!" I stare at the tiny image on the back of the card, stunned.

"Do you still want this one?" The lady raises the bag. "The one on my card is from last year's summer collection but I can make it for you if you prefer."

"Sorry, yes, I still want that one. But *this one* is on my vision board. I'm a writer and this is the dress I hope to wear to my book launch one day."

I wait to feel like an imposter, but I don't.

"Wow, you've written a book. That's so dope. Well, you've got my details, so whenever you're ready."

I'm surprised by Shona's lack of reaction—surely the universe is trying to tell me something.

I turn to her. "Hey! Shona! This lady—sorry, what's your name?"

"Nana."

"Nana designed my dream dress."

Shona looks up from her phone, her expression twisted with worry. She gnaws her lip. "Don't freak out . . ." Then hands me her phone.

And just like that, my world implodes.

39

My chest is pounding. I feel as though I'm having a heart attack.
This cannot be happening.

> **EX-GIRLFRIEND WRITES REVENGE BOOK ABOUT *THE VILLA*'S VILLAIN**

How the fuck did this end up on The Tea Lounge? My brain cannot take in what I'm seeing.

There's a screenshot of my press release and the announcement I tweeted and—

FUCK!

It's a video taken at the Clapham house party.

Bile rises as I unmute the recording with a trembling thumb.

"How can you pick a stupid dating show over me?!" I'm yelling.

Wale and I are arguing at the bottom of the stairwell, surrounded by dozens of people holding up their phones. We're just like one of those toxic couples that you see on those trashy reality shows. My heart stings at how incriminating this looks. The video paints Wale in a very negative light, everything people expect him to be: a time waster, an F-boy, a liar. Finally, it ends with Wale running after me, followed by a smattering of laughter.

"Fuck. This is bad." Suddenly, I feel light-headed.

Shona grabs my hand. "I'm so sorry, hun. Someone at the party must have tipped them off."

"I need to go."

"Wait!" But I'm already running out of the store, my bag smacking hard against my side. I need to get to Wale before he sees this. I dial his number.

Come on, come on, come on.

"Hey, babe. You all right?" He clearly has no idea what's going on.

"Wale, where are you? I need to talk to you in person." I go from running to power walking to running again. I can see a bus stop in the distance.

"I'm at home. You sound flustered. Is everything okay?"

"Don't worry about me. I'll explain everything when I see you. Can we talk ASAP?"

"Sure. Where should I pick you up?"

"Text me your address. I'll come to you. We can talk in your car. Oh, and Wale, before I go, promise me something?"

"Yeah, sure. What is it?"

"Please don't go on any social media. Please."

I end the call before he can ask any questions. I'm wracked with worry by the time I reach the bus stop. The few seconds I wait for the bus are agonizing. I check Uber. Luckily, there's one close by. I book it immediately. The minute wait feels like an hour.

In the taxi, I hold back hot tears. My mind is racing. What if Greg catches wind of it? What if he tells Wale?

I get out my phone again. I have hundreds of notifications—*shiiit*. The post on The Tea Lounge now has over eight thousand likes. Unable to resist, I scroll through the comments.

> **j3zzi3** So, the guy only went on The Villa for clout! What a loser!
>
> **camhi_rose** THIS is what I call karma! Yass, girl! Secure the bag! 💰💰💰

draya_1994 Hm that's Wale's ex, yeah? No offense but Kelechi is way finer 👀

sweetlolly Wale is what's wrong with Black men today. That man does not respect Black women! KMT

brusque_key Ahh, so Wale likes his women thick THICK

ricosmooth Dayum! She was punching above her weight, no? (No pun intended)

I swat a tear away with the back of my sleeve. I've spent nearly my entire life as a plus-size, curvy woman. I know what that comes with. The fat jokes, the fat-shaming, the stares. I've experienced it all. And this is why, strangely, I'm much better equipped to handle public critique.

Because I'm never blindsided.

But Wale will be.

The car stops outside a tired-looking maisonette, the curtains drawn. I scramble out of the car and stand on the opposite side of the road.

I ring him. "Hey, I'm outside your house . . . Hello? Hello?" I lower my phone. He hung up.

A surge of panic soars through me as his front door swings open. Wale takes long, quick strides toward me, his jaw tight.

"What the fuck is this?" He thrusts his phone in my face.

"Wale, I can explain." My voice comes out a strangled cry.

"What is there to explain, Temi? You lied to me! Kojo was right. You've been using me the entire time."

"No, it's not what it looks like!" There's a rawness in my voice. I have to make him listen to me. I *have* to.

"So, you didn't write a book called *The Ultimate Payback*, then?"

I squeeze my eyes shut. "Yes. But I wrote it for myself. To help process our breakup. No one was meant to see it—"

"Then how the fuck did it get out?" His voice is harsh. I've never seen him this hurt.

The Re-Write 217

I force myself to take a breath. There's no way I can spin it. "I sent Mayee the manuscript," I admit in a quiet voice. "Wale, I was scared she was going to drop me."

Aghast, Wale puts his hands behind his head. "You're fucking unbelievable, you know that."

"I didn't think anything would come from it," I cry. "I literally wrote the book in four weeks; my manuscript was probably riddled with plot holes. I sent it to Mayee to appease her, that's all. I genuinely didn't think that Dionne would love it. I feel awful."

Wale shakes his head, his face contoured with disbelief. I'm not getting through to him. He's too hurt.

"Wale, I'm so sorry."

He spits out a mirthless laugh.

"I swear on my life, I was going to back out. I'll call Mayee now and tell her I can no longer go through with it."

There's a sore hoarseness to my voice. How do you convince someone of your intentions? It's almost impossible. I wish I had some sort of physical evidence, like a drafted email or voicemail. If only I could rip out my heart so that he can see my emotions, raw.

Across the street, a man walking his dog slows down to watch.

"Temi, you don't get it, do you?" Wale chokes out. "You lied. To my face. You will do *anything* to get published. Anything. And I went out of my way to do all those nice things for you . . ." His voice cracks. "God, I'm so stupid."

"I can give you back the laptop—"

"You really don't get it, do you?" he says.

I've never seen him this angry. His anger is always contained. I've wronged him—he's livid—and I don't know how to make it right.

"Everything okay there?" the man with the dog says.

I suddenly become aware of my surroundings—another man has stopped in his tracks and there's an older woman watching from her balcony. All it takes is one person with a phone and history will repeat itself.

"Wale. People are watching. Let's go to your car and talk."

"*Talk?*" Wale looks at me, incredulous. "This"—he jabs at his phone—"tells me everything that I need to know." And then his face crumples. Tears begin to well. "I've been pouring my heart out to you, Temi," he says. "Why would you do me like that?"

"Wale!"

The sound of a Nigerian female voice slices through the air. Wale's mum is standing by his front door, clutching her paper-thin nightgown to her chest. Seeing her in the flesh almost pushes a feral cry out of my throat.

"I have to go," he says, his voice drained.

He turns to leave and, in one last desperate attempt, I grab his wrist. He stares down at my hand.

"I'm so sorry," I whisper. "I promise you, I'll fix this."

I don't know what I expect him to say. How can he respond when his worst fears have come to pass? And I'm the reason.

Wale says nothing. He pulls back his hand and walks away.

40

The journey home is a daze. It's like I'm bleeding out and slowly losing consciousness.

It is only when I take out my keys that I realize that I left my dress at the shop. What does it matter. I won't be going to the gala anyway. Wale wouldn't want me there.

I slip off my shoes, tutting at the thin streak of light coming from the living room. *Well, that's going to bump up this month's bill.*

I push the door open.

"SURPRISE!"

It's Mum and Dad. They're standing with jazz hands under a massive CONGRATULATIONS banner, a few stray balloons by their feet. Mum pulls a party popper while Dad beams behind his phone, recording my reaction.

I look between them. Then at the ridiculously cute cupcakes on the table. I feel my lips quiver and I burst into tears.

. . .

It's been over a minute since telling my parents the book deal is off. We're all sitting on my one sofa, me in the middle. I feel as though I've just confessed to a crime. I had to tell them everything, including the fact that Wale is both my ex-boyfriend and my celebrity client.

I wish they weren't here so I could mourn in peace. But they used their spare key to slip in when they realized I wasn't at home. It's hard to know what they're thinking. They've been awfully quiet.

"Why did you take the job in the first place?" Dad says finally, trying to understand my logic. "And you should have told your agent the truth before you accepted the publishing deal."

"*And* you should have been honest with Wale," Mum says in a disapproving tone. "I know he hurt you, dear, but how would you feel if it was the other way around?"

I push my glasses up, pressing my fists against my eyes, my blood heating under my skin. I don't need to be told what I should have done. I already feel like a monster.

I lurch to my feet. I've had enough.

"Okay! I get it!" I flail my arms. "I'm one big disappointment. I know!"

"We're not saying that—" Mum begins.

"But you're thinking it. Just say it! I'm a disappointment of a daughter."

Mum stares at me, aghast. "Why would you say that, Temi?"

Dad puts his hand on her forearm—a quiet signal to allow me to speak.

So, I do. Every rooted belief roars out of me. Everything that has built up from when I was a kid. I talk at one hundred miles per hour while looking down at them, my arms everywhere. I tell them how sorry I am that I never became the child that they hoped for, and how sorry I am that they wasted their hard-earned wages to send me to a top private school. I tell them how sorry I am that I'm not like Rosemary. That I'm sorry for chasing a pipe dream.

By the time I stop, tears are rolling down my face. My throat aches from all the yelling.

Mum and Dad stare up at me in silence. Neither of them seem ready to speak.

"How long have you felt like this?" Dad says finally.

I wipe a stray tear with my sleeve. "I dunno." I sniff. "Since I was a kid. I just feel like I'll never be good enough, no matter how hard I try. And even though it's inspiring seeing how successful you both are, I also feel a lot of pressure, you know?" A tear rolls down my cheek. "I'm grateful for all you've done for me; I will always be. But I can't help but feel it's all conditional. Maybe it's all in my head. I was kinda hoping that becoming an author would put an end to that."

There's a beat of silence. The anger dissipates from my body. I've gotten everything off my chest but I don't feel any lighter.

"Come. Sit." Dad pats the space between him and Mum, still sunken from my weight.

The second I return to my seat, they immediately wrap their arms around me. Mum strokes my hair while Dad angles his body toward me.

"First of all, we love you," Dad says.

I squeeze my eyes shut. I think of Wale and his dad and how desperately he craved that word.

"You are our daughter, and we love you not for what you do but for *who you are*. If we made you feel like a disappointment, then your mum and I are sorry—we're your parents. We're not always going to get it right." He pauses. "Did I ever tell you about the time I got fired?"

I lift my sunken head. I've never known my dad to be out of a job.

"You may be too young to remember but that time I had the entire summer off—?"

"So, you weren't on sick leave?!" I can recall the summer as if it were only yesterday. I was about six or seven and Dad had said he would be home because he had hurt his knee. I was convinced he had pulled an extensive sickie because he walked around the house just fine. At the time, I thought he just wanted to stay at home to play with me.

"And it took me eight attempts to pass my driving test," Mum says, grimacing as if she doesn't want anyone to hear her secret.

"Seriously? Eight times?" I swear the woman can drive with her eyes closed.

She nods and then her expression changes to something more sober. "And I've nearly had to fold my business a couple of times," she adds quietly. "It's honestly miraculous that it's still going."

I wrap my arms around them and, with happy tears welling, I sink into their warmth. It's so easy to forget that my parents are flesh and bone.

"We're not perfect and we don't expect you to be." Mum nestles her head against mine.

"And clichéd as it sounds"—Dad puts a hand on my knee—"we just want the best for you. And we're proud of you."

"Oh, yes. Very proud," Mum says. "It takes a lot of courage to go after your dream."

To lift my spirits, Dad suggests that we eat some cupcakes. It doesn't take the heartache away, but I welcome the red-velvet flavor. Then, step by step, they help me hash out a plan of action. I'm so lucky to have them.

"Okay, tonight, get some rest. Then first thing tomorrow I'll email Mayee saying I need to speak to her urgently," I recite. "When I speak to Mayee, I'll explain everything, apologize, take full accountability, answer any questions. As for Dionne"—I let out a long exhale—"Mayee would probably want to speak to her."

"Just so you're mentally prepared"—Mum takes my hand in hers—"Dionne may never offer you another book deal."

I swallow the burning lump in my throat. "I know." My voice cracks. "Don't worry. I'm expecting the worst."

The worst being that I'll lose my editor *and* my renowned agent. That I'm blacklisted in the industry and no major publisher will want to work with me. It's an excruciatingly painful pill to swallow, but I've brought this all on myself. I have to face the consequences.

My parents must have read the worried look on my face because they hug me again.

"You'll bounce back," Mum whispers.

"And as always," Dad says, "we'll be here."

41

I'm the first of the three to join the Zoom meeting. Seeing my anxiety reflected back from my screen is making me even more nervous.

I emailed Mayee first thing this morning. I hardly slept, so I drafted and sent the email at 5 a.m. Then, wretched with worry and with intense pressure building at the back of my skull, I waited for the call.

It came at precisely 8 a.m. A flush of sticky heat washed over my body as Mayee's name flashed up on my phone. I imagined my parents sitting beside me and, after taking an enormous lungful of air, I answered.

It was difficult to gauge Mayee's true reaction. She was painfully quiet and I kept having to check she was still there. I felt like a sinner in a confessional. I couldn't stop apologizing. After I stopped filling in the silence, Mayee said she would inform Dionne on my behalf and then the three of us would have a meeting, most likely in the afternoon. She didn't sound angry, but she was far from pleased.

I'm downing a long glug of water when Mayee's face pops up on the screen. Today, her jet-black hair is slicked back into a ponytail.

"Hey, Mayee." I wipe my mouth with the back of my sleeve.

"Hi" is all she says. Her red lips are drawn, her face stiff.

I'm debating whether it would be overkill to apologize again when Dionne's face appears.

"Sorry I'm late," she says. "Meeting ran over. Thanks for setting this up, Mayee." And then her eyes dart to where I am on the screen. "So. Temi. It seems like you had quite an eventful evening yesterday."

My first instinct is to apologize. "Dionne, I'm so sorry. I should have been honest with you. I take full responsibility. But I can't, in good faith, move ahead with publishing *The Ultimate Payback*. It just wouldn't be right—for me or for people I care for. I'm sorry for not being fully transparent with you when we met and for wasting your time."

Dionne gives a slow nod. I can't quite read her expression. But she is far from the bubbly person I met at Ocean's office. "Thank you for your apology," she says sagely. "I'm sure this won't come as a surprise, but I'm going to have to withdraw my offer. Thankfully, you haven't signed a contract yet, so we don't have to get legal involved."

I knew it was coming but it still really, really hurts. Tears sting the back of my throat.

"I understand." My voice wavers a bit. I choke down a sob. What makes this so painful is that I had intended on telling them the truth. And no matter what I say, it will seem as though I have only confessed because of the viral post. If I'd had control of the narrative perhaps Mayee and Dionne would have been more empathetic. More understanding. Now, I may never again get this close to becoming a published author. I may never be offered a second chance. I might have to find a new career.

The tears I tried to push down surface again as I accept I won't be working with Dionne or my dream publisher.

I notice what looks like sympathy fill Dionne's eyes. She doesn't rush to end the meeting. "Is there anything else you'd like to say?" she asks.

"I really am so sorry," I say again because that's all I can say.

Dionne stares at me. She looks truly devastated too. "Mayee, unless you have any other questions, that will be all from me."

Mayee shakes her head. "Thank you for meeting at such late notice."

"No worries." Dionne pauses. Purses her lips. I wait for her to say a final goodbye. Instead, she says, "Temi, all this aside, I think you're a brilliant writer. And I'm still open to receiving a manuscript from you in the future."

The dam breaks.

"Thank you," I croak, letting my tears fall. "Thank you."

The faintest smile passes over Dionne's face. "All the best," she says. She logs off.

I'm about to leave, too, when Mayee says, "Temi, hang on a sec."

My heart beats wildly in my chest. Dionne may have given me a second chance but that doesn't mean Mayee will or has to. Hastily, I wipe my tears to prepare myself.

We stare at each other, our squares side by side, the tension mounting with each passing second. Mayee's eyes are feline. She doesn't blink, she glares.

"Temi, what the hell?"

I jolt. This is the first time I've heard Mayee snap.

"Do you know how embarrassing that was? Me having to tell Dionne about this mess? Why didn't you tell me Wale was your ex?"

"I'm sorry, Mayee." I can't stop apologizing. "I really am."

Mayee massages her temples as if she is getting a headache. She has every right to feel pissy—I've caused her so much trouble. She lets out an agitated breath.

"We need to have a conversation about our relationship."

Sweat beads on my neck. This is it. The moment I've been dreading. Mayee is finally going to let me go. I reach for my glass of water. I need to hold on to something.

"I want you to be honest with yourself," she says. "Do you think I'm the best person to be your agent?"

I blink. I wasn't expecting that.

"Of course!" My voice is high from the shock. "You're one of the top literary agents. Any writer would be lucky to have you."

"But do *we* make a good fit? Am I right for you?"

I'm about to blurt "Of course!" again but I can tell Mayee wants me to seriously consider this question. What she's really asking is "Why weren't you honest with me?" An author should feel safe to be open with their agent. After all, they are representing them. And from the start I haven't been.

"Mayee, it's not you. It's me." I fight a grimace at how clichéd my words sound but, sometimes, clichés are true. "I've faced so much rejection in my life, I couldn't bear the thought of losing you, so I put up a front. I pretended that everything was okay and that I had my shit together when really I've been struggling. I should have been transparent with you from the beginning. I should have told you about Wale, that I had barely started writing *Love Drive*. And I never should have sent you *The Ultimate Payback* in the first place. I know you're probably sick of me saying sorry, but I am. I'll understand if you no longer want to represent me going forward."

I feel a tiny sliver of relief to have gotten all that off of my chest without bawling. Whatever happens, at least I can look back and say I took full responsibility.

Mayee twists her wedding ring in deep thought. The line between her brows has gone. "Do you know why I signed you?" she says eventually.

I shake my head.

"Take a wild guess."

I rub my burning nose. "Because of my potential?"

"Exactly. I signed you because I believe in you. I believe you have what it takes to be an author. And despite everything, I still believe that. You're an incredible writer, Temi. Nothing can ever change that."

I glance down, touched by Mayee's words. I sorely needed to hear that.

"I wouldn't normally do this but I'm willing to give you a second chance." My head snaps up as I let out a loud gasp. She raises a finger. "*But* only on the condition that, one, you will be transparent with me going forward, and two, you'll write another book."

"I'll do whatever it takes." I can't help it: joyful tears start to spill. So, this is what it feels like to be the prodigal son. "I promise. I won't let you down."

Mayee barks out a single laugh. "Too right, you won't. I have to dash to another meeting now, but before I go, we need to talk about the memoir."

God, the memoir.

"I've spoken to Greg," she says carefully. "We think it would be best to take you off the project."

42

Despite being given a second chance, I feel empty. Not only have I been pulled from Wale's memoir but we've made mainstream news as well. After the call, I realize I have a WhatsApp message from Shona—a link to an article on *The Daily Biz* followed by

> **Shona:**
> HAVE YOU SEEN THIS?!!!

I cannot bring myself to read it. When is this going to blow over? I promised Wale that I would fix things and I haven't. The post is still up on The Tea Lounge and the last time I checked it had nearly thirteen thousand likes. At least it's now further down the grid.

I go to check again. It's now over fifteen thousand.

Telling myself I cannot feel any worse, I scroll through the comments. It seems to never end. Some people have connected the fact that I'm the girl he took the picture with at the barbershop and have begun speculating.

emma_gazelle Is this a PR stunt?

Many are still lambasting Wale, while some have come to my defense, condemning those who have fat-shamed me. And then I see a comment that makes me stop in my tracks like a rabbit in the headlights.

kelechi_iwobi Can people stop tagging me under this post! Wale and I are cool! You guys don't know half the story!!!

My mind circles back to the radio interview—when Wale said he met up with Kelechi after the show and explained everything.

And then my eye homes in on one word: "story." If I sit back and do nothing, God knows where we'll be trending next. I need to control the narrative. I need to rewrite the story.

I hastily exit Instagram, tap on the camera icon, and then video. My stricken face fills the screen. I'm too exhausted to put makeup on, so I add a filter instead.

I press record. "Hey, guys—"

I hit stop. *Hey, guys* is something someone with a fanbase would say. I try again.

"Good afternoon, everyone, my name is Temi Ojo."

Delete. Too formal.

After my third attempt is met with me staring blankly at the camera, I abandon the plan, too frustrated with how hard it is to nail the right tone.

You're a writer, Temi. So, write.

Quickly, I hop back on to Instagram and create a new post. Trying not to overthink it, I type, white text lengthening over the black background. When I finish, I read over what I've written. I'm tempted to edit it but it doesn't need to be perfect. The sentiment of the message is clear:

Wale, I fucked up.

43

> Yesterday, The Tea Lounge posted that I will be publishing a book inspired by my ex, Wale Bandele. While I am angry but not surprised that this was posted without my confirmation, I have to take some accountability for entangling Wale in this mess. I wrote the book to help deal with our breakup. It was never intended for publication. But being a published author is a dream of mine, and, unfortunately, I gave in to temptation. I'm so ashamed for this moment of weakness.
>
> Although flawed, Wale is one of the sweetest, kindest souls I know and I'm immensely sorry for the hurt I have caused him. Before yesterday's announcement, I had already made the decision not to publish the book. I immensely regret not withdrawing my submission earlier. Lastly, as you have no context for the video and the events leading to our breakup, I would greatly appreciate it if people could stop sending hate our way. Please be kind.
>
> Temi

My post has been up for less than ten minutes when I get a call from Shona.

"Babe, you're on The Tea Lounge again!"

"I know. It's the only way that I can get through to Wale. He hasn't been picking up my calls."

"He won't listen to me either." She pauses. "How you feeling?"

I feel desperate. "Shona, I don't know how I'm going to make things right. Wale hates me and Mayee has pulled me off the memoir." I feel my eyes moisten again; I cannot stop crying. "I'm not even sure if he's going to publish it anymore. I feel terrible. His memoir is more important than this whole mess."

"Then write it anyway." Shona sounds absolute.

"But I've been taken off the project—"

"So? You're doing this for Wale, not for them. Finish the memoir, Temi, and let Wale decide if he still wants to put it out to the world."

My mind snags on the word "finish." I used to hear it all the time at Bonsai. When I left, I still had three projects ongoing. I felt so bad for my clients. I failed them by leaving so suddenly. I had failed to cross the finishing line. But this time, things will be different. I *will* finish what I've started. I *will* make the deadline. This time, I, Temiloluwa Ojo, will win.

44

```
Wale_Memoir_Draft1.doc
Target word count: 50,000
Current word count: 45,062
New deadline: One week to go . . .
```

Vaseline. Earpods. Water.

As though I'm getting ready to live in a bunker, I gather all the things I need to write. My bum is going to be glued to my chair for a very long time. I put on one of DJ Raphael's neo-soul mixes, put my phone on "Do not disturb," and set a timer for two hours. When I get there I'll give myself a fifteen-minute break before going at it again. Finally, I open my laptop, locate the document, and begin to write.

Whether it's the motivation to do right by Wale or the need to escape into a different world, I write with fearless gusto. I'm like an overzealous student determined to crack the piano. I now have to cram what I planned to write in two weeks into one. The sooner I can gift Wale his memoir, the better.

So, I write from morning until evening, and quickly the days and nights blur into each other. Although I try not to get into the habit of looking at WhatsApp—each minute is too precious—when I do, I only check one thing—but my messages to Wale have remained unread.

It's been a week and I'm editing the section on Wale's home life. I've titled it:

People assume that I'm emotionally detached
The truth is I have unresolved childhood trauma

It's been the hardest section to write, the memory of how vulnerable he was that evening too raw. And yet, I write. Even though it hurts and even though it's now the day of the gala. Earlier today, I had a quick look at Wale's Insta Stories. He has been posting behind-the-scenes pictures and videos all day. It looks amazing. I'm glad he's not hiding away despite what's happened.

I'm in the process of reading the manuscript—*surely, I can't be finished?*—when there is a knock. I open my front door.

It's Shona and Fonzo.

"Girl, what's wrong with your phone?" Shona says as she hoists the sides of her mermaid dress, wafting designer perfume as she bustles inside. She looks like African royalty: full-on glam, oversize brass jewelry, her fresh box braids tied into several Bantu knots.

Fonzo, who looks equally dapper in his teal Ozwald Boateng–esque suit, wipes his suede loafers on my doormat.

"Err, aren't you supposed to be at the gala?" I call after them as they pile into my room.

"I've been calling you!" Shona cries.

"Sorry. I've been busy writing." Truthfully, I've also been dodging her. All week she's been trying to get me to go to the gala.

Shona places her hands on her hips. "Get changed. You're coming with us."

"But I've nearly finished Wale's memoir." I gesture at my laptop. "Besides, I don't have anything to wear."

On cue, Fonzo hangs a suit carrier on my door frame. I was so stunned to see them, I didn't even notice he was carrying it. He zips it open and, lo and behold, there's my dress.

Oh, it's beautiful.

"You're welcome," says Shona. "Now, chop, chop." She claps.

With a groan, I slump in my chair. It swivels and rolls backward. "He doesn't want me there, Shona."

"I told him that you're on the guest list. He didn't object."

Well, that is surprising, but it doesn't change anything.

I fold my arms. "I'm not going."

Shona and Fonzo turn to one another.

"Plan B?" Shona says.

"Plan B," agrees Fonzo.

Shona crosses her arms. "What if I told you we know who tipped off The Tea Lounge?"

This is unexpected . . . "I'm listening."

"It was Kojo!" they cry at the same time.

Kojo had crossed my mind—after all, he was at the house party—but so were a lot of people.

"First of all, Kojo was at the house party," says Shona, reading my mind. "And if you look at the angle from which the video was taken, it's from above, so the person who was recording must have been standing in the curve of the stairwell."

"Unlike me, Kojo didn't run after Wale," Fonzo chips in. "He stayed behind."

"Second of all, if you watch the video until the end, you can hear him laughing." Shona opens her clutch and pulls out her phone.

I raise my hand to stop her. "I'd rather not watch it again."

"We also did some digging." Fonzo picks up where Shona left off. "We think the person who exposed the press release must be following you on Twitter. So, we went through your followers—it didn't take long 'cause you only have about two hundred or so—and guess who's following your account?"

My eyes widen. "Nooo."

Fonzo nods repeatedly. "Yup. He uses the name @therealestalpha. I recognized it instantly as it's the same name he uses for his Instagram account. Kojo was trying to get back at you."

The Re-Write

My skin turns scorching hot. I'm livid. This guy is out for blood.

"Kojo also knew about *The Ultimate Payback*," I murmur, thinking aloud. I turn to Fonzo. "We bumped into each other at Starbucks about two months ago. He had a snoop on my laptop while I was in the toilet."

"All signs point to Kojo," Shona says, putting her hands on her hips. "He sounds guilty as F to me. Anyway, get dressed, Temi. We have to go. Like now."

"Sorry, but if your plan B was to get me to change my mind, I haven't; I'm still not going. And even if Kojo is behind the post, it doesn't change anything. At the end of the day, I lied. I don't want to ruin Wale's night by showing up. You guys shouldn't even be here—Wale needs you. Now if you'll excuse me"—I swivel around and tuck myself under my desk—"I've got some editing to do."

Shona breathes out a resigned sigh and says, "C'mon, Fonzo. Let's go." She stoops over to hug me from behind.

"I appreciate you, though," I whisper, and I think I hear her say, "Plan C."

"Huh?" I say with a frown.

Then I realize what plan C is. While Shona is holding me from behind, Fonzo snatches my laptop.

"Oi! Come back here!"

He makes a mad dash out of the door.

Shona continues to hold me down. Gosh, she's a lot stronger than she looks.

Finally, she lets me go. "You have twenty minutes. Chop, chop."

45

Fonzo steers his car into the parking lot of the venue—a picturesque, historical-looking building brought to life with yards of red carpet rolled out in front, two large fig trees on either side. Inside, a live band is playing an Afrobeats song and I can hear the buzz of chatter coming from the people milling outside.

Shona and I clamber out from the back seat. Twenty minutes only afforded me the time to have a quick shower, change, and put my contacts in before I was bulldozed out of my flat. Thankfully, Shona came prepared with a bag stocked with cosmetics, so I was able to do my hair and makeup during the forty-minute drive to the venue. I've gone for a retro look: smoky eyes, red lips, big hair.

Bending toward one of the wing mirrors, I do a last check (I applied my eyeliner while we were going over a speed bump). I fluff my hair and put on my earrings—oversize Ankara wax fabric studs.

"You ready?" says Shona, placing a hand on my back.

"Not really." My voice is small.

I reach for her. Hand in hand, we head to the venue, walking briskly down the red carpet. We pass a stream of stylish guests and influencers, some of whom are posing for the photographers. We end up practically running in case any are pap.

"I'll catch up with you later," Fonzo calls as he straps his camera around his neck.

When we step inside, my jaw drops. The interior is breathtaking, and I momentarily forget how nervous I am. Crystal chandeliers, marble polished floors, a grand staircase. Flanked with Grecian pillars, the lobby is festooned with massive ceramic urns blooming with fresh delphiniums and white lilies. There are hundreds of lavishly dressed people, many of whom are admiring Fonzo's photography propped up on easels. Waiters wander in between them serving champagne and canapés. I'm gazing at a photograph of a man feeding an older woman when Aunty Shirley steps into my eyeline.

"My sweet darling, look at you!" She gives me a hug, steps back, and holds my hands. "Nice. Very nice. Give us a twirl."

She's dressed in a black blouse and slacks. Of course—she's managing the catering.

"This is my friend Shona," I say, gesturing to her.

Aunty Shirley says, "Oh, we're very much acquainted. Thanks for helping us in the kitchen today."

"No problem." Shona cranes her neck. "Do you know where Wale is?"

"He's in the tech room sorting out the walkie-talkies." Suddenly, Aunty Shirley notices something behind us. "Why in the world are they serving—sorry, excuse me." She dashes off.

Shona tugs me to follow her.

I pull back, gripped with nerves. "I think I should go home. Tonight is Wale's night. I don't want to ruin it."

Shona looks me in the eye, her brows creasing with concern. "What if you had a reason to be here?"

"What do you mean?"

She smiles. "I have a plan." She whips out her phone and dials someone. "Hey, Fonzo. We're going to need Temi's laptop."

A few minutes later, the three of us are in the staff office, the sound of a massive laser printer churning in the background.

My heart is a drumbeat in my chest. "Do you think this will work?" I ask from behind the desk.

Shona massages the knots between my shoulders. "We have to try."

Then the door opens. My stomach flips.

"Shona, are you okay?" Wale says, almost breathless. Shona had called him to say she had sprained her ankle and that he should meet her at the office.

I can pinpoint the exact moment he notices me. His expression goes from one of worry to surprise.

There's a hush of silence. I rise to my feet. We stare soberly at each other from across the room. He looks painfully handsome as always. His tux jacket is embroidered with gold floral patterns and fits him like a glove. And he's wearing a velvety bow tie that matches his lapels.

We seem to be speaking in a silent language because I can tell from his eyes that he thinks I look beautiful too.

And then our bubble pops.

"If your ankle is fine, I need to get going" is all he says.

"Kojo leaked the video!" Shona cries. She begins to tell Wale what she told me, but the disorderly way she's telling the story makes it sound like a conspiracy. My eyes keep flickering to him. He's trying to be patient but I can see he's eager to get back to the gala.

"Look, we're not saying Temi's totally innocent," Fonzo says after Shona loses steam. "But she has taken accountability. Surely that should count for something? She's not even going to publish the book anymore."

"Yeah, I saw her Instagram." Wale's eyes say: *And?*

Shona opens her mouth and closes it again.

"Excuse me," he says, turning to leave.

"Wale! Please! Wait!"

In desperation, I hurry over to him. He can't even bear to look at me and, when he does, his jaw clenches, his body simmering with frustration. I feel defeated. I don't know what to say, but I have to try to make him understand. This may be my last chance.

"Wale, I'm sorry." I gulp back tears. "I know I said it before but I will say it a million times if I have to. I'm sorry for not being honest with you from the start and I'm sorry that you felt taken advantage of. It was never my intention to hurt you—you know how much I care about you.

But once you started opening up, things became . . . complicated. I'd only just earned back your trust and I was scared to lose it again. And I'd become so invested in writing your memoir. And most of all, I was scared of losing you."

I stare at him, breathless, hoping my words are both sharp and soft enough to penetrate his heart. Because that's all I have right now. My words.

The printing in the background stops. And that's when I remember: I have something else.

"I also have this for you." I scurry to the printer and pick up the stacks of paper, still warm from the fresh ink. My fingers tremble as I hand them to him—his memoir.

Wale's gaze slides down. His eyes are glued to the title page: *A Memoir by Wale Bandele*. He doesn't say anything. He's too overwhelmed. The angles in his face have softened. He looks truly moved.

"I just came to give you that," I whisper, hugging my elbows.

I watch his throat bob as he swallows, his lashes splaying over his cheeks.

"Thanks," he eventually says, his voice a croak. He glances up. "I have to go."

My heart is a sinking ship as he walks to the door.

And then he stops. "You're on table two," he says.

46

Table two is Wale's table. He's sitting three seats away, going by his place card. With the night in full swing, he spends most of the evening greeting guests or pacing with his walkie-talkie. When I manage to tear my eyes away from him, I'm either chatting with Kathy and the other people at my table or admiring the exquisitely decorated hall adorned with Chiavari chairs and candelabra centerpieces. And then the food arrives. Aunty Shirley's curry goat with rice and peas does not disappoint.

Still, all I keep thinking is *What does this mean?* Why did Wale tell me to stay? Is it because he's forgiven me? Or perhaps he's just being nice and if I hadn't given him his manuscript, he would have politely told me to leave. And what does this olive branch mean for us? Our working relationship? Our friendship? Our future?

Three courses later, we've managed to whiz through an auction, a spoken-word performance, and a few speeches. We've also watched some heartstring-pulling videos of how this gala will benefit the carers. Breezy Brett is doing a brilliant job as MC and keeps the program ticking along with great sensitivity and wit. He has just asked Wale to come onto the stage.

I join in with the applause. My heart flutters as Wale strides onto the platform, giving Breezy Brett a hug and a dab. I know what's coming next.

He clears his throat. "Good evening, everyone," he says. His smile is dazzling and the audience whistles and laughs. Gosh, he is so heart-achingly charming; it's hard to reconcile this man with the one I encountered a few hours ago. "My name is Wale Bandele and I'm the former events and fundraising officer at ACE. Although many of you may know me as that guy from *The Villa*." He pauses. "To the boomers in the room, *The Villa* is a reality TV dating show."

There is a ripple of laughter.

"Don't worry, don't worry. I'm not about to take my shirt off. Though, tonight is a charity fundraiser . . . Any cougars in the room?"

The laughter is louder this time.

A lady in the back heckles, "I'll take you!"

Wale laughs. "Nah, in all seriousness, thank you everyone for showing up tonight. We're here because we want to support ACE. And ACE is here because of one special person." He gestures to Kathy. A spotlight picks her out of the crowd and her face flashes on the screen. Kathy is clearly surprised to be singled out. "As you all know, Kathy McGiffin is ACE's CEO and founder. But she's also a mother figure, an aunt, a mentor, a friend. She has dedicated her life to supporting carers . . . and I have benefited from that myself so I know just how incredible she is. So, tonight, ladies and gentlemen, please put your hands together as I present the one and only Kathy McGiffin with a lifetime achievement award!"

The cheers and applause are thunderous. An emotional Kathy makes her way to the stage. She hugs Wale tightly, rocking him from side to side. Shona hands her a glass plaque.

Kathy steps toward the mic, shell shocked. Her fingers are visibly shaking and her fascinator is now slightly lopsided. She looks at the audience, then at her award, then at the audience again.

"For a woman who likes a good natter, I'm surprisingly speechless."

Everyone laughs.

"Although I'm honored to have received this award, I would like to dedicate it to my ACE family. To every staff member, trustee, and volunteer. To every fundraiser and supporter. And most importantly, to every carer." Her voice wobbles. Wale reaches for her hand. She holds the bridge of her nose until she gathers herself. "To every carer in the room and beyond who has ever felt forgotten or invisible, this award is for you. ACE sees you and we appreciate you and we're with you. Always."

The clapping is deafening as everyone rises to their feet. Wale wraps an arm around a teary Kathy as she takes everything in. And then, as if I'd called Wale's name out loud, he looks directly at me.

He's . . . smiling. Though I'm not sure if he's smiling at me—he was already smiling before he looked at me. But then he offers me a slow, steady nod that makes my heart feel like it has springs.

I have a chance.

We have a chance.

47

After the awards ceremony, the program draws to an end. People are mingling and chatting; some are getting warmed up on the dance floor. Then, through the crowd, Wale and I lock eyes. He shakes the hand of the person he's talking to with a smile, then excuses himself. We meet in the middle. A disco ball is spinning from the ceiling, casting speckled light.

"Hey," I say quietly.

"Hey," he says softly, his hands in his pockets.

"Thanks for allowing me to stay. It was such a beautiful night."

"Appreciate it." He looks down at his shoes, then back at me again. "You look gorgeous, by the way."

"Thanks. You too." I feel my cheeks blush. I purse my lips. "Wale, I'm—"

"I know, Temi. You're sorry. But what you did really hurt me." There's a glossy sheen to his eyes. I swallow. "It hurt 'cause I care about you."

His words feel like a hug and a stab at the same time.

In the background, a Lovers Rock song begins to play. A guest walking by stops to congratulate Wale and shakes his hand.

Wale turns back to me. "We need to stop doing this. Hiding things from each other."

I nod. "No more lies. No more cover-ups. From this day forward, I'll give you the plain, honest truth."

Wale studies me. "Cool. I promise to give you the plain, honest truth too."

We stare at each other.

So, does this mean . . . ?

"Mic check one two, one two."

The amplified voice of Uncle Les cuts over the music and our silent exchange. Wale and I turn.

I can't help but laugh. "Wait. Is Uncle Les going to DJ?"

Wale gives me a sidelong smile. "Yeah, for ten minutes he is. Or until Aunty Shirley heckles him off. Whichever comes first."

Uncle Les taps the mic. It makes a screeching sound. "Apologies," he says over the audible mutterings. "I'm going to start with a special request. You might want to grab your lover."

The crooning of New Edition's "Can You Stand the Rain" fills the hall. *Our song.*

I whip around, my mouth open. "Did you . . . ?"

Wale gives me a knowing smile.

I nudge him. "Go on, then. I dare you to do those moves in the middle of the dance floor."

"I've got a better idea," he says. He bows and extends a hand, and in a mock-*Bridgerton* voice says, "Milady."

With a giggle, I take his hand and he guides me to the dance floor, where a few couples are already slow dancing.

En route, I catch Kathy's eye. She's getting her picture taken. She gives me a wink. I wonder how much she knows.

I sling my arms around Wale's neck and, when he places his hands on the curve of my back, tingles emanate out and up my spine. Joyful relief rises in my chest. Slowly, we sway. And I lose myself in the lyrics, in his neroli scent, in his warmth. I couldn't have asked for more. This is the perfect ending.

"I'm sorry." His voice is a rasp in my ear. I lift my head from his chest. I thought we had put a line under things. "I'm sorry for taking you off the memoir project," he says in response to my questioning brows. "It was Greg's decision—"

I bring a finger to his lips. "Shh," I hush. I give him a tiny smile.

Wale's eyes seem to drink me in. He nips the tip of my finger playfully, then gives it a peck before enveloping my hand in his. "Honestly, thank you for the manuscript. It's not even due for another week. I can't wait to read it—"

"Awww, look at you guys!"

We peel apart.

Kelechi is standing in front of us.

I gawk.

Kelechi is even more drop-dead gorgeous in real life. She's wearing an elegant black halter dress and her teeth are blinding white.

"You must be Temi?" She hugs me first before turning to embrace Wale. Then she claps her fingers. "Yay! You guys are back together. Thank God, I was wondering how things were gonna play out after that video leak. Anyway, I just thought I'd stop and say hi and—ooh, girl, I love your dress. Wale"—she gives him a high five—"well done, man. You absolutely smashed it tonight."

"Thank you."

She gives me a quick glance and then swivels back to Wale, her perfectly sculpted brows arched in warning. "Now, listen to me"—she points a finger at him—"you've been given a second chance. Hold on to her this time, yeah?" She smiles sweetly between us. "Enjoy your evening."

I hook my arms around Wale's neck again, my mind cycling. How much did Wale tell Kelechi? Or was she just referring to what she'd seen in the video?

Wale returns his hands to the small of my back. Boyz II Men's "End of the Road" is now playing. Not a fitting song choice, but it doesn't matter.

"I had a conversation with Kelechi after the show," he says. He leans back slightly so that he can look at me and tucks a curl behind my ear. "As well as apologizing, I told her about us. Told her my heart was still with you."

So, Wale *was* in love with me this entire time.

When I was watching the show, it seemed as though I was the last thing on his mind, when in fact I was behind his inability to commit. It's strange how our actions sometimes don't reflect our truest feelings. It's like *The Ultimate Payback*. I wrote it out of anger. Anger at him and at myself. But Dionne could see the love story at its heart, even if I hadn't written it into being yet. Despite everything, I was still stupidly in love with Wale.

Wale lowers his head and presses his forehead against mine. Our mouths are inches apart. My breath is caught in my throat.

And then we're interrupted again. This time by a stricken-looking Shona.

"Wale! Come, quick! Kojo's here!"

48

We barrel out of the hall, Shona and I behind Wale, holding hands.

"I took him off the guest list," Shona cries.

Fonzo is by the bar, gesticulating. Kojo is lounging on one of the stools with a nonchalant expression. Not only did he have the audacity to gate-crash Wale's event, but he's also wearing a suit. My entire body is vibrating with rage. Every time I try to put Kojo behind me, he keeps creeping back.

"Kojo!" Wale walks slowly toward him—he's a man who's not to be messed with. Shona and I stop and watch from a distance.

Kojo turns to him. His lips curl into a snarl. "Here comes Mr. TV star," he says.

Wale places a hand on Fonzo's shoulder. "I'll take it from here."

Fonzo gives Kojo a long, hard glare before stepping aside.

"You need to leave. Now," says Wale with firm assertiveness. "Otherwise, I'm calling security."

Kojo's expression twists with disbelief. He laughs, but it's tinged with hysteria.

"Man tryna call security on me now. I'm not doing anything, so what's your problem?"

Wale holds his composure; his stance self-assured. "I'm not going to go back and forth with you. I'm giving you the option to leave of your own accord."

Kojo pushes his stool back, the legs making an abrupt screeching sound. "Have you really forgotten what I've done for you?" he says. "You would be nothing without me. Nothing!" He towers over Wale. He's a lot bigger than him and, truthfully, he looks rather intimidating.

Fonzo steps forward.

"I got it," says Wale, holding out a hand. "Kojo, leave."

Kojo squares up to him, his shoulders broad. "Make me," he says.

"Call security," I urge Shona.

Shona pulls out her walkie-talkie. By now, there are other people watching in the lobby. A few of the younger ones even have their phones out.

Oh, for fuck's sake. Not again.

Kojo takes a step closer to Wale, encroaching on his personal space. "I said—make me," he repeats, his voice lower, deeper, harsher.

I swivel around. "Where the heck is security?" I'm wretched with anxiety; my pulse is racing.

Wale doesn't back down. He squares his chin. "Kojo, you and I know we cannot afford to be moving mad like this. Black men are judged enough as it is. Just leave without making a scene."

"Pussy."

There are a few gasps.

Wale doesn't do anything; he stares back at his former friend, his glare unflinching. I can tell that word stung by the tic in his jaw. Throughout his life, he has grappled with being sensitive. Too soft. Too emotional. Not man enough. Whatever he does, he cannot let Kojo get a rise out of him. It will cost him dearly. He has so much to lose.

Each passing second is like the ticking of a time bomb. My heart is beating so fast, I feel as though I'm about to pass out.

Finally, Wale draws out his walkie-talkie. "Security, there's a man in the lobby who is disturbing the peace and refusing to leave."

Right on cue, two men in black suits barge past me. They grab Kojo by his arms and physically restrain him.

"Hey, man! Get the fuck off me!" Kojo yells.

His arms flail; he is screaming expletives. The man is truly unhinged.

The commotion attracts more and more people, including Kathy, Aunty Shirley, and Uncle Les. At last, the security team gets Kojo under control. They pin his arms and drag him toward the exit. There are actual cheers as they leave. I lock gazes with Kojo as he passes. I *want* him to see me.

Even though he deserves a lot more than the humiliation of being thrown out of a private event, I take small solace in seeing him helpless. Wale, with admirable restraint and without any physical violence, has managed to hold on to his dignity. His values. And, most importantly, he didn't allow Kojo to reclaim his power—to control the narrative.

If there's one thing I've learned over the last few weeks, it's how crucial it is to write your own story, otherwise someone else will do it for you. Perhaps if I had reported Kojo after he assaulted me, we wouldn't be in this position. I may never get justice but there's nothing like sending a warning.

You will never hurt me again.

Kojo cuts his eyes at me, then glances away.

I watch him until he's shoved out of the door by security.

"All right! All right! Nothing more to see here!" Kathy shoos people back to the ballroom.

Of all songs, "Macarena" blares from the speaker and everyone scuttles back to the dance floor, ready to leave this ugliness behind. Wale strolls over to us.

"Who the bloody hell was that?" Kathy cries.

"No one," Wale says. "Well, an ex-friend."

Aunty Shirley kisses her teeth. "Hmm, he lucky he didn't cross me. I would have given him two good slaps and a thump around the head."

Fonzo blinks. "Sounds violent." He turns to Wale. "You okay, man?"

Wale nods. "Thanks for having my back."

I place a hand on Wale's elbow. "You handled yourself really well."

"Took the words straight out of my mouth," Shona says. "Like a real man."

Wale wraps an arm around my shoulder and pulls me in, the feel of him safe and comforting. He kisses the side of my head. Despite what's just happened, Fonzo and Shona swoon.

"Our plan worked!" Fonzo says.

Shona loops her arm into Fonzo's and, with a grin, says, "Does this mean you two are getting back together?"

I immediately look at Kathy, Aunty Shirley, and Uncle Les. They only know me as his ghostwriter.

"I had a feeling," Kathy says, wagging a finger. "When I saw you both on the dance floor."

"Oh, I knew," Aunty Shirley says with absolute certainty.

Uncle Les scoffs. "How you know?" He lifts his chin.

Aunty Shirley looks between us, a knowing smile spreading across her face. "He walk different," she says. "His spring came back."

49

By the time the gala is over, Wale is trending on The Tea Lounge. But for good reason this time. Not only are people praising him for the charity's gala—

> **THE VILLA STAR RAISES HUNDREDS OF THOUSANDS FOR CARERS' CHARITY**

—but also for how maturely he handled his altercation with Kojo. Kelechi, who was in the lobby, filmed what happened, and obviously it didn't take that long for The Tea Lounge to jump on the bandwagon. Kojo is getting dragged in the comments section and rightly so. Karma is a bitch.

Wale steers his car in front of my flat. He pulls up the hand brake.

"So . . . good night," he says. It's about 1 a.m. and the pitch-black streets are illuminated by a few lampposts.

I unbuckle my seat belt and lean in to give him a hug.

"Is that it?!" Aunty Shirley heckles from the back seat.

"Kiss her, man! We were young once," Uncle Les says.

Wale looks at me as if to say, *Why did I volunteer to drop them home again?*

I giggle. And then, suddenly feeling very shy, I give him the quickest peck. Aunty Shirley and Uncle Les react like children. Wale smiles like a teenager after his first kiss, wide and hopeful.

. . .

For the first time in weeks, I go to bed feeling relaxed. I have no deadlines hanging over my head. No worries. No secrets. And—the best thing of all—I've got my man back. The relief is almost physical—like the tightness and suppression of the last few months have left my muscles, letting me walk freely again. I wish Wale had dropped off Uncle Les and Aunty Shirley first, so I could have invited him into my flat. Spending the night together would have been perfect. But they live practically next door to each other, so logistically it made sense.

Snuggling my duvet under my neck, I close my eyes and allow my mind to wander. I imagine Wale showing up at the door, still wearing his shirt with his top buttons loose. I imagine him taking my face in his hands and kissing me. Hard. I imagine being suddenly swept off my feet with a yelp before he carries me down the corridor, our kisses growing heavier, more urgent. I imagine him laying me on my bed and the two of us giving in to our feelings.

A few hours later, I wake up to the sound of repeated buzzing. I can hardly open my eyes, and when I do, I realize that it's very early in the morning. There's barely any daylight streaking between the blinds.

Lazily, I feel around for my phone. The vibration stops.

With relief, I slump my head back onto my pillow. I'm about to go back to sleep when the vibration starts up again. This time, I sit up and reach for my phone.

It's Wale.

"Hey, you okay? It's like"—I glance at the screen—"five o'clock in the morning."

"I love it," he says. "I love it, I love it, I love it."

"Love what?" I ask, rubbing sleep from my eye. He sounds excited. Euphoric.

"My memoir! *Duh!* Temi, you killed it. I can't stop buzzing."

Now I'm awake.

"You read it?! How? The manuscript is over two hundred pages long. You must have been shattered after you got home."

"I didn't go home."

"What?"

"Well, I did—after I dropped off Uncle Les and Aunty Shirl. But I didn't go inside. I read it in my car."

My mouth falls open. I cannot believe Wale stayed up all night to read my manuscript. I put a hand on my hair bonnet, momentarily speechless. "But why?" I manage to say. "You could have read it tomorrow or the day after or whenever you have time."

"I know," Wale says. "Trust me, I didn't plan to. But after I read the first page, I couldn't stop. Yeah, it's my story, but it's *how* you told it. You just . . . got it. Your writing, man—it's phenomenal. All the jokes land and you one hundred percent nailed my voice. I even teared up a little. God, I would have thought you were a carer too. You're so talented, Tems."

Speechless, I hold back a sob.

When I was let go from Bonsai, though I truly was relieved, my confidence still took a hit. I started to doubt myself as a writer. And the many rejections I received from publishers didn't help. Truthfully, it was the main reason why I went on to work at a call center. I wanted a job far removed from writing, in case I realized that I was actually no good at it and I had to find a new dream. It was the fear that kept me up all night.

But Wale wasn't just telling me that he loved my writing because it would make me happy. He'd *showed* me. I mean, what sane person would stay up all night reading over two hundred pages after organizing an extravagant gala?

But he did.

Tears begin to well.

"Are you okay?" he says, filling the silence.

I feel my lips quiver as I take in a shuddering breath. I sniff. "I'm just overwhelmed, that's all."

"I wish I could be there to hold you," he says softly.

I sniff again. "Me too. Wait, are you running?" In the background, I can hear hurried steps. Wale sounds slightly breathless too. "Wale, don't tell me you've just left your house at five o'clock in the morning."

Suddenly, there's a knock on the door.

What the hell?

I leap out of bed and jog down the corridor. I open the front door.

"Your wish is my command," he says into his phone.

Wale is standing in my doorway. He's still wearing his outfit from earlier, minus his jacket. Just like in my fantasy, a few of his shirt buttons are undone. He gives me a dazzling smile, ends the call, and slips his phone in his pocket. And then he steps forward, cups my face in his hands, and kisses me.

The collision of our lips and seeing Wale in the flesh throw me and I have to sling my arms over his neck, phone still in hand, to stop myself from toppling backward. He laughs as he kisses me, his hand on my bum, his breath ragged. We stagger out of the doorway, barely remembering to pull it closed behind us. My hands are in his hair, pulling his shirt out of his trousers so I can touch his smooth, firm chest. The kiss is stronger, longer, harder. It's as if no words in the dictionary will ever be enough to tell me how he feels, to express how he wants me to feel. We are both each other's oxygen. We kiss each other as though we need it to live.

Wale begins a slow descent of kisses from my lips down to my collarbone, and I arch my neck, reveling in how deliciously good it feels.

I draw a breath. "How did you get here so fast? Were you in your car the entire time?"

Wale nibbles the soft skin near my shoulders. "Have you ever read or watched something that made you so excited that you needed to talk to someone about it right away? Well, that's exactly how I felt after I read through the memoir. But I didn't wanna freak you out by knocking on your door so early in the morning. So, I called you from my car instead."

"Come here, you." I bring his mouth to mine.

Wale bends his knees and hoists me into his arms—one arm under my thighs, the other wrapped around my waist.

I squeal with laughter and he silences me with a kiss. He carries me to my bedroom, where he puts me down carefully on my bed. His tenderness melts me. I snatch off my pink "Div" hair bonnet and shake out my curls. For a long moment, he stares down at me, as if I'm a precious stone that's only just been discovered.

"You're so gorgeous," he whispers, taking me in.

Without breaking eye contact, I unbutton the rest of his shirt. He tugs it off. My body screams at the sight of his exquisite toned arms made more beautiful with his sleeve of tattoos. I sit up slightly and he helps me out of my top, his eyes widening at the sight of my boobs. And then he works his way down, winding my bottoms and knickers past my ankles.

"Tonight"—he kisses the inner part of my thigh—"you have three wishes. Anything you wish for is my command."

Pressure builds as Wale kisses his way up my leg, teasing me with his slowness.

I've had sex with Wale countless times. But something about this moment is uniquely special. Perhaps because we're both different people. We communicate better. We're open. Honest. We also understand each other a lot more. We know each other's fears, triggers, and insecurities. And what we desire from each other at this present moment. We become one more intimately than ever before.

Wale gave me three wishes, but I orgasm five times before 7 a.m.

50

We doze off in each other's arms, my head against his rising chest. For the first time in months, I'm in a state of total peace. I feel so blessed. I've been given a second chance by Wale, by Mayee, and my relationship with my parents is great. I feel as if I've evolved, not just as a writer, but as a person too.

Wale has barely gotten any sleep when he rolls out of bed and stumbles into his clothes.

Rubbing my eyes, I check the time on my phone. "Dude, it's like eight o'clock in the morning. You don't have to leave." I catch the last flash of brown skin before he buttons up his shirt.

Wale tidies his hair with his hands in front of the mirror. "I know. But there's still some stuff that needs packing away at the venue that has to be out by nine. You free this afternoon?"

"Yeah. What you thinking?"

"Meet me at one at Anansi Books. I've got some notes."

"Notes?"

"Yeah. On my memoir. It's a solid draft but I've got a few comments."

"Yeah. Of course." I knew that.

He stoops over and gives me a long kiss, then grabs his phone and heads toward the door. "See you later, beautiful."

"Wale!"

He turns around.

"Um, I want to tell you something. But once I say it, I don't want there to be a long discussion about it or for you to bring it up again. I want to move on and put the past behind me."

Wale looks at me with concern. He goes to kneel beside my bed and takes my hand in his.

I draw a breath. "It's about Kojo." He braces himself. He inhales slowly and dips his head for me to carry on. "I was really inspired by the way you handled him yesterday. You didn't allow him to get a rise out of you. You controlled the situation and, in turn, retained your power. I know I said my case would go nowhere if I reported it to the police—and I very much still believe that—and I don't have the mental capacity to go through the whole justice system. But I would like some closure on what happened. Based on my terms. Which is why"—I breathe a gulp of air into my lungs—"I've decided that I'm going to report Kojo anonymously to Crimestoppers. Who knows? Maybe it might help another woman in the future."

Wale's grip around my hand tightens. He's peering at me with such pride and I can sense all the things he wants to say but isn't, out of respect for my decision. Finally, he says, "That's very brave of you," and he pulls me into him and holds me for as long as I need him to.

. . .

Later in the day, I go to meet Wale as planned. And when I stroll into Anansi Books, it's filled with sunlight. Aunty Shirley looks fresh-faced as she grins at me from behind the counter.

"He's waiting for you."

Wale is sitting in a black sweater facing the entrance. I feel a wash of déjà vu. Only we're two completely different people now.

With the widest of smiles, he rises to his feet. My heart expands; my happiness is too big to contain.

"You're wearing Sasha," he says, bobbing the side of my glasses.

I give him a wink. "I know."

We slide into our seats. On the table are two plastic cups. A distinctive nutty smell tickles my nose.

"You're too cute," I say with a smile. "Thanks." I take a sip. God, that tastes good. "Now, about these notes."

Wale laughs. "I want to show you something." He rummages into his rucksack before pulling out a notebook. It's one of those vintage-looking bound journals made out of tanned leather. "I wasn't too sure when to share this with you. But I think now is a good time." He opens it and slides the book over to me. "When I returned home after *The Villa*, I started journaling again."

Gingerly, I pull it close. Wale has already revealed so much. What else could he possibly have to say? I glance up at him for a beat and then I read.

> August 16th
>
> I messed up. She will never take me back. I don't think she'll even talk to me ever again. For flip sake, that damn show was such a bad decision. She probably won't even apply for the ghostwriter job, but if she does, I have to show her that I've changed. That I'm a better man now.

"I'm confused. How did you know that Mayee recommended me for the job?"

His smile touches his eyes. He doesn't answer straight away. "Well, I told Greg that Mayee represents this amazing British Nigerian author who just so happens to be a ghostwriter—"

It takes me a second to wrap my head around what he's saying.

"So, wait. Did you plan this?"

Wale is still smiling, the amusement growing in his face. "Only as far as asking Greg to send Mayee the job spec. The rest—fate took care of that. And, obviously, I didn't plan on you writing a revenge book about me." He laughs.

"So, it wasn't a coincidence?" All this time, Shona was right.

Wale laces his fingers with mine and holds my gaze. He looks as though he wants me to hang on to his every word. "While I was on the show, I couldn't stop thinking about you," he says. "It was driving me nuts, and stupid me thought dating another girl would help. But all it did was make me miss you more. None of them came close to you, Tems."

Warmth radiates from my chest.

"I even tried to leave the show a couple of times. But the producers kept persuading me to stay."

"You wanted to leave? For me?" My voice is so small, I can barely hear myself.

Wale tearfully swallows as he nods, his grasp tightening. "But I knew once I came back, I would have to earn your forgiveness. You had every right not to speak to me ever again—I wouldn't have blamed you. Saying sorry over and over wouldn't cut it. I had to *show* you that I was working on being a better man and that I was committed too. I didn't only talk about my mental health during therapy. I talked about us."

All this . . . for me?

"The memoir worked in my favor," Wale goes on, his voice fraying. He clears his throat. "When I was presented with the opportunity, my first thought was *Who the hell would want to read a book written by me?* But then Greg said we could hire a ghostwriter. And, of course, you came to mind. To be honest, Tems, as much as I would like the public to see a different side of me, I don't think I would have gone through with this project if you hadn't come on board."

A single fat tear rolls down my cheek.

"Remember, a few weeks ago, when we sat here?" Gently, he lifts my glasses and brushes a delicate thumb against my lashline. "When I looked you in the face and said people assume that I'm too scared to love? Well, I'm telling you now, I'm not. I was just hesitant to say it. But not anymore. I love you, Temi. I always have."

My tears are flowing now. I was so desperate to hear him say this. I needed to know he was as far along with his feelings as I was with mine.

That he could do what Seth couldn't—be loud and vocal about how he felt about me when I needed to hear him say it the most.

I wipe my nose. Wale gets out a tissue and dabs my wet cheeks. I inhale deeply. "Whew," I say, breathing out.

He smiles. "I threw a lot at you. Take your time."

So, I do. I sit quietly for a moment, taking everything in.

And then I lean over and kiss him passionately. Maybe it's too much for a public setting. But I don't care. Wale Bandele loves me and I love him.

"I love you too," I tell him, relishing the feel of his beard against my palms. "I loved you then and I love you now. You're pretty much the love of my life."

We kiss again.

"So," he says, sitting back in his chair, "how do you feel about being with a celebrity?"

"Finally! You admit that you're a celeb! And it's fine. You're not that famous." I bat a hand. "Besides, half the internet already knows who I am and next season you'll be old news. Wait, does this mean you want to carry on doing the whole social media thing?"

Wale shrugs. "For the meantime. I'm gonna play the long game," he says, nodding. "I think the gala has taught me that I can carve my own lane for myself. I haven't got a fully fleshed-out plan yet but I would like to do something with Black male carers in the future."

As if I needed another reason to love this man.

"And how about you—what's next?" he says, brushing light strokes on the back of my hand. "Have you got an idea for your next book?"

"Not yet," I say. "But I'll get there."

"*We'll* get there," Wale corrects me. He nudges his knee against mine under the table. "Speaking of books, I never did ask . . . *The Ultimate Payback*, how does it end? Did your characters get back together?"

Dionne's suggestion comes to mind. Despite my original ending, Sophie and Wayne were always meant to find their way back to each other. I just needed to get out of their way.

And with a smile of someone who now, without question, wholeheartedly believes in fate, I reply, "It's a romance, what do you think?"

Epilogue

Seven months later...

"Do you have any other questions?" I ask, glancing up from my laptop. I'm sitting in a Costa opposite a seventy-nine-year-old Jamaican woman who bears an uncanny resemblance to Maya Angelou. Her name is Lucinda Jones. And she is also my client.

Lucinda ponders for a moment, the lines on her face deepening as she purses her matte-red lips. "No, I think you've covered everything for now, thank you. I'm so excited to be working with you."

"Likewise."

"Shirl told me great things about you and how you're so professional. I was a bit hesitant at first given your age. But I can confidently say that I'm in safe hands." She gives me a warm smile. "It's important that my grandchildren know about our family history; where they come from."

I will be ghostwriting Lucinda's memoir—she was part of the Windrush generation that saw hundreds of thousands of people arrive in the UK from the Caribbean. She's the second client I've had since deciding to become a freelance ghostwriter seven months ago. I realized that if I took Bonsai's soulless environment away, I actually enjoyed telling other people's stories. And writing Wale's memoir proved to me that I could go at it alone.

I down the last dregs of my tea and rise to my feet. "I'll be in touch,"

I tell Lucinda, giving her a hug. Then I grab my bag and head out, admiring the blossoming cherry trees en route to my next meeting.

. . .

"Temi, thanks for stopping by," says Mayee, grinning from behind her desk. I sit on the velvety chair opposite. Her office has the perfect view of London and a treadmill in front of the window to make sure she makes the most of it. "I've got an update on *Writing Miss Wrong*," she says.

I squeeze the strap of my tote bag. Mayee had sent my manuscript out to publishers only last week. My belly rises with hope. *Could this be . . . ?*

Mayee, who hasn't stopped smiling, stalls for a moment before saying, "Two editors want to meet with you—including Dionne."

I try to speak but no words come out.

Over the last several months, I have worked on this new novel. *Writing Miss Wrong* is about a struggling male ghostwriter who goes back in time to rewrite the history of the first ever Black plus-size pinup actress. It was Mayee who helped me come up with the concept during one of our several brainstorming sessions. We realized that paranormal romance is my thing, so that's what I should be writing, regardless of *Wildest Dreams*' fate. After our moment of honesty, our relationship has gone from strength to strength. I tell her everything—when I'm struggling, when I want a second opinion on an idea, and when I desperately need a deadline extension. Again. Writing this novel has been a much more pleasurable experience. I owe her everything.

"Thank you," I manage to utter.

Mayee jerks. "Why are you thanking me? You did all the hard work."

"But you gave me a second chance," I remind her. "You didn't have to."

Mayee walks around her desk and perches on the corner. She puts a hand on my shoulder. "I'm proud of you, Temi," she says softly. "I really am."

She gives me a moment. And then she tells me all the positive things Dionne said about my manuscript. Apparently, she never mentioned the past. Not once.

. . .

As soon as I return home, I get ready. I put on Cleo (my oversize red statement glasses) and a gorgeous, geometry-patterned dress designed by Nana Badu. I still have my dream dress on my vision board, waiting to be made. One day, I'll wear it to my own book launch.

Despite arriving at Anansi Books early, the place is buzzing—shelves have been pushed toward the back to make more space. Uncle Les is hovering beside the DJ. He looks as though he's waiting his turn to spin the decks. Aunty Shirley and a few familiar faces from her church are wandering about serving Afro-Caribbean snacks.

I spot Wale chatting to Greg and Kathy, and my stomach flips at how heart-achingly handsome he looks in his traditional Nigerian attire. We got our outfits made out of the same fabric so that we match.

"Congratulations!" I cry, hugging him from behind.

Wale spins around. His face brightens. "Hey, you." He tugs me closer for a kiss and steps back to look me up and down. "Girl, you're wearing the hell out of this dress."

I laugh. "You don't look too bad yourself." I consider telling him my news, but this is his day; I'll tell him later. I greet Kathy and Greg.

"We're just talking about Wale's five-a-side-for-carers program," Kathy says, filling me in.

"We've got some interest from a few footballers." Greg takes a swig of his drink. "Can't share any names just yet but things are looking promising."

Kathy crosses her fingers. Her smile is so wide I can see the crowns in her teeth.

"It would be a dream come true for us to work together again," she says to Wale over the loud music. "And if you ever want to pack in this social media stuff, we've got a brand-new desk with your name all over it."

Wale twirls the end of his beard. "Ooh, not gonna lie. The new office is a flex. Greg, you're gonna have to try and match that."

They laugh and then excuse themselves, lured by fresh trays of mouthwatering canapés. Wale turns to me, a twinkle in his eyes. He rocks forward and backward a little—a small signal that he's still internally admiring me.

"So"—I spread my arms—"how does it feel?"

He shakes his head repeatedly and blows air out of his puffed cheeks. Then his gaze lands on the massive easel by the entrance, a blowup picture of his book on the large canvas. Following my feedback to his publishers, they decided to change the title. *Not Just a Pretty Boy from South*. It has a better ring to it. A Wale ring.

"It feels . . . insane," he says, running a hand over his freshly trimmed hair. "But do you know what's even more insane?" He pulls me in by my waist, bending to brush his nose against mine. "You," he says, his voice warm and breathy against my lips. "I'm only here today because of you. This book, Tems, is just as much yours as it is mine. Have you seen my dedication?"

"I have but I can pretend as though I'm seeing it for the first time." I grab one of his many books from the shelf, flick it open, and loudly clear my throat. "'*To my one and only—thank you. This is ours.*' Aww."

Wale beams. "Hashtag Wami."

"No! Hashtag Telé!"

"Fine," he relents with a playful huff. "Hashtag Telé." He wraps an arm around my shoulder and I hang on to his finger.

It's become our couple's name as declared by Black Twitter. After posting a few Insta Stories of us together, it didn't take long for The Tea Lounge to announce that we were an item again. As expected, people rushed to share their unsolicited opinions in the comments section.

Some thought we were a fake couple and just dating for clout. But what has been a nice surprise is the overwhelming online love and support we've received. A lot of people are glad to see Wale dating a curvy, plus-size woman.

"Hold that pose!"

We turn our heads.

Fonzo snaps our photo. He lowers the camera strapped around his neck. Shona is walking beside him, holding two gift bags. They've bought us his and hers journals.

"So, how's the first month been?" says Wale. He returns the Moleskine notebook to its bag. "You're both here and alive—a good sign. Are you guys still pretending to be perfect?"

Shona looks up at Fonzo; they have so much love in their eyes.

"He's the perfect housemate," she says, drawling her words. "He cleans up after himself, folds and puts away my laundry—including my knickers."

"I used to work at Primark," Fonzo says quickly. He waves at Aunty Shirley and Uncle Les. "Come. Let's go and say hi to my parents."

I watch them go, giddiness unfurling inside of me. I'm so glad that Shona has found her person.

"Speaking of parents . . ." I crane my neck. I stop myself from asking, *Was your dad able to take time off work?* Today is Wale's day and I won't allow him to be down. Not even for a second.

After his dad read his memoir, he avoided Wale for a few days, deliberately taking on extra late shifts to prevent bumping into him at home. Then, when he finally did, he quietly told him he was sorry. It was the first time Wale had received an apology from him. Ever. I've met him on a few occasions. He likes to keep to himself, not one to hang about and chat. Wale's relationship with him is still strained but he is open to starting afresh, if his dad is.

Wale looks around—more and more people are piling in—and then he pauses, smiling broadly. I follow his gaze.

His mum and his brother are talking to my mum and dad. Our families haven't met before. This should be interesting.

"The celebrity couple," Dad says when we reach them. We greet each one of them in turn, my heart squeezing as I watch Dad pat Wale's back as if he's his own son. Ayo, who has become my own brother, has flown from Australia to be here. He gives his older brother a long hug.

"Aunty!" I throw my arms around Wale's mum. "Look at you! You look stunning."

Wale's mum glances down at her African kaftan dress, her fuzzy gray hair hidden under a matching headscarf. She's wearing blush and glittery gold eyeshadow, which have beautifully reversed the hard years in her face.

"I followed the same method you showed me," she says, her hand still on my forearm. "But I gave up on the mascara. Kept poking myself in the eye."

We're all laughing when a familiar male voice calls Wale's name.

He's here.

Wale's dad steps into our circle, his lips drawn taut into a hard-to-read expression. His jacket is still zipped up and he's holding two plastic bags. He gives me a nod of acknowledgment first and stares directly at his eldest son.

"I just bought ten copies," he says. "When you're free, you'll sign them, ehn?"

Wale's eyes glisten as he stares back at his dad. I reach for his hand and hold it, lightly stroking the inside of his wrist.

"Thanks, Dad," he says after a quiet moment. "Of course I will."

His dad nods again.

He may not ever say it with words, but Wale's dad just told him he loves him in his own way.

"Group photo!" Fonzo cries.

As always, Fonzo is camera ready, and it doesn't take him long to get us all into position. Wale stands behind me, his hands cradling my hips, his beard prickling my skin. His mum reaches for my hand and I give hers a squeeze.

I imagine myself on the other side, staring adoringly at this picture-perfect moment of two families merging into one.

Honestly, I couldn't have written this story if I tried.

Acknowledgments

Wow. I made it. Several times I wondered whether I would ever reach the end. Writing this book was a marathon—*The Re-Write* involved *many* rewrites. But with the help of my village, I got there.

First and foremost, thank you, God. Thank you for the emotional and spiritual journey you took me on to write this book. I now understand Romans 5:4 ("... *endurance develops strength of character.*") You led me through the fire but I wouldn't have it any other way.

My darling, beloved husband, Martin: thank you for riding with me, for keeping the faith when I was at my lowest, and for making the editing process fun—avocado! (Inside joke.) I would not be where I am today without you. To my precious, beautiful son: you are a blessing, my motivation. We practically wrote this book together—when you were in my belly, and later, latched on my boob! Thank you for being you. I love you dearly. My wonderful parents: thank you for your steadfast faith and for keeping me in your prayers. My equally wonderful in-laws: thank you for your encouragement and for being so gracious to babysit whenever I needed extra support. To my inspirational siblings and my wider family: thank you for championing me, always. Much love.

To my phenomenal agent, Nelle Andrew: as you know, I had to overcome a few mental and physical challenges to write this book. Thank you for handling me with care and for having my back. I appreciate you more than you know. And thank you to everyone at

Rachel Mills Literary. I'm grateful for all the work you do behind the scenes.

To my godsent editors, Lydia Fried and Jeramie Orton: there will never be enough words to express how much you both mean to me. Thank you for helping me find the heart of this story, for your time and patience—how you manage to remain enthusiastic despite us doing several rounds of edits is beyond me! Because of your thoroughness, I am a better writer today. And massive thanks to Harriet Bourton and Pamela Dorman for your ongoing support and understanding.

To Olivia Mead, Rosana Safaty, Georgia Taylor, Natalie Grant, and everyone in the UK and US publicity and marketing teams: thank you for being my internal cheerleaders and for keeping *The Re-Write* on people's radar! Honorable shout-out to Rosie Safaty: everything you touch turns into magic! I'm super grateful for your passion and hard work. Josie Stavely Taylor, Jaya Miceli, and Jason Ramirez, thank you for the beautiful UK and US covers; I can't stop staring at them! A special thank-you to Karen Whitlock, my copyeditor, for going through my manuscript with a fine-tooth comb and for ensuring all the dates and deadlines lined up. Ellie Smith: thanks for doing an excellent job overseeing the proof process. And to everyone at Penguin and Pamela Dorman Books, and Penguin Random House as a whole, thank you for your overwhelming support. Last but not least, special shout-out to Narrative Landscape for putting me on the map in Nigeria!

To my lovely beta reader, Deborah Balogun: thank you for being such a STAN and for believing in the story even when it was in its draft stage! Thank you for being so generous; your feedback was invaluable.

To all the writers who checked in on me while I was writing this book: Nikki May, Jendella Benson, Annie Garthwaite, Josie Silver, Beth O'Leary, Aliya Ali-Afzal, Suzie Oluwabunmi, Amita Parikh, Vanessa Haye, Rachel Faturoti—thank you! Honorable mention to Shani Akilah and Bim Salami for always being a voice note / phone call away.

To my incredible friends: you know who you are. I'm so blessed to have you in my life. Thank you for your genuine support, your words of affirmation, and prayers.

I should also thank the masterminds behind *Love Island*. This book wouldn't be here without its existence! And thank you, Malcolm D. Lee—the genius behind my two favorite films, *The Best Man* and *The Best Man Holiday*. Huge sources of inspiration!

To the unsung heroes of society: unpaid carers—I didn't want to give anything away in my dedication but this book is also for you. You are all angels on earth. I hope by reading this book, you feel seen.

Last but not least, my lovely readers: whether it's reaching out with kind words on social media or telling a friend about my book, from the bottom of my heart, thank you for rocking with me and for being such active supporters. There aren't enough love stories by Black British authors and, with your help, we're changing the status quo. With this said, I would really appreciate it if you could recommend *The Re-Write* to people in your networks. And if it lands in the hands of a Black man, even better.

ALSO AVAILABLE

Yinka, Where Is Your Huzband?
A Novel

Yinka is a thirtysomething British Nigerian woman whose mother's constant refrain is: "Yinka, where is your *huzband*?" Yinka believes love will find her when the time is right. Still, when her cousin gets engaged, Yinka commences Operation Find-A-Date. Will Yinka find a *huzband*? What if the thing she needs to find is herself? This is a love story that makes you smile but also makes you think—and explores what it means to find your way between two cultures, both of which are yours.

"Yinka is a lovable and relatable disaster—which is to say, she isn't actually a disaster at all. . . . I adore her."
—Emily Henry, #1 *New York Times* bestselling author of *Book Lovers*

PENGUIN BOOKS

Ready to find your next great read? Let us help. Visit prh.com/nextread